W9-BLK-603

*For my grandfathers*

# PROLOGUE

A week before the January thaw finally arrived in February, I found myself hanging like a bat from a rafter inside a church steeple, face-to-face with a bell made by Paul Revere.

If you'd have told me a month ago that I'd find myself in this position, I would have said you were crazy.

But then, a month ago my life was completely different. A month ago, my career as a middle-school private eye hadn't begun.

And by the way, it didn't begin inside a steeple. Absolutely truly not.

It began the day my report card made it home before I did.

# CHAPTER 1

"What is THIS supposed to mean?" my father demanded as I followed my brother through the front door, our arms full of boxes. My father stalked across the entry hall, waving a slip of paper at me with his good hand.

Hatcher flashed me a sympathetic look and vanished upstairs. I didn't blame him; I'd have done the same thing in his place. No one wants to face the wrath of Lieutenant Colonel Jericho T. Lovejoy.

"An F plus in pre-algebra?" The chill in my father's voice could have single-handledly reversed global warming. "F *plus*, Truly?"

Yes, that's really my name. It's a family thing.

"Does that mean you almost passed, or that you failed spectacularly?" My father pinned me with one of his signature glares.

I hadn't counted on this—I thought it would take at least a week for mail from Texas to reach the East Coast. And I'd counted on being able to snag this particular envelope from the mailbox before anyone else spotted it.

"Um," I said.

"This is unacceptable, young lady."

Silence is the best strategy when my father gets like this.

"I don't understand it," he continued, pacing back and forth. "Not one bit. Lovejoys can do anything! We're naturally good at math."

Actually, there's a whole long list of things I can't do and that I'm not good at. Usually, though, math isn't one of them. It's one of my favorite subjects, in fact. But how was I supposed to concentrate on stupid pre-algebra when my world had been turned upside down? The F plus wasn't my fault; it was his, and I said so under my breath.

My father stopped midpace. "What was that?"

"Nothing, sir," I mumbled.

My father isn't one of those hypermilitary dads—when we lived on the base in Colorado, I had a friend whose father used to do actual room inspections for her and her brother every Saturday morning in full dress uniform, white gloves and all; still, all of us Lovejoy kids have been trained to add "sir" to the end of our sentences when we're talking to our dad, especially when we want to be on his good side.

And with a math grade like mine, that was definitely the side I wanted to be on.

My father grabbed his coat from off the banister. I resisted the urge to offer some help as he swung it awkwardly around his shoulders. No point adding fuel to the fire. "Wait until your mother hears about this."

That wasn't a conversation I was looking forward to. When my father's mad, at least everything's out in the open and you know where you stand. With my mother, whenever one of us messes up, she just looks at us sorrowfully and shakes her head, like we're the biggest disappointment in the history of the world. Which I probably am.

"Finish unpacking the car," my father said. "I'm heading back to the bookstore. And don't forget, you and Hatcher have Kitchen Patrol tonight."

And with that he left, slamming the door behind him.

I slumped down on the hall bench and banged my forehead against one of the boxes I was holding. It was so unfair! The math grade, the move—everything! Why couldn't we have just stayed in Texas?

This time, there wasn't even the prospect of moving someplace decent again in a year or two either. This time, I was stuck. Forever. In population you've-got-to-be-kidding-me Pumpkin Falls, New Hampshire.

# CHAPTER 2

*Bumpkin Falls would be a better name for it*, I thought bitterly. I still couldn't believe we'd traded Austin for this peanut-sized blip on a map. And a very cold blip too. Winter lasts six months out of the year in Pumpkin Falls, and the likelihood of anything interesting ever happening was about the same as that of me sprouting wings. The nearest mall was an hour away. The town didn't even have a movie theater. It did have a swimming pool, at least. That was some consolation.

I stacked the boxes on the bench, carrying the one labeled TRULY'S BIRD BOOKS over to the bottom of the stairs. I'd take it up to my room later. "Hatcher!" I yelled. "Get yourself down here on the double! Dad wants us to finish unloading!"

I could hear my brother rattling around up there, and wondered what he was doing. Usually, the first thing that happens when we move into a new house, which is often since Dad is in the army, is that Hatcher and Danny run inside to stake out their territory. Mom always lets them, because they're the oldest, I guess. This time, though, there was no territory to stake out. We all knew this particular house like the backs of our hands, and Mom and Dad had decided our room assignments back in Texas.

I opened the front door and was struck by a blast of icy wind. Shivering, I ran to the minivan for another armload of boxes. Dropping two of them on the sofa in the living room, I took the third into the dining room. We were traveling light this time, most of our furniture headed for storage since we wouldn't be needing it. The stuff here was much nicer than ours, anyway.

I rummaged in the box for place mats. I wouldn't win any brownie points with Dad if I shirked Kitchen Patrol—better known as "KP," Lovejoy shorthand for setting the table, helping with dinner, and doing the dishes.

"Where've you been?" I snapped as my brother finally galumphed down the stairs.

"Didn't go so well with Dad, huh?"

"Nope."

"Want to talk about it?"

"Nope."

If there's one good thing about Hatcher, it's that he knows when to leave me alone. He shrugged and vanished out the front door.

Counting out seven place mats and seven napkins, I

arranged them around the table. One set for each of my parents, a set each for my two older brothers and my two younger sisters, and a final set for me, smack-dab in the center of the Lovejoy lineup.

"Truly-in-the-Middle," Dad used to call me, back before he turned into Silent Man. He had a nickname for our family back then too—the Magnificent Seven. The theme song from the old movie used to be the ringtone on his cell phone.

The war changed all that.

Since he came home from Afghanistan, Silent Man doesn't joke around anymore, and there's no fun ringtone, and he hasn't once called me "Truly-in-the-Middle" or referred to our family as the Magnificent Seven. I don't know if we'll ever be that family again. "Magnificent" isn't exactly the word I'd use for us these days.

Six months ago, though, things were different. Six months ago, my life was perfect.

We were living in Texas, for one thing, instead of Nowheresville, New Hampshire. We'd moved to Austin after school got out in Fort Carson, Colorado, at the end of June, so that we could get everything ready for Dad's homecoming. He was set to return from his final tour of duty after Labor Day.

We were giddy the day we moved into the new house. My brothers and sisters and I could hardly believe it—a real, permanent home of our own, at last! And a nice one too, with a swimming pool out back and a big family room with a fire-place, and enough bathrooms so that us girls didn't have to share with Hatcher and Danny. No more rentals or tempo-rary base housing, no more barely-unpacked-before-we-had-to-pack-everything-up-again lifestyle, no more switching schools every two years, along with teachers and coaches and neighbors and friends.

For the first time in my life I had a bedroom all to myself, and best of all, I was living in the same zip code as my cousin Mackenzie. Mom found us a house just down the street from Aunt Louise and Uncle Teddy's, which was the most awesome thing about moving to Texas as far as I was concerned.

Mackenzie and I were born a week apart, and the two of us have been best friends since we were in diapers. When we were little, we actually used to pretend we were twins. Not that anyone would ever mistake us for them. Mackenzie totally has the Gifford genes. She's just over five feet tall and cute as a button, with curly strawberry blond hair just like Uncle Teddy's, and just like my mom's and my little sister Pippa's.

I, on the other hand, have straight brown Lovejoy hair and am not even remotely petite. I've always been the tallest one in my class, but this past year, shortly after I turned twelve, I shot up to just under six feet. I felt like the scene in *Alice in Wonderland* after she eats the cake and grows that weird long neck and says good-bye to her feet, which she can hardly see anymore because she's such a giant.

I wish I could say good-bye to my feet. They grew right along with me, unfortunately. I wear size ten and a half now, and my shoes look like something a clown would wear. Especially next to Mackenzie's.

My cousin is a really good best friend. She knows how much it bothers me to be so tall. My father calls me an Amazon. They were warrior women a zillion years ago, and I guess it makes sense for him to call me that, being a soldier and all, but still, that's a nickname I don't want to get stuck with. Anyway, Mackenzie promised to take me under her wing and introduce me to everyone when school started, so for once I'd be ahead of the curve. I'd be the cousin of cute, perky Mackenzie Gifford, instead of just the freakishly tall new girl.

After our family's move to Texas, Mackenzie and I had the best summer ever. I talked her into trying out with me for the summer swim team, and we rode our bikes to the pool every morning for practice, then hung out for the rest of the day at my house or hers. We had sleepovers and backyard barbecues, and she helped me pick out paint for my new room—a really pretty shade of aqua called "Mermaid." We went to the movies and shopping and to Amy's for ice cream at least once a week. July and August were heaven.

Then came Black Monday.

That's what Mom called it, afterward.

I was practicing the piano that morning while I waited for Mackenzie to finish breakfast and come over. Hatcher and

Danny had gone fishing, and Mom was paying bills and keeping an eye on my younger sisters, who had made a fort under the dining room table and were playing zoo with Lauren's hamster, Nibbles, and Thumper, her rabbit.

I didn't pay much attention at first when my mother's cell phone rang.

"J. T.!" she cried happily.

I looked up. She was talking to Dad! As I watched, though, her smile faded and the color drained from her face, until she was as white as the sheet music in front of me. My fingers stumbled on the piano keys, leaving a jangle of sour notes hanging in the air. Something was wrong.

My mother listened for a minute, then stood up abruptly, sending her chair toppling backward onto the floor. She pressed her cell phone against her chest and turned to us. "Go upstairs, girls."

My sisters poked their heads out from underneath the table.

"But, Mom—" Lauren protested.

"*Now.*"

"Yes, ma'am," my sisters chorused. Wide-eyed, they scrambled out of hiding.

"Make sure y'all take those animals with you." My mother turned her back on us and raised the cell phone to her ear again.

Automatic pilot kicked in, the kind that obeyed without

question when given an order. I crossed the room, scooping up an armload of critters and hustling my protesting sisters up to the room they shared.

"What's happening?" Lauren asked me. "Is everything okay?"

I wasn't sure, and I didn't want to scare her. She's only nine. "It's probably nothing," I said, and steered her and Pippa over to Pippa's Barbie house.

I waited until they were busy building a new zoo, then slipped out of the room. I heard the front door open, and tiptoed over to crouch at the top of the stairs. I didn't care if it was bad news—I needed to know what was going on.

"Dinah, I'm so sorry." It was Aunt Louise. Uncle Teddy was with her, and he had his arms around Mom. She must have called and asked them to come over.

I squeezed my eyes shut tight. *Please, Dad, still be alive! Please, please, please!*

"He only had a few days left!" my mother sobbed. "Just a few days!"

My heart nearly stopped.

"He's just wounded, Dinah," Uncle Teddy murmured. "He'll be safe at home again soon."

My heart started again. Wounded was better than dead.

"What happened?" asked Aunt Louise. "Was it a helicopter accident?"

My father was an army pilot.

Mom shook her head. She drew a shaky breath. "IED," she replied.

My stomach lurched. I knew what that meant. Every military kid with a parent serving in a war zone knew what that meant: "Improvised Explosive Device"—a homemade enemy bomb.

I saw Aunt Louise and Uncle Teddy exchange a glance.

"How did he sound when you talked to him?" Uncle Teddy asked gently, and my mother let out a soft sound, halfway between a sigh and a moan.

"Not like himself!" She started to cry again, and Aunt Louise patted her shoulder. After a few moments, my mother drew another shaky breath, then added, "He's in the hospital in Kabul, but he's being transferred soon to Germany. I want to book a flight just as soon as possible."

"You leave that to me," my uncle told her.

Everything was a bit of a blur after that. As the news of my father's injury spread, the rest of Mom's family started to gather. My mother has six brothers scattered all over Texas, so there were a lot of aunts and uncles and cousins underfoot for a couple of days.

In the end, while Mom flew to Germany to be with Dad, Aunt Louise, Uncle Teddy, and Mackenzie came to stay with Danny and Hatcher and my little sisters and me. Over the next few weeks there were lots of phone calls at odd hours, and whispered conversations between the adults, and then, finally, a videoconference with Dad. He didn't say much, but I was relieved to see that he looked like himself. Well, mostly. If you didn't count the fact that where his right arm should have been there was a whole lot of nothing.

"Upper extremity loss," the military calls it.

"He's alive," Mom reminded us every time she called to talk to us, first from Germany and later from the military hospital in Maryland. "We need to be grateful for that. Not every family is as fortunate as we are."

She meant the Larsons. Dad's best friend, Tom Larson, had been in the same transport hit by the IED, and he wasn't coming home. I couldn't even imagine how his family must be feeling. We'd spent lots of time with them over the years—we'd even gone to Disney World together last spring break.

"Your father's going to get through this, and so will we," Mom told us.

I didn't see how, though, and I couldn't stop worrying about it.

Not that anyone noticed. You wouldn't think I'd be that hard to overlook, given the fact that I'm now the family Clydesdale. Somehow, though, I still tend to get lost in the shuffle.

My cousin Mackenzie is an only child, and after just a few days of looking after the five of us Lovejoys, I could tell that Uncle Teddy's and Aunt Louise's heads were spinning. I guess they decided that divide and conquer was their only hope of survival, because pretty soon my uncle was busy having lots of man-to-man talks with my brothers, while my aunt turned her attention to us girls. Which mostly meant Pippa.

My baby sister is a Drama Queen with a capital *DQ*. Pippa may just be a kindergartner, but she knows how to grab the spotlight. She can turn on the waterworks at the drop of a hat. And with her halo of blonde curls, two missing front teeth, and pink sparkly glasses—well, hardly anybody stands a chance. Pippa had Aunt Louise wrapped around her pinkie finger in nothing flat.

Mackenzie and I were assigned to keep an eye on Lauren, meanwhile, which pretty much left me to fend for myself. I didn't say anything, though, because I knew everybody was doing the best they could.

By mid-September, my father was deep into physical therapy, learning how to use his new temporary prosthesis—the fake arm he'll have to wear—and adjusting to life as a lefty. I could only imagine how that was going. My father is not the world's most patient person.

"He's a real trouper" was all my mother ever said, but from the tone of her voice I could tell that wasn't the whole story.

Somewhere in the middle of all this, school started. Before Black Monday, I'd actually been looking forward to it, which is kind of unusual for me. Since military families move every couple of years, you'd think I'd be used to changing schools. This is our normal. For me, though, I'd always dreaded that first day, especially since I turned into Truly the Amazon. Austin had felt different, thanks to Mackenzie, and for once I didn't have butterflies stomping around in my stomach during the weeks leading up to it.

After Dad was injured, though, I didn't think about school at all one way or the other. It just kind of snuck up on me. I was pretty dazed that first week, even though Mackenzie took me under her wing just like she said she would. Her friends were all really nice to me and everything, but somehow it all felt wrong, like I was sleepwalking or something.

I tried to act normal, and I tried to focus on my classes, and I made an effort to get involved, the way my mother's always urging me to do whenever she catches me moping after one of our moves. I continued swimming, and I even joined a bird-watching club, ignoring Mackenzie's snarky little comments about my bird obsession.

Which isn't an obsession. Not really. Well, okay, maybe a little bit.

It didn't help that Mackenzie had suddenly become interested in boys. And not just boys in general, but one boy in particular: Cameron McAllister, seventh-grade star of Austin's Nitro Swim Club. All my cousin wanted to talk about was how cute he was, how funny he was, and how she was pretty sure that he liked her back.

Crushes were the furthest thing from my mind. It was all I could do just to get through each day. In spite of my efforts to blend in and be normal, underneath I was anything but. Underneath, I was "Hi-my-name-is-Truly-and-my-father-just-lost-his-arm-in-the-war." I thought about Dad all the time. I couldn't help it. I wondered if he was scared when the bomb exploded. I wondered how he felt about losing his best friend. And I wondered if he'd ever be able to fly again.

The one thing my father loves more than anything else in the world, except maybe us, is flying. Being a pilot was his life. Would he still be able to fly, with just one arm? I had so many questions.

And then he finally came home, and my life turned upside down again.

# CHAPTER 3

"J. T., what are you thinking?" I overheard Mom ask as my father hung up the phone in the kitchen. He'd been back in Texas less than a week. "They made it very clear they want you, despite—you know, everything."

"A one-armed wrestling coach?" Dad scoffed. "That's about as useful as a one-armed pilot. It wouldn't be fair to the team in the long run, and I don't need their pity."

"That's just pride talking and you know it. You have plenty to offer."

My brother and I, who were doing our homework at the dining room table, looked at each other wide-eyed. We probably weren't supposed to be hearing this conversation.

"Did Dad just turn down UT?" Hatcher whispered.

"Um, I think so," I whispered back.

"That can't be good."

The whole reason my parents had decided to settle in

Texas—besides the fact that my mom's family was there— was because my father had two job offers lined up. The airline he was going to fly for was based out of Austin, and on top of that, the University of Texas had offered him a part-time job as an assistant wrestling coach. Dad had been an all-star wrestler for the Longhorns, recruited out of high school on a scholarship, and UT was where he'd met Mom. After college, he'd joined the army, but he and his former coach had stayed in touch, and when UT heard he was retiring, they'd jumped at the chance to add him to their coaching staff.

All of this was before Black Monday, of course. Since the injury, my father's plans for flying had been dashed. Apparently commercial airlines aren't exactly lining up to hire one-armed pilots.

And now it looked like his wrestling days were over too.

Dad wouldn't reconsider, despite Mom's pleas. Lieutenant Colonel Jericho T. Lovejoy has a stubborn streak.

After that, he turned into Silent Man. He barely went out, and none of us kids quite knew how to act around him. We're used to Dad either barking orders or joking around, but while the barking continued, the joking did not. Our fun-loving father seemed to have vanished into thin air. He still got up every morning, still shaved, still got dressed in khaki pants and a white shirt, his usual off-duty uniform. But he rarely wore his prosthesis—the hook at the end of it scared Pippa—so one shirtsleeve was usually empty, and there was an emptiness to the rest of him too. Mom tried to make up for it by being extra cheerful, but by Halloween, her upbeat attitude had wilted, and she was looking strained and pale.

And then Gramps and Lola showed up.

The two of them arrived unannounced in early November, a taxi having deposited them on our doorstep one evening just as we were finishing dinner.

"We thought it would be fun to surprise you!" Lola told Dad, giving him a hug. She stepped back and looked him up and down, then patted his good arm. "You're looking well, J. T. Much better than when we saw you in Maryland."

My grandmother turned and spotted me. "Truly!" she cried, flinging out her arms.

"Lola!" I cried back, flinging myself into them. We've always called her Lola instead of Nana or Grandma or anything like that. Mom says it's because her name is catnip to kids, the way it rolls off the tongue, like "lullaby" or "lollipop."

"How's my most beautiful eldest granddaughter?"

I laughed. "You mean your *only* eldest granddaughter, right?"

"You're still beautiful," she replied, kissing me on the cheek.

When Lola says something like that, I almost believe her.

Lola and Gramps are two of my favorite people in the whole world. They live in New Hampshire, where Dad grew up, and where they own a bookshop. We usually go to see them every summer, but this summer, because of the move and because of Dad's injury, we didn't make it there. Having them turn up in Texas was a nice surprise.

The real surprise came the next morning, though, when they sprang the true reason for their visit on us.

"We've joined the Peace Corps!" Lola announced at breakfast.

We all looked at her like she'd said she was planning to take up belly dancing.

"You're kidding, right?" said my father.

"It's something we've always wanted to do," Gramps explained.

"Since when?"

"There's a lot about your mother and me that you don't know, son," Gramps said loftily.

My dad's hippie-dippie sister is usually the one to drop bombshells like this. Aunt True—who's named after the original Truly Lovejoy, just like me—is always heading off to go trekking in Nepal or sea kayaking in Patagonia or volunteering in some third-world orphanage. She sends us postcards from all over. Our fridge looks like the United Nations made a house call.

I looked at my grandparents, trying to imagine them in the Peace Corps. If they were birds, Lola would be a dove, small and serene. Gramps, on the other hand, with his piercing gaze, bushy eyebrows, and prominent nose—he calls it "the Lovejoy proboscis"—was more of a great horned owl. He was quiet like an owl too. Quiet like me. Gramps was the one who'd gotten me hooked on birding. Whenever we get together for a visit, he takes me on walks and tells me the names of all the birds we see. He sends me bird books every Christmas and every birthday, and he's the one who got me started keeping a life list, which birders do to record all the different species they've spotted. His is about the size of a dictionary, though, while mine is just a few pages.

Lola cleared her throat. "The thing is," she continued, "we've decided it's time to turn the bookstore over to the next generation. You'd be doing us a big favor if you'd consider taking the reins, J. T."

Gramps nodded. "Things haven't been going so well, and we think the business needs a fresh approach. Your sister says if you're in, she's in."

Dad looked stunned. "Run Lovejoy's Books? With True? In *Pumpkin Falls?*"

"Unless you plan to pick it up and move it, yes, in Pumpkin Falls," said Gramps, sounding a little testy. He's very proud of our family's connection to the town. There have been Lovejoys in Pumpkin Falls since before the American Revolution.

My father swiveled around, pinning my mother with one of his signature Lieutenant Colonel Jericho T. Lovejoy glares. "Did you know about this, Dinah?"

Mom bit her lip. "Well——"

"It's either turn it over to you and your sister or sell," Lola said briskly. "We've been avoiding this for a while now, but it's time to face facts. Not that selling would be the end of the world, but the bookshop has been in the family for nearly a hundred years."

Dad grimaced. "No pressure or anything, right?"

My grandfather placed his hand on top of Dad's remaining one. "Would you at least consider the possibility, son? Nothing would make your mother and me happier."

I could tell that running a bookstore with his sister wasn't exactly on my father's list of "Top Ten Things I Most Want to Do When I Grow Up." For one thing, he's not the biggest bookworm in the world, plus he and Aunt True don't always see eye to eye on things. Hardly ever, in fact.

At first, Dad flat-out refused. He said it was all a plot, hatched by Mom and his parents, and that he wouldn't be backed into a corner, even if it meant selling the bookshop. But with no pilot job, and no coaching job either, what choice did he have? By Thanksgiving, it was a done deal. Our new house went on the market a week later, and the movers came right after New Year's.

And now here we were: stuck in Pumpkin Falls, in the middle of the coldest winter on record, moving into the house my father grew up in, in the town he couldn't wait to leave.

# CHAPTER 4

"Gimme a hand with the salad, Drooly?" Hatcher called from the kitchen a few minutes later.

Most of the time I don't mind it when my brother calls me that. It's been his nickname for me forever. Tonight, though, I wasn't in the mood. I barged through the door ready to let him have it, then stopped abruptly.

"What?" said Hatcher innocently, batting his big brown eyes at me. He was wearing Mom's favorite apron, the pink one with DON'T MESS WITH TEXAS on it, and he'd stuffed the top with dish towels to give himself a bust. A couple more wadded into the seat of his pants added an exaggerated bottom. He did a little dance, wiggling his rear end at me, and I couldn't help it, I laughed.

Which was the whole point, of course. Hatcher's always trying to crack me up.

Mom says that except for his hair color, he's pure

Gifford. Her whole family loves practical jokes, and telling funny stories, and they've all got these big, loud laughs just like Hatcher's. My brother is the definition of happy-go-lucky. Nothing much bothers him, and he's always looking on the bright side, just like Mom. "Cheerful as a sunflower," she calls him.

I, on the other hand—well, nobody's ever called me a sunflower. Hatcher and I look a lot alike, with our freckles and brown eyes and stick-straight brown hair (his is shorter than mine, of course, thanks to Dad's vigilance with the clippers), but that's where the resemblance ends. He's sunshine; I'm shadow. Like I said, I'm the quiet type. Except for the times when I stick my foot in my mouth, and when you wear size-ten-and-a-half shoes, that's a whole lot of foot. Unfortunately, my foot spends a lot of time there. I'm kind of famous in my family for blurting out the wrong thing at the wrong time.

Hatcher danced over and placed a colander on my head like a crown. "Duty calls, milady," he warbled. "Prepare to wash and chop."

My smile vanished. Grumbling, I crossed to the fridge and started pulling out salad fixings. KP was my least favorite chore. The plan was for Hatcher and me to alternate weeks with Danny and Lauren, to help Mom out now that she's going back to college. It's always been her dream to be an English teacher, but between juggling all of us kids and our constant moves with the military, it was pretty much an impossible one. Now that we were finally putting down roots, she had decided to finish her degree. It's really convenient for her, what with Lovejoy College being right here in Pumpkin Falls.

The college was founded in 1769 by one of our ancestors: Nathaniel Daniel Lovejoy, my great-great-great-zillion-times-great-grandfather, who built this house and who looks down his Lovejoy proboscis at us from his oil portrait hanging over the fireplace in the living room. His wife, Prudence, whose nose is a normal size, stares back at him from her portrait above the piano. There are more Lovejoys scattered over the walls in other parts of the house too, so many that I can't always keep track of their names. Nathaniel Daniel is pretty hard to forget, though. What were his parents thinking?

Even Pippa thinks it's a stupid name. "Nathaniel Daniel looks like a spaniel," she sing-songed the first time she heard it.

"When's everybody due back?" asked Hatcher.

I shrugged. "Soon, I guess. Mom said they'd be home for dinner." Lauren and Pippa had gone along for the ride while she and Danny registered for classes—my mother at Lovejoy College, and Danny at the high school over in West Hartfield. Not only is Pumpkin Falls too small to have its own movie theater, it also doesn't even have its own high school, which means Danny will have to drive himself nearly half an hour to school each day.

My brother slid the lasagna into the oven and gave me a sidelong glance. "So, what's the deal with the grade?"

I made a face and sliced into a tomato. "I don't know, Hatch. Ever since I found out we were moving again, I couldn't concentrate on anything. I tanked a couple of tests."

"Did you think Dad wouldn't find out?"

"I thought I'd beat him to the mailbox, that's for sure."

"Moron," he said, punching me in the arm. It was a friendly punch, though, and I gave him a rueful smile.

By the time dinner was ready I was feeling a whole lot happier. My mood took a nosedive again a few minutes later, though, when Dad walked through the door, scowling.

Mom was right behind him. "Mmm, that lasagna smells delicious," she said, taking off her coat and hat and hanging them on a hook in the mud room.

"Supermarket's finest," said Hatcher.

She swooped in to kiss each of us on the cheek. "Sounds good to me. I think I'm going to like this new KP arrangement."

I gave my father a speculative glance. Mom was way too upbeat for someone who knew about an F plus. Maybe he wasn't planning to tell her about my report card after all.

My mother watched, her lips pressed together, as my father struggled with the zipper on his jacket. I could tell she wanted to help, but we've all learned to wait until asked unless we want to get our heads bitten off. It takes a lot for Dad to ask for help with anything.

"Danny's all set for tomorrow, and so am I," Mom said lightly, squatting down to help Pippa with her zipper instead. "It's kind of funny to think we'll all be starting school together."

My little sister flung her arms around her. "You can come to my clathroom, Mommy," she lisped, thanks to her missing teeth. "I'll let you thit right nextht to me."

"Thanks, Pipster," my mother replied, ruffling my sister's curls. "I really wish I could—but I have to go to my school." Straightening up, she glanced around the kitchen and frowned. "Where's Lauren?"

"Out in the barn," Danny told her. Gramps and Lola's house has a really cool old barn that they use as a garage. Gramps has his woodshop out there, and they turned part of the hayloft into an art studio for Lola. "She's still in the car. She said she wanted to finish her chapter."

"For heaven's sake, it must be ten below out there!" Mom exclaimed. "Get her in here, would you?"

Danny went to do as she asked while the rest of us sat down at the table. When he and Lauren returned, we said grace and then dug in. I glanced over at my father now and then as we ate, bracing myself for the ax that I knew would eventually fall. We made it all the way to dessert without a peep about my report card.

"Did we get any mail?" my mother asked as Hatcher passed around a plate of the Pumpkin Falls General Store's famous maple walnut blondies.

I froze.

My father looked over at me and raised an eyebrow. "Do you want to tell her, or shall I?"

I sighed. "Go ahead."

"Excuse me?"

"Go ahead, *sir*."

He reached into his shirt pocket and pulled out the envelope, then passed it wordlessly to my mother.

"Truly," said my mother, shaking her head sorrowfully when she spotted my math grade, just as I knew she would. "I'm so disappointed in you."

Hatcher kicked me under the table. I glanced over to see him tap his two forefingers under his chin. That's our shorthand for "chin up." I sighed again. What I really wanted to tell my mother was that it was all Dad's fault, that he was the reason we'd had to leave Austin, which was why I hadn't been able to concentrate on stupid pre-algebra. But I couldn't say that, naturally.

"I know, Mom," is what I said instead. "I'm sorry. I promise I'll try harder."

"You certainly will," said my father, his voice as crisp as the creases in his starched shirt. "In fact, I've decided on a plan of attack."

Of course he had. Lieutenant Colonel Jericho T. Lovejoy is big on plans of attack.

"I'll tutor you until your grade is acceptable again," he continued. "I'll expect you at the bookstore by 1530 hours every afternoon after school."

1530 is military-speak for three thirty p.m. "But—" I began.

He ignored me. "You can stay and help your aunt and me when we're done with tutoring, then Danny can pick you up on his way home from practice."

"But—" I tried again.

"We're about to start inventory, and we could use an extra pair of hands," he continued. He glanced down at his own left hand, which was awkwardly gripping his fork, and frowned briefly. "I'd enlist your brothers, but they'll be too busy to help right now, what with wrestling season starting."

The table fell silent as he jabbed his fork into a bite of lasagna. Hatcher and I exchanged a glance. Wrestling was a sore topic these days. Before Black Monday, Dad had always helped coach Hatcher and Danny when he was home, but now—well, now he could barely even say the word.

"But—"

"No buts, young lady. That's an order."

Lieutenant Colonel Lovejoy is big on orders, too.

"What about swim team tryouts?" I burst out, unable

to contain myself any longer. I did remember to add "sir," though. Lola and Gramps had checked for me, and the tryouts were scheduled for the end of the month.

"You bring your grade up, then we'll talk swim team," my father replied coolly. "Until then, young lady, this is a done deal."

# CHAPTER 5

*Good-bye sunshine, hello snow,* I thought glumly the following morning, staring out the window of our minivan as we pulled out of the driveway. It's not a very long walk to school from where Gramps and Lola live, but Mom had offered to drop us off on the way to her first class because of the storm.

Heaps and heaps of the white stuff had fallen overnight, at least a foot of it, and it was still coming down. Just to torture myself, I'd checked the weather in Austin this morning: sixty-two degrees and sunny. It was practically summer there. The thermometer outside Gramps and Lola's kitchen window, meanwhile? A frigid seventeen degrees.

If we were thinking maybe school would be canceled, though, we were wrong. My father snorted when Hatcher brought it up at the breakfast table.

"A snow day in Pumpkin Falls? Don't get your hopes up,"

he'd told us. "A little precipitation never stops anything here in the Granite State."

A little? Staring out at the yard, which was barely visible, I caught a flash of red by the bird feeder as a male cardinal swooped down from a nearby tree. Cardinals are already on my life list, of course—they're a really common bird—but they're still one of my favorites. I just love those bright red feathers, especially this time of year.

"How about cold, then?" Hatcher clearly wasn't going to give up. He'd tapped the newspaper lying on the table in front of Dad. Half the front page of the *Pumpkin Falls Patriot-Bugle* was devoted to a picture of the town's famous waterfall, along with a headline that screamed FALLS FREEZE FOR FIRST TIME IN A CENTURY! I couldn't believe this was what passed for news here. A frozen waterfall? Seriously?

"Nope, cold won't do it either," Dad had replied calmly. "Better get your jackets on."

A snow day would have been really nice. I wasn't feeling ready to face a new school again. After our move to Austin, I'd thought I was finally done with that.

The snow crunched beneath the minivan's tires as Mom turned off Maple onto Hill Street and headed down toward town. Tourists call Pumpkin Falls picturesque because of the waterfall and the covered bridge and the old-fashioned bandstand on the village green—village white, this morning—that anchors the center of town. They flock here like migrating geese every fall to tour the college campus, famous for its cluster of white clapboard buildings, and to take pictures of the steeple on the church, with its giant clock and the bell made by Paul Revere, and to buy maple syrup and maple sugar candy and souvenirs at the General Store. Mostly they come to gawk at the fall foliage, though. Everybody calls them leaf peepers, but I call them stupid. Who cares about a bunch of leaves?

We skirted one end of the village green, passing several big, square, Colonial-style houses, the post office, the Pumpkin Falls Bed & Breakfast, the Pumpkin Falls Savings & Loan, and, right by the iron gates and big driveway leading onto the campus, the official residence of the president of Lovejoy College. I knew this because the sign out front said so.

"The wheels on the bus go round and round . . ." From her booster seat in front of me, Pippa belted out a tuneless rendition of her favorite song. Lauren was seated next to her with her nose in a book as usual, and Hatcher was in the front passenger seat, talking to Mom. I was in the way back in my seat of choice by the right-hand window. Usually Hatcher is beside me because Danny likes to ride shotgun, but Danny was long gone. He'd gotten up at zero dark thirty this morning to drive himself to West Hartfield.

I'd noticed that Danny wasn't complaining much about the move to Pumpkin Falls. Probably because Gramps and Lola had given him their car to use while they were in Africa. He'd hardly stopped grinning since he got the keys.

"Round and round, round and round," droned Pippa.

My mother glanced in the rearview mirror. "Could you maybe keep it down a little, please, peanut?"

Pippa cranked it up a notch instead. "ROUND AND ROUND, ROUND AND ROUND!"

My mother sighed. We eased to a stop across from the world's teeniest public library, then turned onto Main Street, which Gramps always rather grandly refers to as "the heart of the business district." If this was the heart, I figured it must be on life support. There were only a handful of businesses besides the bookshop, and if you ask me, which nobody ever does, the only one that's the least bit interesting is the Pumpkin Falls General Store.

Dad says it's the biggest tourist trap north of Boston, but my brothers and sisters and I love it. They're not kidding about the "general" part. You can buy anything there. Need a mop? They've got it. Tulip bulbs? Those, too. From plumbing supplies and fishing tackle to printer ink, livestock feed, kitchen gadgets, snow shovels, postcards, T-shirts, underwear—if you can think of it, the general store probably has it. At Easter, they even sell baby chicks and ducklings. Plus there's a penny candy counter and an old-fashioned soda fountain with homemade ice cream that's almost as good as Amy's in Austin. One of my favorite things to do whenever we visit Gramps and Lola in the summertime is to sit out on the store's front porch in one of the rocking chairs, eating a strawberry ice-cream cone.

Mom slowed as we approached Lovejoy's Books. A big sign across the front window read CLOSED FOR INVENTORY. Someone was standing outside, and Pippa stopped singing long enough to shout, "Daddy!"

"No, honey," my mother told her. "I think it's Aunt True."

It was kind of hard to tell from the back, because whoever it was was wearing a big hooded jacket. Then I realized they were shoveling snow, which meant it probably wasn't Dad. Stuff like that is still awkward for him, even with his new prosthesis.

Aunt True spotted us and waved the shovel. We waved back. Mom pulled over to the curb and lowered her window.

"Howdy!" she said. "Working hard, I see."

My aunt grinned. "You bet. Everybody ready for school?"

Pippa and Lauren nodded happily. Hatcher and I shrugged. Kindergarten and fourth grade are still something to get excited about, but once you hit middle school, it's not as much of a thrill.

My aunt smiled at me. "Your dad says that you'll be joining us at the bookshop later, Truly."

"Yes, ma'am."

"That's way better than stupid day care," Lauren grumbled. Mom's class schedule means that my sisters have to go to after-school care, and Lauren is not happy about it.

Aunt True reached over my mom's shoulder and plucked

Lauren's book away. *"The Long Winter,* huh?" she said, reading the title. "Good choice for a day like today." She gave it back. "I love Laura Ingalls Wilder. I have all her books—maybe there's one you'd like to borrow. How about you come over for tea at my apartment one afternoon soon?"

"What about me?" said Pippa. Her lower lip trembled, poised to turn on the waterworks if the answer was no.

"You're invited too, of course," Aunt True told her.

My aunt is living above the bookstore. Gramps and Lola own the whole building, and she moved into the apartment upstairs when she came home to Pumpkin Falls to help out.

To be honest, Aunt True is a bit of a mystery. She's visited us a few times over the years, and she always remembers to send presents at Christmas and birthdays, but I don't really know her very well. Everybody says we look alike, but I think it's just because we're both tall. Well, maybe that and the freckles. She sure isn't quiet like me, though. If I had to compare Aunt True to a bird, I'd have to pick a loud one.

Mom I've always thought of as a robin. They're such cheery, dependable birds. And Dad's an eagle for sure, what with his strong jaw, piercing gaze, and prominent nose. He got stuck with the Lovejoy proboscis, just like Gramps. So far, none of us kids have shown signs of sprouting it, although I've caught Hatcher staring at his profile in the mirror a few times recently. He's worried it's going to appear out of the blue one of these days, like chest hair or zits.

My gaze settled on Aunt True's hat. Multicolored and lumpy, it had braided yarn ties dangling from the earflaps and was obviously hand-knit. It was identical to the ones she'd brought back for Danny and Hatcher and me from her trip to Peru. We were smart enough not to wear ours in public, though.

Parrot, maybe? Yeah, that fit. Aunt True was a parrot, loud and bright and squawky.

"Bye, kids! Have fun!" she called as we drove off.

Fun? I sincerely doubted it. I felt a prickle of nausea as we made a left onto School Street—how original—and pulled up in front of a brick building with the words DANIEL WEBSTER SCHOOL carved in stone above the entrance. A bunch of kids were milling around outside, trying to make a snowman, but the snow was too dry and powdery.

We went directly to the front office inside, where the principal came out to greet us.

"You must be Dinah Lovejoy," he said, shaking Mom's hand. "I'm John Burnside—J. T. and I were at school here together many moons ago. I was so sorry to hear about his injury."

That's another thing about small towns. Everybody knows everybody, and everybody knows everybody's business.

"I'm looking forward to catching up with him as soon as you're settled in," Mr. Burnside continued. "I hear he and True are going to be running the bookshop?"

"That's right," Mom replied.

"Excellent, excellent. Wish you could have been here for the good-bye party for Walt and Lola. It was a humdinger." He cocked his head and looked me and my siblings over. *Flamingo*, I thought. Tall and bony, with thinning red hair and a skinny neck that popped up out of his shirt collar like a periscope, Mr. Burnside reminded me of the large pink birds we saw last spring break in Florida. I half expected him to tuck one leg up under him, the way flamingos often do. "We certainly are looking forward to having Lovejoys here at our school again."

"And they're certainly looking forward to being here, aren't you, kids?" said my mother, nudging Hatcher, who nodded and gave the principal one of his big sunflower smiles.

"You'll practically double our school population!" Mr. Burnside joked.

That almost wasn't a joke, as it turned out. Daniel Webster School had fewer than a hundred students, with kindergarten through eighth grade all crammed under one roof.

"It's like the one-room schoolhouse in *Little House on the Prairie*!" said Lauren, sounding excited.

Mr. Burnside laughed. "Not quite."

After sorting out all the paperwork and locker assignments, our new principal offered to show my little sisters to their classrooms. Pippa was acting clingy, so my mother went with them.

"Got your lunch?" she called back to me over her shoulder. I nodded, and she blew me a distracted kiss.

"Daniel Webster doesn't have a real middle school, but they put the seventh and eighth graders upstairs so they can pretend like we do," said the bubbly girl who'd been assigned to escort my brother and me to our classrooms. "You're Lovejoys, right? My name is Annie Freeman and I'm in fourth grade. I live on a farm with my family up near the ski run on Lovejoy Mountain."

Not only had Nathaniel Daniel founded the college, he'd also named a mountain and a lake after himself. I guess he figured why not, since he was one of the first settlers in the Pumpkin River Valley. "Mountain" is a pretty grandiose name for the big hill on the far side of the covered bridge, though. Especially for someone like me who spent two years in Colorado, where the real mountains live.

Hatcher's classroom was at the top of the stairs. "You'll like Mr. Mazzini," Annie told him. "He's the most popular teacher in the eighth grade." She grinned. "Of course, he's the only teacher in the eighth grade, except for Mr. Bigelow, who doesn't count, because he teaches science to everybody."

"Good luck," Hatcher said to me, rolling his eyes as he went into his class.

"Thanks," I said. I was going to need it. My brother knows exactly how I feel about the first day at a new school.

"Ms. Ivey is a great teacher too," Annie continued, turning

to look at me. Her braids bounced around on her head like a bouquet of antennae. "She's young and really pretty, and she's funny, too. At least that's what my brother, Franklin, says. He's in your class. I have Mrs. Ballard, who's okay, I guess." Without pausing to take a breath, she chattered on. "So you're from Texas? They say 'howdy' there a lot, don't they? I went to Texas once, to San Antonio for the national spelling bee championship—I'm the best speller in the school, and I won first place in the Grafton County tournament, not that I'm bragging or anything." The girl gave me a sidelong glance to see if I was impressed, but didn't wait for a reply. "I guess our mountain is named after you, huh? Well, your family, I mean. And the college and the bookstore and the lake and everything?"

I nodded silently, wishing the little magpie would shut up. She didn't, of course.

"I love the lake! I go to Camp Lovejoy every summer," she continued. "Last year, I was in a cabin with this girl from Connecticut—that's spelled C-O-N-N-E-C-T-I-C-U-T—and she wet her bed almost every night."

As Annie chattered on, I tuned her out, wondering instead what Mackenzie was up to. It was two hours earlier in Texas, but I decided to send her a text anyway:

SEND HELP! TRAPPED IN HICKSVILLE, USA!

There was no reply. She was either asleep or in the shower. I sighed and slipped my cell phone back in my pocket. Ever since I'd woken up this morning, I'd been hoping this would all go away, and I'd find myself back in Austin. But it was painfully obvious that that wasn't going to happen.

It was time to go into stealth mode.

Hatcher calls this my defense mechanism. It's not that I'm shy—I'm not. Quiet, yes. Shy, no. My growth spurt has put me in the spotlight, though, which is my least favorite place to be. Stealth mode helps, but there's no way I can be completely invisible. I'm too hard to hide. There aren't too many seventh-grade girls who are almost six feet tall—it's like trying to hide a Winnebago in a parking lot full of Mini Coopers. Still, it's not impossible to fade into the wallpaper if you really try. I just stay quiet, speak when spoken to, and generally try to keep a low profile.

So far, it's worked pretty well. Of course, I've had plenty of time to perfect it. This is the sixth school I've attended so far. I went to kindergarten in Alabama, spent first and second grade at Fort Hood near Killeen, Texas, third and fourth in Germany, fifth and sixth in Fort Collins, Colorado, and half of seventh in Austin, Texas. I think it's fair to say that when it comes to stealth mode, I'm a pro.

"This is it," said Annie, her dark braids bobbing again as she skipped ahead to hold my new classroom door open for me.

"Thanks."

"You're w-e-l-c-o-m-e," she replied, smiling broadly.

Despite the fact that my stomach was churning and Annie was mildly annoying, I couldn't help smiling back. I'd have to remember to introduce her to Lauren. I had a feeling that the two of them would really get along.

"Welcome!" said Ms. Ivey, coming over to greet me. Annie was right; Ms. Ivey was really pretty. Her slightly upturned nose crinkled in a friendly way when she smiled. *Definitely a chickadee*, I thought as she took the enrollment form I was holding.

"Trudy Lovejoy, is it?" she said, glancing at it.

"Truly," I corrected her.

"What a pretty name! Truly original." She smiled at me again, and just like with Annie I couldn't help smiling back, even though it's kind of a dumb joke and I've heard it a zillion times before. I felt myself relax just a teeny bit. Pumpkin Falls might be a hick town, but so far the people I'd met were all really nice.

"Truly Gigantic," said someone from the back of the room in a stage whisper.

*Okay, maybe not all of them*, I thought, reddening.

"That's enough, Scooter," Ms. Ivey said sharply, and the ripple of snickers ceased. "Is that any way to welcome a new classmate? Where are your manners?" She scanned the room. "Let's see, Truly, why don't you take a seat next to Cha Cha Abramowitz."

She propelled me toward a petite girl who was curled up

in her chair with her legs folded gracefully under her. No bird here—Cha Cha Abramowitz was all cat. She had catlike eyes, too, large and green, and a short fluff of dark hair. Ms. Ivey introduced us, then made a beeline for the back of the room, where an argument had broken out. I was guessing the boy named Scooter was at the bottom of it.

"Truly, huh?" said the girl, who had a surprisingly deep voice for such a small person. "That's kind of unusual."

"And Cha Cha isn't?"

She grinned. "It's Charlotte, actually. My little brother couldn't pronounce it when he was a baby, and his nickname for me kind of stuck. Plus, my parents own a dance studio, so it fits. I don't mind, really."

"I don't mind my name either," I told her, which was a total lie. It's a pain to always have to explain to people that no, it's not a typo, my name isn't Trudy, it's Truly. It *should* have been Trudy, but the moron who was processing immigrants the day my great-great-great-grandmother got off the boat from Germany couldn't read. He took one look at her passport—which our family still has, framed on a wall at Gramps and Lola's house, which even I can decipher, which proves the guy really *was* a moron—and wrote down Truly instead of Trudy on her official papers. There's been a Truly in the family ever since. My Aunt True is really a Truly too, but she's always gone by True. Which is probably a good thing, now that we're both living in Pumpkin Falls. Too many

Trulys in this tiny town might make it explode or something.

"Looks like you could use a little help with pre-algebra," Ms. Ivey said, not unkindly, when she looked over the results from the math section of my placement tests a little while later.

"Uh, yeah. My father's going to tutor me."

She nodded. "Excellent."

Behind us, the door to the classroom flew open.

"Lucas?" trilled a blue sleeping bag. Or what I thought at first was a blue sleeping bag. On closer inspection, I saw that it was actually a slender woman in a puffy, ankle-length down coat. Her face was partially hidden by its hood, but I caught a glimpse of bright blue eyes. As they came to rest on a pale, skinny boy sitting near Cha Cha and me, I thought, *Blue jay*. Her gaze had that same intent look I'd seen on jays just about everywhere we'd lived.

"There you are!" said the woman, sounding relieved. "The weather forecast is predicting more snow, so I thought I'd better stop by on my way to work and bring you some extra mittens." She held up a pair of red ones.

"Thank you, Mrs. Winthrop," said Ms. Ivey, neatly intercepting the boy's mother as she started across the classroom toward him.

"Be sure Lucas puts them on before he leaves this afternoon!"

"I certainly will, Mrs. Winthrop," said Ms. Ivey, plucking the mittens away and gently maneuvering her back toward the door.

"I'll have hot chocolate waiting!" Mrs. Winthrop promised, waving at Lucas.

Ms. Ivey closed the door firmly behind her. But Mrs. Winthrop wasn't done yet. She tapped on the glass window and blew her son a farewell kiss.

Scarlet-faced, Lucas slunk down in his seat.

"Lucas!" mimicked someone from the back of the room, his voice going all high and squeaky. "Did you remember to put on clean underwear this morning?"

"Stuff a sock in it, Scooter," boomed Cha Cha, "or I'll remind everybody about the time you came to school wearing Jasmine's tap shoes."

"I think you just did," I blurted, the words popping out before my stealth-mode filter had a chance to activate.

The classroom erupted in laughter. Lucas shot Cha Cha and me a grateful look. I glanced over my shoulder at the boy called Scooter. He was looking directly at me, scowling. Definitely a bird of prey.

So much for stealth mode. I'd just made my first enemy in Pumpkin Falls.

# CHAPTER 6

"A bunch of us are going sledding after school," Cha Cha told me a little while later, as we were heading downstairs to the cafeteria. She was as short as Mackenzie, and I could tell by the looks some of the other kids were giving us that we made a funny-looking pair. "Want to come?"

I hesitated. Stealth-mode protocol called for me to lie low until I was part of the school scenery, instead of a very tall novelty. I'd been trying that all morning, though, and Cha Cha wasn't letting me get away with it. She was determined to be friends.

"It will be fun!" she urged.

"I can't," I told her. "I have to go to the bookstore."

Cha Cha knew all about Lovejoy's Books. It turns out she and her family had been at the going-away party for Gramps and Lola. Pretty much everybody in town had been invited, I guess.

She frowned. "Can't you go later?"

*You don't know my father*, I thought. Lieutenant Colonel Jericho T. Lovejoy doesn't do later.

"There's this tutoring thing," I replied, and then, as Cha Cha looked at me expectantly, I caved, spilling the whole story about my math grade, and my father's reaction, and how it meant I'd be tutored every day for the foreseeable future.

"Well, if you have to be stuck someplace, the bookstore isn't such a bad spot," she said when I was done.

I looked at her in surprise. Cha Cha didn't strike me as the bookworm type.

"It's one of my favorite places in town," she continued, holding the cafeteria door open for me. "When I was little, I used to like their Story Hour better than the one at the library, because your grandmother made treats to go with whatever we were reading. You know, like cupcakes with little candy carrots on top when we read *Peter Rabbit*. Plus," she added, "my brother and I love Miss Marple."

Miss Marple is Gramps and Lola's golden retriever. Named after the elderly detective in Agatha Christie's mystery series, she's the store mascot. Her picture is on the bookmarks given out with every purchase.

"Everybody loves Miss Marple," I agreed as I followed Cha Cha to a table by the window.

"Hey, Cha Cha, can I eat with you?"

I looked over to see a tiny boy standing beside us. His face, which barely reached the tabletop, wore a hopeful expression.

"Sure, Bax, have a seat," Cha Cha told him, patting the bench beside her. "This is my brother," she told me as he clambered up. "Baxter, this is Truly."

"Hi," said Baxter shyly.

"Hi back," I replied.

"Tell Truly what grade you're in," Cha Cha said, and her little brother proudly held up one finger.

Baxter Abramowitz was kitten to Cha Cha's cat. He had the same slight build, the same curly dark hair and green eyes and dimple in his cheek. As I watched him eating his peanut-butter-and-jelly-sandwich, it struck me how different Daniel Webster was from any other school I'd ever been at. Not just because all the grades were together in one building, but because it was obvious that what my brother Hatcher calls "the universal cafeteria classification system" didn't seem to have made it as far as Pumpkin Falls. I looked around at the tables, trying to sort out who was who. Usually the jocks sit together, and the drama kids sit together, and so do the gamers, and the skateboarders, and the band kids, and so on. This was the first cafeteria I'd seen since elementary school where everybody sat together in a jumble.

Across the room, I noticed that Annie and my sister had found each other on their own. The two of them were talking a blue streak over their sandwiches. Or more accurately, Annie was talking, and Lauren was listening. What was weird, though, was that they were sitting at what I would normally have thought of as the jock table. Hatcher was beside them, and although Pippa was perched on his knee, he was talking to a bunch of guys who were clearly athletes, including Scooter Sanchez.

"Over here!" boomed Cha Cha all of a sudden, her deep voice making me jump. She waved wildly at a girl just entering the cafeteria, a girl who looked familiar, which was odd, since I was pretty sure we'd never met.

"Jasmine of the tap shoes," Cha Cha told me as she introduced us. "She and Scooter are twins."

My eyebrows shot up. "Ohhhhhh."

"Don't judge me," Jasmine replied quickly, flashing me a smile.

*Raven*, I thought, resisting the urge to reach out and touch her shiny dark shoulder-length hair. I smiled back. "I promise I won't."

"Where were you this morning, Jazz?" asked Cha Cha, and Jasmine bared her teeth at us.

"Orthodontist," she replied.

"Aren't you supposed to get those things off soon?"

Jasmine nodded. "One month left to go. Dr. Wilcox says I should have them off in time for Winter Festival."

"Nice," said Cha Cha, slapping her a high five.

Our table filled up quickly. Besides Cha Cha and Jasmine and Baxter and me, there was Lucas Winthrop, who hadn't spoken a word all morning, Annie Freeman's older brother, Franklin, who was just as friendly as Annie but not nearly as talkative, thank goodness, and Amy Nguyen, whose mother is my mother's academic advisor at the college, as it turned out.

"I'll tell her to make sure your mom gets straight As," Amy said with a friendly smile.

Usually on the first day at a new school, I end up either sitting by myself at lunch, or with someone who's been assigned to be nice to me. This was—different. Good different, though not different enough to make me stop wishing I was back in Austin.

I took a bite of my tuna-fish sandwich and quietly observed my new classmates. Franklin was talking about his family's farm, which from what I could gather was famous for its maple syrup. If his sister Annie was a magpie, thanks to her nonstop chatter, Franklin was definitely a wood thrush. His warm brown skin and eyes were the same shade as the thrush's cinnamon-colored contour feathers. They were also the same color as the syrup his family's farm produced.

"Who's that?" I asked Cha Cha, pointing to a boy across the room who was sitting next to Scooter. I recognized him from our homeroom.

Cha Cha turned around to see. "Oh, that's Calhoun."

"Calhoun who?"

Franklin shrugged. "He just goes by Calhoun."

"Some people call him R. J.," Jasmine added. "His dad

does, anyway. Calhoun is my brother's best friend."

"He moved to Pumpkin Falls last year, when his father took a job at Lovejoy College," Cha Cha explained. "Dr. Calhoun is the president."

Jasmine reached over and helped herself to a piece of Cha Cha's brownie. "I am so not looking forward to science class this afternoon," she said, changing the subject.

"No kidding," said Cha Cha.

"Why? What's happening?" I asked. "We have somebody else for science, right?"

Jasmine nodded. "Mr. Bigelow. It has nothing to do with him, though." She shuddered. "It's frog dissection day."

Lucas Winthrop's already pale face went about three shades paler.

"Eew," I said. We'd done that back in Austin, right before winter break. It was completely disgusting. Maybe if I asked, I'd be allowed to skip the lab and go to the library instead.

"Not going to faint just thinking about it, are you, Lucas?" teased Franklin, his dark eyes alight with amusement.

The tips of Lucas's ears grew pink. He stared down at the table.

"Of course he's not going to faint!" said Jasmine, clapping Lucas on the back. "Just remember what we told you— deep breaths, okay?"

Lucas nodded unhappily. I watched him out of the corner of my eye, trying to decide what bird he was. Lucas Winthrop was even quieter than me in full stealth mode. A humming-bird, maybe?

The bell rang loudly a few minutes later and I cleared away my lunch things and followed Cha Cha and Jasmine and the others back upstairs to the science lab.

"Good news, my friends!" said the teacher, before we could even sit down. "You've been given a reprieve!" He chuckled. "Or perhaps I should say the amphibians have been given a reprieve."

Short, bald as a grape, and slightly overweight, the science teacher was definitely a duck, I thought, watching as he waddled over to greet me.

"You must be Truly Lovejoy," he said. "I'm Mr. Bigelow. You picked a fine day to join us—you're in for a treat." Turning back to the rest of the class, he clapped his hands. "Bundle up and meet me down by the front office in exactly five minutes! We're going on a field trip!"

"No frogs?" whispered Lucas.

"That's correct, Mr. Winthrop. No frogs."

Lucas looked visibly relieved.

Mr. Bigelow didn't leave us in suspense as to our destination.

"We're off to see the wizard—I mean the falls," he joked, and a collective groan went up around the room.

"Seriously, Mr. B?" said Franklin. "The waterfall?"

"Not just any waterfall, a *world-famous* waterfall," Mr.

Bigelow replied. "Don't you read the newspaper?"

Was he talking about the *Pumpkin Falls Patriot-Bugle?* I wondered. He didn't seriously expect us to take some podunk newspaper's word for it, did he? I doubted anyone outside of the Pumpkin River Valley had even heard of the falls.

"The last time the falls froze over was 1912, and they may not freeze again for another hundred years," our science teacher continued. "This is history in the making, my friends! Grab your jackets, and those of you who have cell phones with cameras, I'm setting aside my no-cell-phone rule for the afternoon. Bring them along—you're going to want pictures. I guarantee you'll tell your grandchildren about this someday!"

*Fat chance*, I thought as we headed for our lockers.

Outside, I was glad to see that the snow had stopped. As we followed Mr. Bigelow toward town, Scooter and Calhoun and some of the other boys started jostling each other. Ms. Ivey, who had come along to help chaperone, was keeping a close eye on them. I noticed Lucas sticking to Franklin and Jasmine like a burr. For protection from Scooter and Calhoun, probably.

"That's our family's place," Cha Cha told me proudly as we turned the corner onto Main Street. She pointed across the street to a large building that stood between a Kwik Klips hair salon (*"We cater to student budgets!"*) and Earl's Coins and Stamps, which had been there for as long as I could remember, and which I couldn't believe was still in business because really, who collects coins and stamps anymore?

"The Starlite Dance Studio," I replied, reading the sign. "Cool," I added politely.

I peered in the window as we passed Lovejoy's Books. My father was nowhere to be seen, but I spotted Aunt True. She had her back to us and was doing something to one of the bookshelves. Inventory, probably.

The next block contained an antiques store, a laundromat called the Suds 'n Duds, and Lou's Diner, which smelled wonderfully of fresh donuts.

"Our field trip just might include a stop here on the way back," Mr. Bigelow said, pausing to sniff the air. "If you all behave yourselves, that is."

Just then the diner door burst open and Lucas's mom appeared, looking anxious.

"Is everything all right?" Mrs. Winthrop asked breathlessly. "Are you evacuating?"

Out of the corner of my eye I saw Scooter elbow Calhoun. Poor Lucas. They'd be making hay with that one.

"Everything's fine, Amelia," said Ms. Ivey. She gave her arm a soothing pat. "Just a field trip to the falls, nothing to worry about."

"Field trip? In this weather?" Mrs. Winthrop wrapped her arms around her light blue waitress uniform and shivered. "Lucas should have an extra scarf." She dashed inside and reappeared a moment later with a bright red one, obviously hers, and obviously a match to the bright red mittens she'd dropped off earlier, which Lucas was dutifully wearing. Much to Lucas's chagrin, his mother managed to dodge Ms. Ivey this time, and in a flash he was wrapped up tight as a burrito. "There," Mrs. Winthrop said, kissing the top of his head. "That should keep you cozy." Turning to the rest of us, she added, "Be careful, kids—it's slippery with all this snow."

The minute the door to the diner closed behind her, the boys at the back of the line exploded with laughter.

"Are we *evacuating*?!" howled Scooter. "Ooh, Lucas, are you all *cozy* now?"

"Scooter!" warned Ms. Ivey, marching over to deal with him.

"Poor kid," I murmured, as Lucas drooped off after Mr. Bigelow.

Cha Cha nodded. "I know. Talk about a helicopter parent! My mother says Mrs. Winthrop really should have a bunch more kids to keep her busy. Lucas is an only child, and she hovers over him, like, well—"

"A helicopter?"

"Exactly."

We smiled at each other.

The bell in the church steeple struck a single note as we made our way past the Pumpkin Falls Savings & Loan, the library, the post office, and Town Hall.

"That's where my parents work," Jasmine told me, pointing to a white clapboard house across the village green. The sign out front said SANCHEZ & SANCHEZ. "They're both lawyers."

"So do you live upstairs?"

She shook her head. "There's an apartment upstairs, but my parents rent it out to one of the college professors. We live on Oak Street, just up the hill from your grandparents' house."

We continued on, and Jasmine and Cha Cha started talking about the Winter Festival, which apparently is a big deal this year since it's celebrating its one hundredth anniversary, plus it's scheduled for Valentine's Day weekend so it's an even bigger deal. As the two of them talked, I spotted a pair of juncos and heard the distinctive *chick-a-dee-dee-dee* that let me know there was a black-capped chickadee or two flitting through the nearby evergreens. Hearing them reminded me that I needed to put out more sunflower seed and suet in the backyard and make sure the electric heater in the birdbath was working properly. Gramps had left me full instructions on taking care of his beloved feathered backyard visitors.

A few minutes later we reached our destination.

I've always really liked the covered bridge in Pumpkin Falls. Whenever we'd come to visit Gramps and Lola, spotting the bridge was a game our family would play in the car after the long drive north from the airport in Boston. Each of us kids would jockey for position, straining for a glimpse of it as we came down the hill and around the final corner toward town. The first one to yell, "I see the bridge!" after it came into view won a dollar to spend at the General Store's penny candy counter.

Seeing the bridge used to be exciting. Now, though, all it did was remind me that I was stuck in a town tiny enough to actually *have* a covered bridge.

Still, I had to admit that its cardinal-red exterior looked pretty against the snow-covered landscape. I paused and snapped a picture of it with my cell phone to send to Mackenzie, then followed my classmates as Mr. Bigelow funneled us through the entrance.

"Stay to the right, please!" he told us. "Single file—leave plenty of room for cars."

Our footsteps echoed through the bridge's wooden interior. Overhead arched a puzzle of interlaced rafters, and to the right was a solid waist-high partition topped with a lattice of crosspieces, like a row of large *X*s.

We spread out along the partition. I leaned against it and looked down at the river, then at the falls.

Which were frozen, just as promised.

It was oddly quiet. Usually you could hear the roar of the Pumpkin River as it tumbled over the falls and rushed underneath the bridge, but now there was silence. Even Scooter didn't have any smart-alecky comments. A stone's throw from us, the frozen waterfall spanned the river from bank to bank, white as the marshmallow frosting on my favorite birthday cake.

"Listen up, everyone!" said Mr. Bigelow. He clapped his hands, and the sound bounced off the bridge's wooden floor and walls. "I want you to start by just observing. Feel free to take pictures if you'd like, sketch if you'd like, jot down notes if you'd like. I'll give you five minutes!"

Beside me, Lucas pulled out a small notebook and a pencil and began to draw. I glanced over his shoulder and watched him for a minute or two; he was pretty good. Then I turned my attention to the river. Most of it was frozen, and the parts that weren't were remarkably still—so still that I could see the reflection of the bridge's red paint. I took a picture of that, too. Directly below us, some water was still flowing between the clumps of ice, and I watched for a while as it swirled lazily around the stone pillars holding up the bridge. Then I glanced over Lucas Winthrop's shoulder again. He was adding a graffiti-speckled rafter above his sketch of the waterfall.

Curious, I glanced up. The rafters were decorated with names, hearts, arrows, dates—the oldest one I spotted was 1899—and interlinked initials, sure signs that Cupid had been here. Directly overhead I saw SAM LOVES BETTY; JOJO AND CARL; and E & T FOREVER drawn inside a slightly lopsided heart. I took a few more pictures.

I was so busy looking up that I didn't notice Scooter and Calhoun until they were practically on top of me.

"Whatcha looking at?" Scooter demanded.

"Nothing," I replied coolly.

He looked up, too, then nudged Calhoun. "Got a pen?"

Calhoun fished in his jacket pocket and produced one.

"Gimme a boost—I'm going to add 'Truly Gigantic loves Lucas,'" Scooter told him, and Calhoun snickered.

"Morons," I muttered.

Calhoun bent over and laced his fingers together. As Scooter placed a foot in his grip and Calhoun started to hoist him into the air, Mr. Bigelow suddenly materialized.

"Don't even think about it, boys," he said. "Besides the fact that it's incredibly dangerous, defacing the bridge is a very big no-no, and the town will charge you a very big fine."

Scooter removed his foot from Calhoun's grasp and held his hands palm up in the classic *Who, me?* gesture.

Mr. Bigelow squeezed in between us and leaned on the railing, looking out at the falls. Several of my classmates drifted over. "Drink it in, kids, drink it in," he said. "The minute the January thaw arrives, which should be any day now, this will all be water under the bridge." He waggled his eyebrows at his stupid pun, and a chorus of groans went up around me. I could tell that my classmates really liked Mr. Bigelow, though. I was beginning to, as well.

"So," he continued, "who knows why the early settlers built covered bridges in the first place?"

Franklin's hand shot up.

"Yes, Franklin?"

"To keep snow off the bridge?"

"Indeed!" said Mr. Bigelow. "A buildup of heavy snow could collapse a wooden bridge like this one, which would have been disastrous for a town like Pumpkin Falls, cutting it off from the outside world. Instead, the slope of the roof allows the snow to fall harmlessly into the river." He looked around. "Anyone else?" None of us rushed to answer, so he continued, "Covering a bridge also protected it from the elements, preventing rot. Our thrifty Yankee forbears liked the idea of extending a bridge's useful life by a couple of decades." He winked. "Plus, I wouldn't put it past them to have figured out that someday covered bridges would attract tourists."

"So how do waterfalls freeze, exactly?" asked Jasmine.

"Why, thank you for asking, Miss Sanchez!" said our science teacher. "Water freezes at thirty-two degrees Fahrenheit—you all know that. But for moving water, it's a little more complicated."

He went on to explain that as water cools below the freezing point, the molecules slow down and start to stick together, forming crystals. Ms. Ivey passed around a handout with diagrams showing those stuck-together bits, which were called "frazil."

"You'll note they're roughly one millimeter in diameter," Mr. Bigelow went on. "Very tiny, but small is mighty in this case. As the frazil clump together, they form snow in the air, ice in the water. Now in the case of moving water, they first accumulate against solid surfaces—like those rocks over there along the riverbank, or the bridge's supports below us." He pointed to the top of the falls. "See those icicles up there?"

We nodded.

"Those started as clumps of frazil. And so did that," he added, pointing to the broad ledge of ice that had formed at the bottom of the falls. It appeared to be holding up the entire mass of frozen water that had once been the waterfall. "Look at all the different formations! Chandeliers of icicles! Undulating folds! And all those nodules and layers and cauliflower lumps! It's like something out of a fairy tale." He sighed happily. "Isn't nature spectacular?"

I fished my binoculars out of my backpack (a birder is never without her binoculars) to inspect the waterfall more closely. Now I could see that the ledge of ice at the bottom was actually an inch or two above the river.

"Water is still getting through underneath that ledge, right?" I asked. "It's not frozen solid, I mean."

"Ah, our new student has sharp eyes," said Mr. Bigelow. "And binoculars! Extra points for bringing binoculars. You are correct, Truly. Water is still flowing through, though at a much slower speed than usual."

I panned across the face of the waterfall, then stopped. Hanging down from the top of the falls was something that looked like a large, frozen tube. With the aid of my binoculars, I could see a fine spray of mist emerging from the end of it, like clothes out of a laundry chute.

"What's that?" I asked, handing my binoculars to my science teacher.

"Oh my," Mr. Bigelow breathed when he spotted it. "Students, you all need to see this." He passed the binoculars down the row of my classmates. "That, my friends, is very rare! You can actually see the waterfall in the process of freezing from the outside in. At the moment, water is still flowing through it, like a pipe. Eventually, though, if this cold weather continues, it will freeze into a solid column of ice."

I stood there for a long time, gazing at the waterfall and thinking, oddly enough, of my father. Had his injury frozen him from the outside in? And was the father I'd known all my life still in there somewhere, a trickle of him at least?

# CHAPTER 7

"See you tomorrow," said Cha Cha.

We were standing outside Lovejoy's Books, finishing up the donuts Mr. Bigelow had bought for us at Lou's Diner, just like he'd promised. The rest of our class had gone back to school, but our teachers had let the two of us remain behind downtown since I was headed to the bookstore anyway and Cha Cha was going to the dance studio. Their receptionist was on maternity leave, and Cha Cha's mother had texted her to see if she could fill in for half an hour while she taught a tango class.

"Have fun sledding later," I replied.

"Thanks. Have fun with pre-algebra." She laughed as I made a face, then waved good-bye and crossed the street.

I waved back, then stepped inside the bookshop—and right into the middle of an argument.

"No cat, and that's final!" said my father in his Lieutenant

Colonel Jericho T. Lovejoy you'd-better-not-answer-back voice.

Aunt True laughed, which startled me. Laughter is not the usual response to one of my father's orders. "Who made you boss?" she retorted.

The two of them were too wrapped up in their quarrel to notice me, so I quietly slung my jacket and backpack onto the old church pew by the door that served as a bench.

My father's face was the same color as Lucas Winthrop's mitten-and-scarf set, a sure warning sign that an explosion was imminent. This didn't seem to faze Aunt True in the least.

"We're running this place together, J. T., remember?" she continued.

"We're already saddled with a stupid dog," my dad told her. "We don't need a cat, too."

The "stupid dog" in question was curled up on her bed by the sales counter, watching this exchange anxiously.

"Memphis has been with me through thick and thin," replied Aunt True. "He'll get lonely upstairs all by himself."

Aunt True had been dog-sitting until we got settled. Miss Marple was scheduled to go home with us tonight, and Lauren could hardly contain herself. She's always wanted a dog, but our constant moves—one of them overseas—had ruled that out.

"Besides," Aunt True continued, "the two of them are already great friends."

It was possible that she was stretching the truth. Memphis

was perched on the sales counter staring balefully down at my grandparents' dog, his coal-black tail lashing back and forth. By the wary expression on Miss Marple's face as she glanced up at him, I figured it for an uneasy truce at best.

"The two of us are a package deal," Aunt True stated firmly. "If Memphis goes, I go."

Hearing her bicker with my father reminded me of Hatcher and Danny. It was weird to think that to Aunt True, my dad wasn't a lieutenant colonel in the United States Army, but just her baby brother.

The muscles in my father's jaw twitched. He swiveled on his heel. "Fine," he said, stalking off toward the office. "But one whiff of litter box and he's out of here."

Aunt True spotted me and smiled. "Truly!" She came over and gave me a hug. "Cup of tea?"

"No, thanks," I replied.

"You'd better be off to the dragon's lair, then." She nodded toward the office door. "Watch your step in there; he's a little cranky today. Bossy older sister, out of his element, too many pets. You know the drill."

She disappeared toward the back of the store and I headed into the office. "Truly Lovejoy reporting for duty," I announced with a smart salute, hoping to get a smile out of my father.

No such luck. He was too busy frowning at a piece of paper clamped in the steel pincers at the end of his prosthesis.

"I've got you set up over there," he said, waving his left hand at the other desk.

I slid into the beat-up leather swivel chair in front of it and stared glumly at the book that was waiting for me. *Pre-Algebra for the Clueless!* blared the familiar bright blue-and-black cover from the Clueless series.

"We'll start at the beginning and work our way through," my father said, still not looking up.

"But—" I began. It wasn't like I was a complete moron at math, after all.

"A firm foundation is the key to success," he continued, ignoring my protest. "That and review, review, review. Oh, and there are worksheets, too."

Of course there were. I sighed and opened the book. At the beginning, just like he'd ordered.

An hour later, my head was spinning. I was algebra-ed and Lieutenant-Colonel-Jericho-T.-Lovejoy-ed out. "Can I go help Aunt True now, please?" I begged, handing over my latest worksheet.

My father inspected the results, then nodded. "Dismissed."

I scuttled out before he could change his mind.

Aunt True was nowhere to be seen, but I could hear rustling in the back of the store. I found her in the room that Lola and Gramps called the Annex, where all the used books were kept. Most of the books in the store are new, but my grandparents have always had a spot where they shelved used ones.

My aunt looked up. "How'd it go?"

I made a face, and she laughed.

"Maybe this will be more fun." She passed me a hand-held scanner and steered me to a back corner of the room. "If you could start on this shelf over here, that would be great. Just take one book at a time and scan the bar code, okay? The computer will do the rest. Any books without bar codes—and there are bound to be some—go in this basket. I'll deal with them later."

She walked me through the scanning procedure a couple of times to make sure I knew what I was doing, then patted me on the shoulder. "I'll leave you to it, then. Your father and I have a meeting with the accountant in a few minutes." She started to walk away. "Let me know if you find any treasures," she called back over her shoulder. "Lovejoy's Books could use all the good news it can get right now."

I took the scanner and started in on my assigned task. Half an hour later, I pulled a book off the shelf that would change everything.

# CHAPTER 8

I'm not sure why I took my discovery home with me.

I probably should have just given it to Aunt True, or to Dad. By the time I found the envelope tucked inside an old copy of *Charlotte's Web*, though, they were already in the meeting with their accountant and Danny was double-parked outside, honking the horn. So I just stuffed the envelope in my backpack, grabbed Miss Marple, and left.

Dinner was the usual Magnificent Seven mayhem, as my father used to call it before Black Monday.

"Toot Soup!" cried Danny, as Hatcher ladled some into his bowl.

"Don't start," my mother warned.

Too late. My little sisters were already giggling. "Toot Soup" is what my brothers call bean soup, because of the inevitable sound effects it produces. Knowing we'd be busy with the first day of school, Aunt True had made a pot of it for us and dropped it by, along with a salad and some bread.

Eyes dancing behind her sparkly pink glasses, Pippa spooned up a bite, then made a rude noise. Lauren snickered.

"Pipster," said my mother severely. "Do you want to eat in the barn with Miss Marple?"

Pippa thought this was a great idea. Between trying to settle her down, Hatcher and Danny's instant replay of their first wrestling practices, and Lauren's glowing report on her new friend Annie, I was squeezed out of the dinner conversation as usual.

I'd brought the envelope with me to the table, but even if I'd had the opportunity to tell everybody about it, in the end something held me back. I decided to keep the secret to myself for a little while longer.

After dinner, I went directly upstairs. One of the only good things about moving to Pumpkin Falls is Gramps and Lola's house. The house Dad grew up in is so big, half the town could move in and we'd never bump into one another.

All of us kids have a bedroom of our own, and there are still a couple left over. Hatcher and Danny have taken over the entire third floor, and I even have my own bathroom, which was where I was headed. It's the warmest spot in the house.

Locking the door behind me, I sat down on the floor by the radiator. It's one of the old steam-heat kind, like all the others in the house. They hiss and rattle and clank so much it sounds like a bunch of baby dragons are on the loose. But they do the trick as far as keeping the house warm, which I guess is the main thing when you live in a climate as cold as this one. I leaned back against the claw-foot tub and pulled the envelope out of my pocket.

It was sealed shut, and as far as I could tell had never been opened. Why would someone leave a letter stuck in an old copy of *Charlotte's Web*? Had they meant to mail it, and forgotten? Or had they left it there deliberately for someone to find? There wasn't an address on the envelope, or even a real name—just the capital letter *B*. But the envelope had a stamp on it, like it was all ready to send.

So why hadn't it been?

I traced the *B* on the front with my forefinger, wondering if I should open it. I was pretty sure that was some sort of a crime, though. Mail tampering or interfering with the US Postal Service or something. I didn't want to get arrested. On the other hand, if I didn't open it, how was I supposed to figure out who it was meant for? What if it were something important?

"Truly?"

I jumped as someone hammered on the door. It was my brother.

"Hatcher!" I hollered. "You about scared me to death!"

"Quit barking at me. Someone's on the phone for you."

I scrambled to my feet and returned the envelope to my back pocket. Maybe it was Mackenzie. She'd know what to do.

It wasn't Mackenzie, though; it was Cha Cha.

"I'm calling to see if you want to sign up for a practice slot," she said. "They're going fast."

"Practice slot for what?"

"Cotillion."

I had no idea what she was talking about.

"Didn't Ms. Ivey tell you about Cotillion?" she asked as I hesitated.

"Um, maybe?" I'd come home with a stack of newsletters and sign-up sheets and flyers, all of which were still in my backpack upstairs in my room.

I, meanwhile, was now perched on a rickety old wooden chair in a tiny closet tucked under the front hall stairs. The closet contained the only landline in the house, an ancient rotary-style phone that looked like a relic from some old movie. Dad says it's the same one that was here when he was a kid, and that it's always been in the makeshift phone booth under the stairs. Gramps and Lola aren't much for change.

"So here's the deal," Cha Cha continued. "All middle schoolers at Daniel Webster are required to attend Cotillion."

"Which is?" I prodded a stack of moldy phone books with the toe of my sneaker. Above me, a bare bulb dangled from the ceiling. Not exactly the kind of place for a lingering conversation.

"Kind of a tradition in Pumpkin Falls. My mom calls it a rite of passage. Cotillion is a series of dance classes we all take at school, and then the big finale is during Winter Festival, when we get to show off what we've learned at the town's annual dance."

I had no idea how to respond. A dance that the entire *town* went to? What planet was I on?

"We're lucky," Cha Cha continued. "Now that we're in middle school, we get to do ballroom instead of a stupid square dance, like the younger kids have to do. Anyway, it'll be starting up soon."

"You're telling me I have to take a *ballroom dance* class?" I could feel panic rising in me. Dancing is practically at the top of the list of things I'm not good at. "You're kidding, right?"

Cha Cha was very quiet. *Uh-oh*, I thought. Had I just insulted her?

Apparently not. "Nope, I'm not kidding," she said cheerfully. "In fact, my parents will be teaching it."

I could hear music in the background, and people talking. "Where are you?"

"At the Starlite. Anyway, in addition to the class at school, everybody's required to attend two private practice sessions here at the studio with my parents. There's no charge, of course."

"Of course," I echoed, still feeling stunned.

"So how does the Saturday after next sound?"

"Fine, I guess," I said, wondering whether I should tell Cha Cha about the letter. I pulled it out of my back pocket.

"Oops, gotta go," she said, before I could bring it up. "There's a call on the other line. I'll pencil you in for eleven thirty. Let me know if that doesn't work, okay? See you tomorrow!"

"But—"

She'd hung up.

I sighed and replaced the receiver, turned out the light, and headed back upstairs. I hesitated in front of the door leading to the third floor, but a series of random thumps from above signaled that my brothers were practicing their wrestling moves. It probably smelled like the boys' locker room up there, plus they got cranky when they were interrupted. I'd talk to Hatcher later.

"Truly!"

I poked my head into my sisters' bathroom to see my mother holding up a towel for Pippa. Pippa's old enough to get ready for bed on her own, but she likes to have Mom help her. It's part of being the baby of the family, I guess.

"How was your first day, sweetie?" my mother asked, as Pippa climbed out of the tub. "I didn't get to talk to you much at dinner."

Sometimes it feels like I'm more in stealth mode at home than anywhere else.

"It was okay," I replied.

"Make any new friends?"

I shrugged. "Maybe."

My mother smiled. "Good. You can tell me all about it in the morning. I need to get a start on my homework once I'm done here. Oh, and Hatcher said he has a bunch of forms for me to sign, so you probably do too. Go ahead and leave them on the kitchen table for me, okay?"

I nodded.

"Say good night to Truly." My mother gave my little sister a nudge, and she trotted obediently over, holding her arms up for a hug. I bent down and embraced her gingerly, since she was still pretty damp. She smelled good, though, and I nuzzled her hair. Pippa might be a drama queen, but I love her anyway.

"Night, Pip," I said.

"Night, Truly."

I headed down the hall to my room, pausing by Lauren's door. It was open just a crack, and a strange noise was coming from the other side. I peeked in to see her flopped on her stomach on her bed, reading. No big surprise there. That was Lauren's usual after-dinner routine. And before-dinner routine, and every-other-time-of-day routine. She was patting her pet rabbit, Thumper, with one hand while she turned the pages of her book with the other. She didn't look up. When Lauren was engrossed in a book, World War III could start and she wouldn't notice.

Thumper was curled up beside her, wearing a doll-size

nightgown and a resigned expression. My sister loves dressing up her pets. She'd put a baseball cap on Miss Marple too, who was lying on the braided rug next to the bed, keeping a wary eye on the source of the strange noise—a clear plastic hamster ball rocketing around the room and periodically crashing into the furniture. Nibbles was enthusiastic about exercise.

Miss Marple heaved herself to her feet when she spotted me. I motioned to her to stay, but she ignored me. Toenails clicking briskly across the bare wooden floor, she shook off her baseball cap and followed me down the hall to my bedroom. I paused at the door and looked down at her, frowning.

"No, Miss Marple," I told her firmly. "No dogs allowed in here."

Miss Marple sat.

"Go see Lauren," I told her.

She didn't budge.

My sister is the animal lover in the family, not me. It's not that I don't like animals—I do. From a distance. Which is maybe one reason why I like bird-watching so much. Wild birds don't shed and they don't need to be walked or have doggie breath or cages or litter boxes that need cleaning.

Miss Marple gave a tiny whine. One that I interpreted to mean, *I'm afraid of the hamster ball and I don't want to be dressed up in people clothes and I need a place where I can go into stealth mode.*

"Oh, fine," I said, relenting. "You can come in. But just this once."

I was still getting used to my new bedroom. It was cavernous, with high ceilings and big tall windows on two sides. During the day, light poured in from the back and side yards, which was nice, but at night it was kind of creepy, the way the tall windows stared at me blackly. Crossing the room to pull down the shades, I glanced outside to see that the sky had cleared and a full moon was casting a silvery light on the snow.

It was a perfect night for owling.

When I was little and we came to Pumpkin Falls to visit, Gramps used to make up bedtime stories for Danny and Hatcher and me about a family of owls who lived in the barn out back when he was a kid. I asked so many questions about them that he finally bought me a book—*All About Owls*. I still have it. It's on the bookcase by my bed, alongside all the other bird books Gramps has sent me over the years.

Miss Marple settled onto the rug with a wheezy sigh. I pulled down the shades and turned around, pausing for a moment to survey the room. My gaze came to rest on the tiny pottery owl on my dresser, the owl mug full of pencils and pens on my desk, and the black-and-white woodcut of a snowy owl hanging over my bed. The woodcut is my prized possession. I never get tired of looking at it. My mother found it in Germany back when we were living there, and had it framed for me for my birthday.

I guess I kind of have an owl collection.

Owls are my favorite birds. I love their beautiful faces and big round eyes. Plus, talk about stealth mode! Besides the fact that owls have awesome camouflage (their patterned feathers make them really hard to spot), they also have built-in mufflers—velvety-soft filaments on the surface of their feathers and a fringe on the edge that are designed to deaden sound. Owls fly almost completely silently, which is exactly how I'd want to fly if I were a bird.

I went over and sat down on my bed. I ran a finger over the spine of my tattered copy of *Owl Moon*, which sat between the two brass owl bookends Gramps and Lola had given me this past Christmas. *Owl Moon* was my favorite picture book when I was Pippa's age. I still take it out and read it now and then. I always wanted to be that kid in the pictures, the one whose father took him—or was it her?—out on a snowy night to look for owls. But my father was seldom home, and when he was, he was usually in bed early because like practically everybody else in the military he gets up at the crack of dawn, and anyway, we never lived where there were owls nearby.

And now that there might be, he's turned into Silent Man and I'm not a little kid anymore.

I really wished Gramps and Lola were still here. They were both so easy to talk to, and nobody in my family had much time for me lately. Plus, Gramps could have taken me owling.

Thinking about Gramps reminded me that I needed to be

sure and fill up the bird feeders tomorrow. I glanced across the room to the hook on the back of my bedroom door, where my grandfather's old barn coat and wool hat were hanging. I'd found them waiting there when we moved in, along with a bird carving that Gramps had left for me in the pocket. It was a black-capped chickadee with the words *backyard magic* carved on the bottom.

Slipping the mystery envelope out of my pocket, I went and grabbed my laptop off my desk and carried it back over to the bed. I really needed to talk to someone, and was hoping Mackenzie was online.

She was, and a minute later, her face popped up onscreen.

"You got your hair cut!" I said in surprise.

She smiled the same wide Gifford smile I see daily on my mother and Hatcher. "Like it?" She swiveled around so I could check out the sides and back.

"It's really cute," I told her. Of course, everything looks cute on Mackenzie. It's easy to look cute when you come in such a small package.

"It's a lot easier for swimming."

I felt an unwelcome stab of envy. Mackenzie was only on a swim team because of me, and now I might not even be able to swim at all. I changed the subject. "How's Austin?"

My cousin quickly brought me up to speed on what was going on with her family and with everybody at school, including Mr. Perfect Cameron McAllister, of course. According to

Mackenzie, Cameron was even more amazing than ever, and he definitely liked her back because he'd teased her in social studies.

"Mom says that's how you know when a boy likes you," she told me. "So, is Pumpkin Falls as awful as you thought it would be?"

"Worse," I replied. "It's totally Sleepy Hollow here. You'd hate it." I told her about the upcoming Winter Festival, complete with its stupid dance for the entire town, and about stupid Cotillion, and the frozen waterfall that was front-page news, and how Daniel Webster practically qualified as a one-room schoolhouse.

"I think it sounds kind of cool."

"That's because you don't have to live here."

She grinned. "Your room looks nice, at least."

"Yeah."

My room is what Lola calls the Blue Room. It was Aunt True's when she was growing up—her high school yearbooks are still piled on the bottom shelf of the bookcase, right next to my stash of sudoku. Mom and Dad always stayed here before when we used to visit, but now they're in Gramps and Lola's room at the front of the house, so I asked if I could have this bedroom. Blue is my favorite color, and pretty much everything in the room is blue and white, from the braided rug to the bedspread and curtains.

"Tour?" asked Mackenzie.

I held up my laptop and panned slowly around. My grandparents had left all their furniture for us to use, and in addition to a desk and bookcase, I had a white four-poster bed, a rocking chair with a blue-and-white quilt folded over the back, and an old-fashioned dresser topped with a blue lamp and an antique blue-and-white china pitcher and bowl.

"Sweet!" said my cousin when I was done.

I shrugged. I still missed my aqua "Mermaid" room back in Austin. Mom says military families take their homes with them wherever they go. "A house is just a place to put your home," she'd remind us every time we moved. But we Lovejoys have been migratory birds for what feels like forever, always borrowing other people's nests. Even though Gramps and Lola's is a nice one to borrow, my family had finally had a nest of its own back in Austin. And it felt really unfair that we'd had to leave it.

"So did you try out for swim team yet?" Mackenzie asked. "Or is Pumpkin Falls too small to have one?"

I made a face. "It has one, but I'm not on it yet." I told her about the fiasco with my report card.

"Seriously?" My cousin's voice shot up about an octave. "Your dad won't let you swim unless your grade improves? That's harsh."

"Tell me about it. And even if he changes his mind, I'll be super out of shape by the time tryouts roll around."

"So when are they?"

"In a few weeks," I replied.

"Can you get your math grade up by then?"

"I don't know. I hope so." I glanced down at my bedspread and saw the envelope. I'd almost forgotten why I'd wanted to talk to Mackenzie in the first place. "Hey, this weird thing happened today at the bookstore." I explained about the letter I'd found, holding it up so she could see.

"And you haven't opened it yet?" she shrieked in excitement. "What are you waiting for?"

"You really think I should?"

"Duh! Aren't you dying to know what's inside?"

I slid a finger under the envelope's flap and ripped it open. Inside was a yellowed sheet of paper with a quote on it. I read it aloud:

> *Why, what's the matter, that you have such a February face, so full of frost, of storm and cloudiness?*

"That's it?" my cousin said.

"Yup. Except for some numbers and letters underneath." I read those aloud too: "PR2828.A2 B7."

"Weird."

"I know, right?"

"It isn't signed or anything?"

"There's a capital *B*, just like on the front of the envelope." I held the sheet of paper closer to the laptop camera so she could get a good look.

"It's got to be a message for somebody," said Mackenzie, her blue eyes sparkling. "Maybe it's a secret code—you know, spies or something."

I laughed out loud. "Spies? In Pumpkin Falls?"

"It could happen," she insisted.

"No, it couldn't."

"Why not?"

"Because nothing ever happens here," I told her.

"Well, something just did!" my cousin replied. "You've got a mystery on your hands, Truly!"

# CHAPTER 9

I needed to talk to my mother.

Hoping that she might be able to help me solve the puzzle, I headed downstairs, passing under the gaze of several centuries of Lovejoys as I did so.

"Obadiah, Abigail, Jeremiah, Ruth," I chanted, reading the names on the brass plates embedded across the bottom of each of the frames. I slowed as I reached the last two in the lineup—Matthew Lovejoy and his wife, the original Truly. The stair tread creaked loudly as I took another step down, passing Matthew in his Civil War uniform—Union Army, of course—and coming face-to-face with my namesake's portrait. I squinted at it. Did I look like her? I guess our hair was sort of the same color, and we both had brown eyes, but if she'd had freckles like me, the painter hadn't added them.

My mother's voice drifted out from the kitchen, mingling with the clatter of dishes and silverware. "Someone's in the kitchen with Dinah, someone's in the kitchen, I know-oh-oh-oh. . . ."

*Uh-oh*, I thought, suddenly struck by a pang of guilt. Hatcher and I were supposed to have taken care of the supper dishes again tonight, but I'd gotten sidetracked by the envelope.

"Someone's in the kitchen with Dinah"—my mother held the high note for a long moment, then swooped down to the final stanza—"strumming on an old banjo." Her voice was soft and sad, so different from the way Dad used to sing it. He'd always belt it out, tossing us a wink as he slipped his arm around Mom's waist and waltzed her around the room.

Singing and waltzing weren't so much on Dad's agenda these days. At all, in fact.

As I reached the bottom of the stairs, the doorbell rang.

"Could somebody get that?" Mom called. "I'll be out in a sec."

"Sure, Mom," I called back.

I crossed to the front door and opened it, letting in a blast of icy air that nearly knocked me off my feet. A tall woman, nearly as tall as me, stood on our doorstep, dressed in a long black wool coat. Her head was wound so thoroughly in a black scarf that only her eyes were visible. They gleamed behind a pair of black-rimmed glasses, darting around the hall.

*Crow*, I thought. Most definitely a crow.

"Um, can I help you?" I said, as the woman brushed

past me and stepped inside. I closed the door behind her.

She craned over my shoulder, peering into the living room as if she were looking for someone.

"*May* I help you," corrected my mother, emerging from the kitchen. She smiled at our visitor and held out her hand. "I'm Dinah Lovejoy, and this is my daughter Truly."

"Yes, I know." The woman shook Mom's hand, then extricated herself from her scarves, revealing a gaunt face sharply divided by a knife blade of a nose and topped with a pouf of teased hair that looked like it had been dipped in a pot of ink. She carefully patted it into place, her mouth pruning up in a thin smile. "Figured I'd drop this by on my way home," she said, holding out a stack of mail. "I'm Ella Bellow."

"Ahhh," my mother replied, as if that explained everything. "Well, thank you so much, Mrs. Bellow."

The woman looked around again. "I thought I might say hello to J. T., too, if he's in. I heard about what happened to him. We all did, of course. Such a pity. I've known him since he was just a nipper."

I'd never heard my dad called a "nipper" before. I filed this away to share with Hatcher and Mackenzie.

"He's working late at the bookstore tonight," my mother told her. "Inventory, you know."

"Yes, I heard he and his sister were taking over the business. Things haven't been going so well at the shop, from what I understand." She paused. "Not that times aren't tough everywhere—Bud Jefferson over at the coin and stamp shop is struggling too."

My mother's face flushed angrily.

"Think your family can make a go of it?" Mrs. Bellow continued. "I mean, what with J. T.'s condition and all?"

"My husband can do anything he puts his mind to," my mother replied stiffly.

Our visitor's mouth pruned up again. "Well, I suppose time will tell. Good evening to you, Mrs. Lovejoy." She nodded to both of us, then left.

My mother closed the door firmly behind her. "Well, of all the nerve!"

"Who was that?" I asked.

"Only the biggest busybody in Pumpkin Falls! Your grandmother warned me about her. She's the postmistress."

"Is the coast clear?" someone whispered.

My mother and I jumped. Turning around, I saw my father peering out from behind the kitchen door.

"I came in through the barn," he said. "Recognized her car in the driveway. I'm not up to one of Ella's interrogations. Not tonight." He shook his head wearily.

"Truly, I think it's time for you to go on upstairs and get ready for bed," my mother told me.

"What?! It's not even nine o'clock yet!"

"It's been a long day for everyone," she added, with a slight but significant nod in my father's direction.

"But—"

"No buts, honey." She gave me a gentle push toward the stairs. "Go on now."

I hesitated. I could tell my mother was worried about Dad, and I was torn between a wish to be obedient and a burning desire to enlist her help with the mystery envelope.

Obedience won out.

"Yes, ma'am," I said meekly. "See you in the morning."

"Good night, sweetheart." She stretched up to kiss my cheek, then followed my father into the kitchen.

I started upstairs, then paused, listening to the murmur of my parents' voices. Something was clearly up. I snuck back downstairs, flinching as I stepped on the squeaky stair tread. The portrait of the original Truly gave me a disapproving look.

"Yeah, I know," I whispered to her. "It's not polite to eavesdrop."

Tiptoeing down the hall, I peeked through the crack between the kitchen door and its frame.

"Did you get any dinner?" my mother asked my father. "I can fix you a plate of leftovers, if you'd like."

"True and I ordered pizza," my father replied. He shrugged his jacket off and flung it over one of the chairs at the kitchen table. "Though heaven knows we shouldn't have spent the money."

My mother leaned back against the sink. "Is everything okay?"

"Okay?" My father gave a short laugh. "It's a mess, Dinah. A real mess. I don't know how my parents kept the business afloat this last year, even with the bank loan."

I drew back, feeling guilty for listening but unable to pull myself away.

A chair scraped against the floor and I heard my father sit down. "They borrowed some money a while back to help the bookstore through what they told me was 'a dry spell,'" he went on to explain. "The note's coming due soon, and I'm not sure how we're going to pay it."

My mother murmured something I didn't catch.

"The accountant doesn't hold out much hope," my father told her, "but True seems to think we can turn things around. She wants to give it six months, but I just don't think it's worth it. Realistically, it will take every extra cent we have to keep the bank from foreclosing on the loan. We're stretched pretty thin as it is. Even with my pension and the insurance money and all, we still have college for the kids to save for, and we're dipping into savings for your tuition—"

"I'll drop out," my mother said quickly.

"You will not. Better we just admit this whole thing has been a mistake, and call it quits."

"I'll get a part-time job, then."

"On top of a full load of classes plus the kids? C'mon, Dinah."

"I'm willing to give it a go if you are," my mother told

him. "I know you, J. T.—you've never backed away from a challenge in your life. You'll have a hard time forgiving yourself if you don't give this your best shot."

My father was quiet. Seconds ticked by. Then, "Six weeks," he said finally. "I'll give it six weeks."

I turned and crept back upstairs to my room, where I lay in bed awake for a long time.

What if six weeks wasn't long enough?

# CHAPTER 10

"Family meeting tonight," my mother announced at breakfast the next morning.

There were only five of us at the table. Danny was long gone, of course, and so was my father.

"What's up?" asked Hatcher, pouring himself some more orange juice.

I knew exactly what was up. The bookstore, that's what. I looked over at my mother, wondering how she'd answer.

"Nothing to worry about" was all she said, though. Checking her watch, she changed the subject. "I've got to run. Sorry I can't drive you again, but my first class starts in fifteen minutes. Hatcher, you know the way, right?"

My brother nodded. Not that it was even remotely possible to get lost in a town the size of Pumpkin Falls.

"Good," my mother continued. "Be sure and lock the house when you leave."

"What about Miss Marple?" Lauren passed a toast crust to the dog, who was lurking hopefully under the table.

My mother's face fell. "Is she still *here?* Your father was supposed to take her with him to the bookstore!"

"We can drop her off on our way to school," Hatcher told her.

"Will you have time?"

He nodded. "No worries, Mom. We've got your six."

That's military-speak for *We've got your back.*

She looked chagrined. "Guess we still have a few wrinkles to work out with this new routine."

After breakfast, I shooed my sisters upstairs to brush their teeth, then headed for the mudroom.

"Back in a sec," I told Hatcher, who was packing our lunches.

I threw on my jacket and boots, grabbed the plastic container filled with sunflower seed, and bounded out the back door. The glare from the sun on the snow-covered yard made my eyes water. Wading through the drifts over to the nearest feeder, I filled it to the brim, then quickly made the rounds to the other ones. Excited twittering and the rustle of wings in the pine trees that fringed the backyard signaled that my efforts hadn't gone unnoticed. When I was finished, I watched for a moment as chickadees and cardinals began to swoop in for their breakfast. I was tempted to linger, but I'd be late for school if I did.

"Time to go!" Hatcher called, as I stomped the snow off my boots back in the mudroom.

I helped him bundle my sisters into their warm things, and then we left, locking the front door behind us.

"I'm blinded!" Hatcher cried, throwing his hands up in front of his face in mock horror at the bright sunlight. "Help me, Lauren! Help me, Pip!"

He staggered down the front steps and flopped onto his back in the nearest snowbank, making my sisters giggle. I zipped my jacket all the way to the top and pulled my hat farther down around my ears. It might be sunny out this morning, but it certainly wasn't warm.

Hatcher and I swung Pippa between us while Lauren and Miss Marple trotted along behind. At the bottom of Hill Street we took a shortcut across the village green, following the narrow footpath that had been trampled in the snow.

Miss Marple broke into a trot as we reached the other side, dragging Lauren behind her down Main Street. A couple of blocks later, she stopped abruptly in front of Lou's Diner.

My sister tugged on the leash. "C'mon, Miss Marple," she said, but Miss Marple ignored her and sat down on the sidewalk instead.

A moment later the bell over the door jangled and a large balding man in a white apron poked his head out. "There you are," he said, not to us but to the dog. "You're running late this morning, aren't you?" He reached into his pocket and pulled

out a donut hole. "Here you go, milady." He tossed it to Miss
Marple, who caught it neatly and gulped it down.

"No fair!" cried Pippa, her pink glasses sparkling in
the sun.

"You want one too, do you?" The man in the apron
grinned at her. "Hang on a sec." He disappeared back inside,
reappearing a minute later with a small white paper bag.
"Don't expect this kind of treatment every morning," he
warned, handing it to Pippa with a wink. "Gotta save some
for the paying customers. I'm Lou, by the way. You must be
the Lovejoy kids. Welcome to Pumpkin Falls!" He rubbed his
hands together briskly. "I'd better run, it's cold out here!"

The bell over the door jangled again as he went back
inside.

"I like Lou," said Pippa, helping herself to a donut. She
held the bag out to Hatcher and Lauren and me, and the four
of us munched on our treats as we continued down Main
Street. I paused in front of the window of the *Pumpkin Falls
Patriot-Bugle.*

Under a big banner proclaiming PUMPKIN FALLS THEN
AND NOW! was this week's front page, alongside a front page
from 1912. Old and yellowed, it sported what looked like an
identical picture of the frozen waterfall, along with an equally
overexcited headline.

"I can't believe what a big deal they're making out of the
stupid waterfall," I said.

"It *is* a big deal," Lauren insisted. "Annie Freeman said that Ella Bellow said that a TV news crew might be coming up from Boston to film it."

"Oh, well, if *Ella Bellow* said it, then it must be true," I replied.

"Who's Ella Bellow?" asked Hatcher.

"The postmistress. She came by last night while you were upstairs doing your homework. Mom says she's the biggest busybody in town."

"Whatth a buthybody?" asked Pippa.

"Somebody who sticks their nose into other people's business," I told her.

My little sister raised a pink mitten to her own nose and pondered this as we headed for the bookstore. The door was locked, and Pippa skipped over to the window and peered in, then knocked on the glass. A minute later Dad emerged.

"You brought the dog," he said, running his hand through his hair. "I guess I forgot." He took the leash from Lauren, who bent down to scratch Miss Marple behind the ears. Then Pippa had to pat her and give her a good-bye kiss, too, of course.

"You'll be late for school," my father said, tugging on the leash. Miss Marple glanced sorrowfully back at us as the two of them disappeared inside.

"I think she'd rather stay with us," said Lauren.

"Daddy doethn't like Mith Marple," added Pippa sadly, slipping her mittened hand into mine.

Hatcher and I exchanged a glance. Silent Man didn't seem to like much of anything or anybody these days.

"He isn't used to her yet," my brother told her.

We made it to school just before the bell rang.

"Hey," said Cha Cha as I slid into my seat.

"Hey back."

"How was the tutoring session?"

I made a Toot Soup noise.

She grinned. "That bad, huh?"

Between the stuff going on with my dad, the bookstore, and the mystery envelope—now stashed in my backpack—I was practically bursting to talk to someone. A real, live in-person someone, not just an onscreen-Mackenzie-who-was two-thousand-miles-away. My mother was juggling way too much right now and didn't have time for me, I wouldn't see Hatcher again until tonight at suppertime, and Cha Cha was right here. It was time to abandon stealth mode.

"What do you know about Ella Bellow?" I asked her.

"The postmistress? Why?"

I filled her in on Ella's unexpected visit last night.

"She's always fishing for gossip," Cha Cha said, wrinkling her nose. "My mother says she has ears like a fox. Eyes, too. She doesn't exactly read the mail at the post office, but she sure keeps close tabs on the return addresses, and she watches who gets what from whom. I got a check for my birthday from my aunt Sylvia in New York last fall, and Mrs. Bellow knew about it before I did!" She gave me a sidelong glance. "So, was she right? Is the bookstore in trouble?"

I told her about the conversation I'd overheard in the kitchen between my parents.

"Six weeks, huh?" she said when I was done. "Then what happens?"

"I don't know," I replied. There'd be no reason for us to stay in Pumpkin Falls without the bookshop, but we'd sold the house in Austin, and there was no job there for my father anyway, so I doubted we'd move back to Texas. Where would we go? What would we do? I got a pit in my stomach just thinking about it. "And there's more, too," I said, thinking of the envelope. "Can you keep a secret?"

"Sure."

Before I could continue, Ms. Ivey clapped her hands. "If you'd open your social studies books to chapter seven, we'll continue our review of the Constitution and the Bill of Rights."

"We can talk more during study period," Cha Cha whispered.

Ms. Ivey crossed the room to our desks. "Truly," she said, "I've been meaning to ask you something. I coach girls' basketball here at Daniel Webster, and we'd love to have you on the team."

Why is that just because I'm tall, everybody assumes I play basketball?

"There are several other players you've probably met, including Jasmine Sanchez and Amy Nguyen," she continued. "Think you'd be interested?"

I shook my head. "Thanks, Ms. Ivey, but I'm a swimmer." At least I would be, if my father ever let me try out for the team. I didn't tell her that, though.

My teacher gave me a rueful smile. "Too bad. I know you'll have fun swimming, but we could really use a player with your height."

"Truly Gigantic," whispered Scooter as Ms. Ivey went back to her desk, careful not to let her hear him this time.

I ignored him.

"Lucas is on the swim team too," Cha Cha told me.

"Really?" I glanced over at Lucas, sizing him up. I never would have pegged him for a swimmer. Those toothpick arms didn't exactly scream, *Michael Phelps*.

The next hour couldn't pass quickly enough for me. Now that I'd decided to abandon stealth mode, I couldn't wait to spill the beans to Cha Cha. Fortunately, Ms. Ivey paired the two of us up for a research project on the First Amendment, which gave us an excuse to sit together in the library during study period.

"So what's going on?" Cha Cha whispered.

I glanced around. Jasmine and Franklin were at the table nearest to us, but they were busy talking and laughing, and from what I could tell weren't paying us the least bit of attention. "This is," I replied, pulling the envelope from my backpack and passing it to my new friend. "I found it stuck inside an old copy of *Charlotte's Web* at the store yesterday."

Cha Cha opened it and read the letter inside. "Wow! It's kind of like finding a message in a bottle."

I nodded.

Cha Cha read the note again. "Those look familiar," she said, pointing to the numbers beneath the quote.

"Really?"

"Uh-huh," she replied. "They remind me of something, but I don't know what." She picked up the envelope and inspected it. "Wouldn't you love to know who this was meant for, and who sent it? Or didn't send it, I mean. Too bad it was never mailed. A postmark would have given us a date at least."

I grabbed the envelope back. "Cha Cha, you're brilliant!" Heads swiveled in our direction, and I quickly lowered my voice. "Stamps are issued on a specific date—my brother Danny used to collect them."

Cha Cha grinned her catlike grin. "Now who's brilliant? We can stop by Earl's Coins and Stamps after school. They should be able to help us."

Ms. Ivey crossed the room toward us. I whisked the envelope and letter underneath my notebook.

"How are you girls progressing?" she asked.

"We're off to a bit of a slow start," Cha Cha admitted.

Our teacher steered us to some books and websites, and

the rest of the study period passed in a flurry of actual study.

Cha Cha and I didn't have a chance to talk at lunch, because there were too many people around and because Franklin Freeman, who didn't usually babble as much as his little sister, went on and on about the record cold snap, clearly worried about what it could mean for his family's maple syrup harvest.

"If the January thaw doesn't arrive soon, it's really going to affect the flow," he said.

I had no idea what he was talking about, but everybody else at the table nodded sympathetically.

*This entire town is obsessed with weather*, I thought. *And frozen waterfalls, and maple syrup.*

After lunch, it was time for science class again, where it turned out our frog reprieve had only been a temporary one.

"Saddle up, cowboys!" said Mr. Bigelow. "It's showtime!"

I explained to him about how I'd already dissected a frog earlier this year back in Austin, but if I was hoping that he'd let me ditch the lab and go to the library instead, no such luck.

"Terrific! You'll be the expert, then." He steered me to the table where Jasmine and Cha Cha were sitting. Franklin and Lucas were stationed on one side of us; Scooter and Calhoun on the other.

"You ladies are the roses between thorns," quipped Mr. Bigelow. He trotted off, returning a moment later to place a tray containing a dead frog on the table in front of us.

"Eew!" squealed Jasmine, recoiling, and Cha Cha mimed sticking her finger down her throat.

"Courage!" our science teacher told them, plopping trays with more of the limp green specimens in front of the boys.

As soon as Mr. Bigelow's back was turned, Scooter grabbed his frog by one of its hind legs, then leaned over and dangled it in his sister's face.

Jasmine shrieked and batted it away. "Scooter!"

Both the dead frog and Scooter were back in their proper places by the time Mr. Bigelow turned around.

"Is there something I need to know about?" he asked, frowning.

Scooter blinked at him innocently, his face as devoid of expression as the frog's.

"Just that—oh, forget it," said Jasmine. "Brothers," she muttered to Cha Cha and me as our teacher walked away.

"Tell me about it," I replied. "I have two of them." Picking up the lab instructions, I began to read them aloud. "Too bad there isn't an app for this," I grumbled when I was finished.

Cha Cha surreptitiously whipped out her smartphone and tapped on the screen. "Um, actually, there is."

Jasmine's dark eyes lit up. "We should totally use it!"

Mr. Bigelow materialized behind us like a genie summoned from a lamp. "No, you totally shouldn't," he said, plucking the cell phone from Cha Cha's hand. "You know the rules— you're doing this old-school, ladies."

"But why should some poor frog sacrifice his life for us?" Jasmine protested. "It's inhumane!"

"It's for a worthy cause," Mr. Bigelow countered. "Try and think of him as a little green hero, sacrificing his life for science."

"A little green hero who smells revolting," Jasmine said, making a big show of holding her nose. She picked up a scalpel with her other hand. "This is just gross."

Behind us, there was a loud thud. We turned around to see that Lucas had fallen off his lab stool onto the floor. His face was nearly as green as the frog on our tray.

Scooter and Calhoun burst out laughing.

"Shut up, you guys! It's not funny!" cried Cha Cha.

Mr. Bigelow rushed over and helped Lucas sit up. "Deep breaths, now, son," he said, bending him forward so that his head was between his knees. "You're okay—you just fainted."

While Lucas was recovering, Cha Cha rummaged in her backpack.

"Maybe this will help," she said, holding up a bottle of Sassy Lassie perfume.

Jasmine and I stared at her, puzzled.

She gave us an impish grin and tapped the lab sheet. "The directions don't say we can't." She gave our little green hero a couple of vigorous squirts, then leaned over to the neighboring lab table and sprayed Lucas's frog too.

My eyes watered. I wasn't so sure that this was an improvement.

Mr. Bigelow shook his head wearily. "And to think that I could have had a career in research." He flapped his hand at us. "Fine. Whatever works."

Forty-five minutes and half a bottle of Sassy Lassie later, the dismissal bell rang.

"I hope I never have to do that again," said Cha Cha, hopping down off her lab stool.

"Me too," echoed Jasmine.

"That's what I said last December," I told them, stuffing my notebook into my backpack.

Lucas Winthrop, who still looked half-wilted, trudged along ahead of us as we went back down the hall to our lockers.

"Poor kid," murmured Cha Cha. "Wait until his mother hears about this."

Jasmine nodded. "He'll probably have to start wearing a protective helmet to school or something."

I smothered a giggle. Maybe having a busy mother who didn't have a whole lot of time for me wasn't such a bad thing after all.

"Can you believe I have to go back to the orthodontist again today?" Jasmine complained, pulling on her jacket. "Stupid wire broke, and it's poking me in the lip." Her cell phone buzzed and she answered it. "I'll be right out, Mom. No, Scooter says his braces are fine." She waved to Cha Cha and me. "Gotta run. See you guys tomorrow!"

As she jogged off down the hall, Cha Cha and I joined the flow of students heading for the front door.

"Are you *kidding* me?" I said in disbelief as we emerged from the building. The sun from earlier in the day had disappeared, and it was snowing again.

"Welcome to winter in New Hampshire," said Cha Cha, sweeping an arm out in a dramatic gesture.

*BLAM!*

A snowball hit me squarely between my shoulder blades. I whipped around to see Scooter and Calhoun standing there laughing. Calhoun had Lucas Winthrop dangling by one of his spindly arms and was busy stuffing snow down the back of his neck.

"Welcome to winter in New Hampshire, *Truly Gigantic*!" Scooter called, mimicking Cha Cha's sweeping gesture.

"Truly big mistake, *Metal Mouth*!" I called back, furious. Two could play at this game. Scooping up a handful of snow, I took aim at Jasmine's brother.

*BLAM!* My snowball hit its target, exploding into a zillion bits.

My counterattack wiped the stupid grin off Scooter's face. Calhoun let go of Lucas and gaped at me, shocked.

*Take that*, I thought smugly.

Cha Cha darted over and grabbed Lucas by the hand. "Run!" she shouted to me.

The three of us took off down School Street. Scooter and Calhoun were hot on our heels. I paused a couple of times to fire off more snowballs for cover, then rounded the corner of Main Street behind my new friends. We dove through the door of Earl's Coins and Stamps and stood there dripping snow and panting.

"May I help you?" said the man behind the counter, just as Scooter and Calhoun charged through the door, snowballs in hand.

The store owner was pretty spry for someone his size. In a flash, he had both boys by the collar and hustled them outside.

"Sorry, Mr. Jefferson," said Cha Cha when he returned. "We got ambushed."

"I can see that," he replied, eyes twinkling beneath a pair of shaggy dark eyebrows. He was pretty much shaggy all over, from his wild tangle of curly dark hair to his rumpled sweater and corduroy pants. No bird for Mr. Jefferson—he was all bear. "So, is this just a safety zone to give you time to catch your breath, or can I actually do something for you kids?"

I looked over at Lucas, then at Cha Cha. We couldn't very well toss Lucas to the wolves. Scooter and Calhoun were no doubt waiting outside, itching for revenge. We'd have to let Lucas see the envelope.

I fished it out of my backpack and slid it across the counter. "I'm wondering if you could tell us anything about this stamp."

"Let's hope so," Mr. Jefferson said cheerfully. "Stamps are my business."

"So are you Earl?"

"Well, technically speaking, yes. But everybody calls me Bud. My father was the real Earl—this store was his baby. And you're a Lovejoy, from the looks of you."

Was it that obvious, I wondered? I nodded. "I'm Truly Lovejoy."

"There's another one?" His shaggy eyebrows shot up. "Your aunt True and I went to high school together. Well, welcome to Pumpkin Falls, Truly. Or perhaps I should say you're *truly* welcome to Pumpkin Falls." He grinned at his own joke. "We were all delighted to hear about your dad and True taking over the bookshop. Not that we won't miss Lola and Walt," he added hastily.

Picking up the envelope, he examined the stamp. "Oh, sure, I remember this one. The Battle of Gettysburg. This was from the Civil War series about twenty years ago." He spun around and ran a finger across the notebooks lining the shelves behind him. "Here it is," he said, pulling one of them out. Riffling through the plastic sleeves it contained, he pointed to a pristine horizontal strip of stamps.

Cha Cha leaned in to take a closer look while I jotted down the year. "There's President Lincoln, and Harriet Tubman, and Ulysses S. Grant," she noted. "These are actually kind of cool."

Mr. Jefferson nodded. "I like to think so."

"My father collected stamps," Lucas suddenly piped up.

"That's right," said Mr. Jefferson. "He used to spend a lot of time in here. The two of us were good friends."

Cha Cha had told me that Lucas's father died when he was a baby, which I guess kind of explains a lot about Mrs. Winthrop being so overprotective.

"You're welcome here anytime," Mr. Jefferson continued.

Lucas stared at the stamps. "My mother likes me to go right to the diner after school."

"I understand," the shop owner told him. "But my door is always open."

Lucas nodded.

I would have liked to stay and look at more stamps—Cha Cha was right, they were kind of cool—but I was due at my tutoring session in five minutes and my father wouldn't be happy if I was late. The three of us thanked Mr. Jefferson and left.

I looked carefully both ways to make sure Scooter and Calhoun weren't lurking behind a mailbox or something, then motioned my friends to follow me across the street.

"So did that help?" Cha Cha asked.

"I guess," I told her. "At least we've narrowed down the date range."

"Twenty years ago is a long time, though," Cha Cha said. "The person who wrote the letter and the person it was meant for might not even live here anymore."

I nodded. "Yeah, I know." It was probably going to be

impossible to track them down. But for some reason I still wanted to try.

As we approached the bookstore, I noticed a man in a dark green hooded jacket peering in the window. He stepped back, started to walk toward Lou's Diner, then hesitated. After a moment he returned to the window and peered inside again. *Odd*, I thought.

Before I could say anything, though, a snowball came sailing out from behind a parked car.

"Incoming!" I hollered, and grabbing ahold of my classmates, I pulled them into the bookstore.

# CHAPTER 11

"Greetings and salutations," said Aunt True as the snowball splatted harmlessly on the glass door behind us. She glanced outside. "A skirmish, I take it?"

We nodded.

She locked the door. "It's your lucky day, then. Due to inventory, the store is officially closed. You have now entered a snowball-free zone, and on top of that, it's snack time!" She smiled as she crossed the room toward us, then drew back abruptly. The smile vanished. "Good heavens, what is that smell?"

"Um," I said. "Us, probably. We dissected frogs today in science class."

She gave me a tentative sniff. "I'm not exactly detecting Eau de Kermit."

"Cha Cha sprayed our frogs with perfume."

Aunt True laughed. "And you would be Cha Cha, I presume?" she asked, turning to my new friend.

Cha Cha held out her hand. "Charlotte Abramowitz," she said. "Nice to meet you."

"Cha Cha's parents own the Starlite Dance Studio across the street," I told my aunt, as the two of them shook hands. "And this is Lucas Winthrop. His mom works at Lou's."

"Happy to meet you both," said Aunt True. "I'm True Lovejoy, Truly's aunt."

Out of the corner of my eye, I could see my classmates giving her a discreet once-over. Aunt True was dressed parrot-style as usual, in a bright orange hand-knit sweater over jeans. Down at her ankles, purple-and-green striped socks disappeared into a pair of leopard print clogs. "I hope you kids are hungry for a snack, because I've been baking all afternoon."

My father emerged from the back office just then. "Truly? You're right on time."

"Hi, Dad." *My family, the freak show*, I thought, as Cha Cha and Lucas politely looked everywhere but the hook that protruded from the end of my father's right shirtsleeve. "This is Cha Cha Abramowitz and Lucas Winthrop. They're in my class at school."

"Nice to meet you both," he said politely. "Now say good-bye to your friends, Truly. Time's a-wasting and math's a-waiting."

I sighed. "Yes, sir."

"Not so fast," Aunt True told my father, pulling a tray out

from under the counter. "I promised them a snack. I've decided that as part of the bookstore's new marketing campaign, we're going to offer tea and treats every afternoon for our customers."

Miss Marple, hearing the word "treats," trotted over to join us.

"Hey, Miss Marple," said Cha Cha, giving her a pat on the head.

My father looked over at Cha Cha, clearly startled to hear such a deep voice come out of such a petite person. "What marketing campaign?" he asked my aunt. His eyebrows dove for each other as he frowned. "We don't have money in the budget for tea and treats."

"Word will soon spread," Aunt True continued, ignoring him. "Hordes of visitors will descend to sample our goodies, and stay to buy our books."

"A bunch of freeloaders will show up, you mean," muttered my father, but I noticed he reached for a cookie.

My aunt passed the tray to my friends and me. I selected a cookie too, and took a bite, which I immediately ejected back into my hand. "Um, Aunt True, what's in these?"

Beside me, Lucas started to cough. Cha Cha, who hadn't taken a bite of her cookie yet, eyed it suspiciously.

"Looks like your culinary skills haven't improved much over the years, sis," my father remarked, grimacing.

Aunt True put her hands on her hips. "I'll have you know

I've cooked to great acclaim on every continent!" she retorted. "This is a recipe inspired by my time in Tibet. I had to make a few substitutions, of course, since the General Store doesn't carry yak milk. Did I add too many hot chilies?"

"Maybe just a few," I told her, slipping the rest of my cookie to Miss Marple. She promptly spat it onto the floor, and my father gave a hoot of laughter.

"And the reviews are in!" he crowed, sounding almost like his old self. "Bad sign when the dog won't eat it, True."

"Maybe a more traditional recipe would be a better idea, Ms. Lovejoy," Cha Cha suggested, discreetly returning her cookie to the tray. "What if you did something in honor of our town, like pumpkin bread or pumpkin muffins?"

Aunt True nodded. "Pumpkin muffins. I like it. No— wait! How about pumpkin *whoopie pies*? Quintessentially New England, but with a twist." She nodded. "That's perfect! They'll be our signature treat." She gave my father a sidelong glance. "I'll make mini ones, which will be more budget-friendly," she added. "People will come from far and wide to sample the treats at Lovejoy's Books."

My father threw his cookie in the trash. "Good, because they won't come from anywhere to sample these things." His brief flash of a good mood had evaporated. He looked over at me. "I'll be in the office. Don't be long."

"No, sir."

Aunt True looked ruefully down at the tray. "I hate to waste these, but he's right. They're pretty awful."

"You could give them to Danny and Hatcher," I suggested. "They'll eat anything,"

My aunt's eyes lit up. "Excellent strategy! Thank goodness for teenage boys."

"We should get going," Cha Cha told me. "I'm due over at the Starlite, and Lucas's mother will worry if he doesn't turn up at Lou's soon."

Hearing this, Lucas blushed.

I peered out the window. "The coast looks clear," I told them. "You should be okay."

"If you're worried about an ambush, that's a problem easily solved," said my aunt. "I have an errand to run, so why don't I just go along and make sure you both arrive at your destinations safely? I need to check on Memphis first, though—he and Miss Marple weren't getting along this afternoon, so I had to separate them."

Cha Cha turned to me as my aunt disappeared out the side door toward the stairs to her apartment. "Real quick, can you show me where you found the envelope?"

"The one with the *B* on it?" asked Lucas.

Cha Cha and I exchanged a glance. Lucas had obviously been paying attention! Cha Cha raised an eyebrow, and her unspoken question hung in the air.

"Oh, fine," I said. It wasn't as if Lucas would blab our secret to anyone—he barely spoke as it was. I explained about the mystery as I led the two of them back to the Annex.

"It was here in the used-book section," I told them, waving vaguely at the bottom shelf and handing the envelope to Lucas. He opened it and read the letter inside while I looked around for the basket of books without bar codes. There was no sign of it. "It was inside a copy of *Charlotte's Web*."

"Do you remember the pages it was stuck between?" asked Cha Cha. "That could be important."

I shook my head. "I wasn't really paying attention."

"And nothing else was in there?"

"Not that I noticed."

Just then, there was a sharp knock on the bookshop's front door.

"We're closed!" I heard my father yell from the office. "Can't you see the sign?"

The knocking escalated frantically. Grabbing the letter and envelope from Lucas, I stuffed them back into the pocket of my jeans and hurried to the front of the store to see what was going on. My friends were right behind me.

"For heaven's sake!" said Aunt True, crossing to the door and unlocking it. "What's the matter?"

"Where's that blasted January thaw when you need it?" fussed a small, plump, elderly person, barging past her into the store. She was bundled in more layers than Lucas Winthrop, but hers were considerably rattier. The two scarves wound around her neck clashed horribly with her threadbare jacket—red and blue stripes and purple plaid do not go well with green camouflage—and her boots, which looked about two sizes too big, were stuffed with crumpled newspaper. A face as wrinkled as a dried plum peeked out from beneath a bright orange hunter's hat. The earflaps were tied securely under her chin. Emerging from beneath the flaps were a few wisps of snow-white hair and the telltale wires from a pair of earbuds.

An elf owl, if ever I'd seen one.

"We're closed," my father repeated.

"Good afternoon, Miss Marple," she said, ignoring him.

Miss Marple got to her feet and trotted over expectantly.

"Don't worry, I didn't forget your treat." There was a rustling noise as the woman plunged an orange mitten into one of the many plastic bags she was carrying. "Oops, that's not it."

The five of us stared at her mittened hand. There was a kitten in it. The tiny creature let out a squeak, and at the sound another furry little head popped out of the woman's jacket pocket.

"How many kittens do you generally carry with you?" asked Aunt True, blinking in astonishment.

There was no response, so my aunt repeated her question, louder this time.

The elderly woman removed one of her earbuds. I heard

the faint, tinny strains of the Beatles' "Can't Buy Me Love."

"Depends," she replied.

Tucking both kittens back into their hiding places, she rummaged in the plastic bag once again, this time pulling out what looked like toast crusts. What I hoped were toast crusts, at least. Miss Marple had had enough food surprises today, what with Aunt True's cookies.

"We're closed," my father repeated for the third time.

"It's a book emergency," said our visitor.

Seeing our blank looks, she wiped her nose on the end of one of her scarves and rooted around in another plastic bag, emerging with a battered paperback this time. "Mystery swap," she added, waving it at us. "You know, bring a book, take a book?" When that got no response either, she heaved a sigh. "Never mind, I'll do it myself."

"Who's that?" I whispered, as she trundled off toward the Annex.

"No idea," Aunt True whispered back.

"It's Belinda Winchester," said Cha Cha.

Dad's head snapped around. "*That's* Belinda Winchester?" he said, watching her walk away. "She was at least a hundred when I was a kid! I can't believe she's still living here. Or still living, period."

"She looks kind of homeless," I said.

"She wasn't when I was growing up," my father replied. "She used to live in a big old house at the end of our street."

"She still does," said Cha Cha.

"I remember her now!" said Aunt True. "A little nutty, had about twenty-seven cats—or at least she did back then—house crammed with stuff?"

"That's her," said Cha Cha.

Belinda Winchester returned a moment later with a different paperback. My father stepped over to the cash register. "How would you like to pay for that this afternoon?"

"*Pay* for it?" the older woman screeched. The furry heads popped out again, their round kitten eyes wide in alarm. "What part of 'swap' don't you understand?" She peered at my father more closely. "Say, aren't you Walt and Lola's boy?"

I'd never heard my father called a "boy" before. He hesitated for a moment, then nodded.

"You're the delinquent who broke my garage window with a slingshot!"

My father reddened. "That was a long time ago, Miss Winchester," he replied stiffly. "And as I recall, I saved up my allowance to pay for the repair."

Aunt True was smiling broadly by now. I could tell she was enjoying this.

Our visitor sniffed. "Don't know as I remember it that way." She stuffed the paperback into a plastic bag. "I'd say this makes us even." And with that she and her kittens stalked out.

Aunt True laughed so hard her knees went weak. She collapsed on the bench by the door, gasping for breath.

My father shook his head in disgust. "Whose idea was it to have a mystery swap? What are we running here, a charity?"

"Calm down, J. T." said Aunt True, wiping her eyes. "It's just a used paperback. And it was a book emergency, remember? With a side of kittens." She dissolved in laughter again.

"We're the ones with a book emergency, especially if we just let our inventory walk out of here," my father told her. "This is a business, not the public library."

Beside me, I heard Lucas suck in his breath.

"No more stalling, Truly," my father said curtly. "Say good-bye to your friends. I want you in the office on the double." He spun on his heel and left.

As Aunt True started out the door, Lucas turned to Cha Cha and me, his pale face alight with excitement. "I know what the numbers on your mystery envelope mean."

# CHAPTER 12

Telling Lucas about the envelope turned out to be a good idea.

Except for the fact that I could barely concentrate on my math tutoring afterward. I stared blindly at the open book in front of me, my shoe woodpeckering against the metal base of my chair.

Across the room, my father threw down his pen. "You've got ants in your pants this afternoon, Truly!"

"Sorry."

"Try and focus, would you?"

"Yes, sir." I wondered just how well he'd be able to focus if he was on the brink of solving a mystery.

"They're library call numbers," Lucas had told Cha Cha and me. "See?" Reaching into his backpack, he'd pulled out a copy of *Your Government and You* and pointed to the sequence of numbers across the sticker on the book's spine.

Sure enough, although the numbers were completely

different from the ones on my letter, the pattern was the same.

Cha Cha had frowned. "So whoever wrote the letter was sending the person it was meant for off to find another book?"

I'd nodded. "It's like a scavenger hunt! We need to go the library."

The problem was, none of us could. My father would have been breathing fire if I hadn't shown up for my tutoring session in about thirty seconds flat, Cha Cha was due over at her parents' dance studio to fill in for the receptionist again, and Lucas's mother was probably having a cow because he wasn't there yet. So we'd agreed to meet at the library after dinner.

I chewed the end of my pencil nervously and glanced at the clock. The other problem was, my mother had scheduled that family meeting tonight. This narrowed my brief window of time even further for making it to the library before it closed. I felt like I'd explode if I had to wait until tomorrow.

I sighed and stared again at the worksheet in front of me. Math is usually something I enjoy, but word problems? *Puh-leez.*

My father pushed back from his desk a little while later and came over to check my work. "You can do better," he told me, pointing out a couple of errors.

"Yes, sir," I replied glumly.

Suddenly, there was a loud squawk from out in the store. "J. T.!" shouted Aunt True. "Come quick!"

My father bolted out the office door. I was right on his

heels, grateful for an excuse to ditch the word problems.

We found my aunt over by the travel section. "Would you look at this?" she said in amazement. She was kneeling on the floor by the basket of books I'd been looking for earlier, holding up the copy of *Charlotte's Web*. For a second I wondered if maybe she'd found another letter inside, but that wasn't what she was excited about. "It's an autographed first edition!" She showed us the inscription, which read: *To my nifty little neighbor Bee, from Andy White.*

"Who's Andy?" my father asked.

"That was E. B. White's nickname," Aunt True told him.

Dad stared at her. "And here I thought the place was on fire or something from all the fuss you were making."

Aunt True scrambled to her feet. "Don't you understand? Some autographed first editions go for thousands of dollars!"

My eyebrows shot up. There were people willing to pay that kind of money for an old book?

"Really?" Now my father sounded excited too. "We might be able to pay off the bank loan if that's the case—or at least make a serious dent in it."

Aunt True looked over at me. "Were you the one who found this book, Truly?"

I nodded. "Yeah, when I was scanning stuff in the Annex."

"You just may have saved the day." She kissed me on the cheek, then waltzed happily toward the front of the store. My father and I followed her. "I'm going to do a little research and see if I can come up with a value for it, then we'll put it in the rare books cabinet for safekeeping."

The rare books cabinet was a locked, glass-fronted bookcase by the sales counter. There wasn't much in it these days—I guess anything of value had long since been sold to help keep the store afloat.

As Aunt True disappeared into the office, there was a knock on the front door.

"Does everyone in Pumpkin Falls have a book emergency today?" my father grumbled, going to answer it.

This time it wasn't a desperate customer, though; it was my mother.

"Big news!" she announced as she came in. The rest of my family was right behind her. "I have a job!"

Pippa did a pirouette. "Mommy ith going to be a danther!"

"No, honey, I'm just *working* at a dance studio," my mother corrected. "Big difference." She turned to my father. "I saw an ad in the *Patriot-Bugle* this morning and answered it."

My mouth dropped open. "You're going to be the receptionist at the Starlite?"

My mother looked over at me, astonished. "How on earth did you know that?"

I explained about Cha Cha, and she laughed. "See? It was meant to be."

"Are you sure you're going to be able to handle it, Dinah?" my father asked.

"It's only part-time, and it's just until the dance studio's regular receptionist gets back from maternity leave," she told him. "And guess what? As one of the perks, Pippa and Lauren get free dance lessons."

Hearing this, Pippa spun around the room again.

Lauren plopped down on the floor near Miss Marple and opened her latest book—she'd moved on from Laura Ingalls Wilder to *The Borrowers*. Danny and Hatcher made a beeline for Aunt True's cookies. I watched, waiting for the fireworks, but my brothers scarfed down the cookies without so much as a peep. Their stomachs must be made of iron.

"Where's True?" my mother asked. "I can't wait to tell her."

My father gestured toward the office with his right hand. Only it wasn't his right hand any more, of course. It was a hook.

Pippa spotted it and froze. Her eyes widened, and I could see Dad's jaw muscles tighten as she ducked behind my mother and started to cry. It just kills him when Pippa does this.

My parents have tried, they really have. And so have Danny and Hatcher and Lauren and me. But no one has been able to convince Pippa that the hook isn't a big scary thing. So Dad's just given up wearing his prosthesis when he's at home. He keeps it in a gym bag and carries it to and from the bookstore every day. It's only temporary, Mom says, insisting that Pippa will get used to it. Plus, Dad is scheduled to get his new more permanent prosthetic arm soon and everyone's hoping she'll like that one better.

"What's all the commotion?" asked Aunt True, emerging from the office. "Another book emergency?"

My mother shook her head. "Not exactly. More of a Pippa emergency." Lowering her voice to a whisper that was barely audible over my little sister's wails, she explained the situation.

Aunt True crouched down beside Pippa. "Well, my goodness, and here I thought there was a hippopotamus loose in the store!"

The wails subsided into hiccups.

"I've seen a hippopotamus, you know," Aunt True continued. "Back when I lived in Tanzania. And I've seen lions and zebras and crocodiles, too."

Pippa peeked out from behind my mother.

"Speaking of crocodiles, do you know the story of Peter Pan?"

My little sister nodded, sniffling. She wiped her nose with the back of her hand.

"We went on the ride at Dithney World."

"And do you remember the crocodile?" Aunt True asked her.

Pippa nodded again. "Tick-Tock."

"That's right. And what did that crocodile do?"

Pippa's forehead puckered as she thought about it. "He thwam after Captain Hook."

Aunt True smiled. "Uh-huh," she said. "Tick-Tock wasn't afraid of silly old Captain Hook, was he?"

Pippa shook her head.

I could see where this was going, and so could my father.

He frowned. "Really, True?"

"Come on, J. T.," Aunt True coaxed. "Where's your sense of humor?"

A corner of his mouth quirked up. I could tell he thought it was funny, even though he was trying not to.

"And you don't have to be afraid either," Aunt True told Pippa. She motioned to my father, who heaved a sigh and reluctantly waved his prosthesis. "See? You can pretend you're Tick-Tock, and that's just silly old Captain Hook."

"Thilly old Captain Hook," Pippa repeated. She didn't look entirely convinced, but she wasn't crying anymore either. A moment later, she started running around the store shouting "Tick-Tock! Tick-Tock!" as my father gamely let her chase him.

"Thanks, True," said my mother, watching them.

"Tell her about your job, Mom," I urged, and she did.

"That's fantastic, Dinah!" said my aunt, then showed her the first edition of *Charlotte's Web*. "What a red-letter day for the Lovejoys! I'd say this calls for a celebration—I'm taking us all out to dinner at Lou's."

My mother hesitated. "We have a family meeting scheduled."

"You can have it at the restaurant," said Aunt True. "Nobody's cooking tonight."

"Are you sure, True?" Mom asked. "There are rather of a lot of us."

"Really?" said Aunt True, blinking in fake surprise. "I hadn't noticed."

I was beginning to really like Aunt True.

After my aunt locked *Charlotte's Web* away in the rare books cabinet, we trooped over to Lou's and crammed in around the diner's biggest table. Lou had to bring over a couple of extra chairs to fit us all in. I took it as a good sign that Pippa asked to sit next to my father.

"Don't see big families like yours much these days," said the restaurant owner.

Like clockwork, our heads all swiveled toward Dad. This was his cue to leap in with a comment about the Magnificent Seven. But Captain Hook's smile had vanished and Silent Man was back.

Mom quickly spoke up to fill the awkward silence. "We love having a big family! I'm one of seven kids, myself." She chattered on to Lou for a couple of minutes, then Lucas's mother came over to take our order.

I looked around the crowded restaurant. I guess if you're pretty much the only restaurant in Pumpkin Falls, you're going to be busy most of the time. The tables and booths were filled with a mix of college students, older people, and local families.

I spotted Amy Nguyen and her brother and parents in one of the booths, and Lucas, who was sitting at the end of the counter by himself, eating a cheeseburger and doing his homework. He waved shyly, and I waved back.

Danny and Hatcher launched into a recap of their wrestling practice for Dad while Mom and Aunt True started talking about some novel they were both reading. Lauren was still buried in *The Borrowers*, so I helped Pippa color her place mat until Mrs. Winthrop returned with our food.

As she set a small plate of greens and dressing in front of my father, I waited for him to say, "Oh, a honeymoon salad!" the way he always used to. He'd grin in anticipation, waiting for the waiter or waitress to ask what he meant by that. Then he'd waggle his eyebrows Groucho Marx-style and say, "Lettuce alone!" It always got a laugh.

Now, though, he just picked up his fork and started to eat.

"You're Truly, right?" said Mrs. Winthrop, handing me my fish and chips. I nodded. "I want to thank you for helping Lucas out today after school. Those bigger boys can be a bit—rowdy."

"You're welcome."

"Lucas said something about going to the library with you later for a project you're working on?"

I nodded.

"Would you mind walking him home afterward?" his mother asked, fiddling with the salt and pepper shakers. "It's just that, you know, it's dark and the roads and sidewalks are icy."

"Don't you worry," my mother told her. "Truly will see your son safely home."

"Thanks."

I watched her walk away. I was wrong about Mrs. Winthrop being a blue jay. She was pure mother hen.

"So what was that all about?" my mother asked. I explained about the snowball fight earlier, and she smiled at me. "That was very kind of you, sweetheart."

"All hail Saint Drooly," said Hatcher in a robot voice, sticking French fries in his ears. He turned to Pippa. "Frankenfryenstein. Want. Ketchup."

Pippa giggled. Not to be outdone, Danny wedged a pair of fries between his upper lip and teeth. "Yesssssss," he said, affecting a fake accent. "Fangs a lot, Truly—Count Spudula approvessss."

"Boys," warned my mother, but it was too late. Lauren was oblivious, of course—too engrossed in her book to notice—but Pippa laughed so hard that milk squirted out of her nose. This startled her and made her cry again, and when I reached for some napkins to help clean her up, I knocked over my water glass, making an even bigger mess. My father shot me a black look as some of the liquid pooled over the edge of the table and onto the leg of his pants.

"For heaven's sake, Truly!" he snapped.

"But it was Pippa's—"

"Don't answer back."

I slumped in my seat. "No, sir."

Mrs. Winthrop brought over some paper towels. As she and my mother started to mop up, the door to the diner opened and a figure in black came in.

"Oh, great," muttered my father. "Just what I need to make my evening complete."

It was Ella Bellow.

Spotting us, she made a beeline for our table. Her lips thinned in disapproval as she surveyed the lake of watery milk. "Waste of money, taking children to restaurants," she observed, shaking her head. "Especially when there are so many of them."

"It's my money, and I don't consider it a waste," Aunt True replied. "Can we help you, Ella?"

Pippa's tears instantly ceased. She looked up. "Ella Bellow?"

I felt a prickle of misgiving.

The postmistress gave my little sister a fleeting smile, but her gaze was riveted to the hook at the end of my father's shirtsleeve.

"Take a picture; it'll last longer," said Hatcher under his breath.

My mother elbowed him sharply. "It's nice to see you again, Ella," she said politely. "And now if you'll excuse us, we were about to have a family meeting."

"Of course," said the postmistress, steering herself to the

closest table. She took a seat with her back to us, but it was obvious that she was all ears.

My mother leaned forward and whispered, "I vote that we take our dessert back to the bookstore and have our meeting there."

"Mom'th whithpering becauth Ella Bellow ith a buthy-body," said Pippa in a loud voice. "Right, Truly?"

The postmistress's back stiffened. The nearby tables went dead silent. Aunt True choked on a bite of cheeseburger, except her coughing fit sounded suspiciously like laughter to me.

"Truly!" my mother whispered furiously. "What did you tell your sister?"

"It's not my fault!" I whispered back. "And anyway, you were the one who said it first!"

My father glared at me. "Truly Lovejoy, don't you dare speak back to your mother."

"Truce!" said Aunt True weakly, waving her napkin like a white flag. Her eyes were watering and she was trying hard to suppress a smile. "All in favor of family harmony, especially in public places"—she tipped her head toward our neighboring eavesdropper—"raise their hands."

Hatcher and Danny raised their hands. So did I.

Mrs. Winthrop, who looked like she was trying not to smile too, finished cleaning off the table.

"Let's change the subject, shall we?" Aunt True contin-ued. "How was your day, Dinah?"

"Fine up until now," my mother replied.

"Look at the bright side," my aunt told her. "It can't get any worse, right? But, seriously, any interesting classes?"

Mom nodded. "Yes, all of them. I especially like my American History for Educators class. Professor Rusty is so interesting."

Dad's eyebrows snapped to attention. He looked over at Aunt True. "I didn't know Rusty was back in town! How long's he been teaching at the college?"

Aunt True suddenly seemed very interested in rearranging her silverware. "Six months or so. Mom mentioned something about it before they left for Africa."

"Who's Rusty?" asked Danny.

"Someone your father and I went to high school with," Aunt True said lightly. "So, what do you say we all get ice-cream sundaes to go?"

I glanced anxiously at the clock, then turned to my mother. "Can I be excused to go to the library? It's going to close soon."

"*May* I," said my mother automatically. "And no, you may not."

"Mom!"

"You know our agreement."

Attendance at family meetings is mandatory. It's one of Lieutenant Colonel Jericho T. Lovejoy's rules.

"I don't need a sundae." I begged. "And it's just down the street—I'll be back at the bookstore before you guys even finish dessert. We only need to look this one thing up."

My mother frowned. "It's for your project with the Winthrop boy, right?" she asked, and I nodded. It wasn't a lie, really. Solving the mystery of the envelope counted as a project, and Lucas was helping me. My mother pressed her lips together, considering. "Well, I suppose it's okay," she said finally. "If you promise to hurry."

"I promise," I said, getting to my feet. "Absolutely truly, cross my heart and hope to fly."

I froze, aghast.

I'd said it completely without thinking, the words no sooner out of my mouth than I would have given anything to snatch them back.

My father stared down at his prosthesis, which was resting on the table. Pain creased his forehead. "I think we'll save the family meeting for another night," he said gruffly, then pushed back from the table and stood up.

Ella Bellow swiveled around in her chair and stared as he walked out of the restaurant.

"Truly, how could you!" said my mother, giving me her trademark disappointed look.

"Nice going, moron," added Danny. "You totally ruined everything."

Even Hatcher looked at me reproachfully.

"I didn't do it on purpose!" I protested. "It just came"—I caught myself before I said "flying"—"out!"

"Cross my heart and hope to fly" is this saying that Dad's

best friend Tom Larson made up, way back when the two of them were in flight school. We always knew when Dad was talking to Mr. Larson on the phone, because that's how they'd end their calls. It was like their own private motto, and over the years it had become our family's motto too. But now it's strictly off-limits because Mr. Larson didn't make it back from Afghanistan, and it reminds my father of that horrible day when he lost both his arm and his best friend.

Once again, I'd gone and stuck my foot in my mouth. I was Truly-in-the-Middle-of-a-Mess.

Aunt True was wrong—the evening could get worse. It just did.

# CHAPTER 13

I didn't wait for Lucas; I just grabbed my jacket and ran.

"Hey!" he called, dashing through the front door of the diner after me. "Wait up!" Panting, he caught up with me as I reached the *Pumpkin Falls Patriot-Bugle* building. "What's the matter?"

"None of your business," I snapped. What was I supposed to tell him? That I desperately wished that everything could go back to the way it was before? Before Black Monday, and before Silent Man, and before we had to move here to this stupid place? That I'd give anything to hear my dad laugh again, and to hear the Magnificent Seven ringtone on his cell phone? I charged ahead down the sidewalk and didn't stop until I reached the library.

"I was worried you weren't coming," said Cha Cha, leaping up from the bench inside the lobby. "They're getting ready to close."

Lucas and I followed her through the main reading area, a cozy room lined with bookshelves and two big, comfortable chairs that flanked a crackling fire. Belinda Winchester was seated in one of them, still wearing her bright orange hunter's cap. Her eyes were closed; she was either napping or listening to music through her earbuds. There was no sign of kittens.

I glanced up the stairs that led to the children's room, wondering if Charlotte's Corner was still there. I'd spent a lot of summer afternoons sitting cross-legged underneath it. Gramps and Lola didn't just run a bookshop; they were book people through and through, and the Pumpkin Falls Library was at the top of their list of places to take visiting grandchildren. Story Hour was always held beneath the bronze sculpture of the doorway of Zuckerman's barn, with Charlotte the spider looking down from her web, and us kids fighting over who got to sit next to Wilbur and who got stuck beside Templeton the rat.

Cha Cha led us to a pair of computer terminals in the teeny reference area. She climbed up on a stool in front of one of them, her short legs dangling.

"Read me the numbers," she said.

I pulled the envelope out of the back pocket of my jeans and opened it. "'PR2828.A2 B7,'" I replied.

She typed this into the search field, pausing a moment and then frowning at the screen. "Again, please. Slower this time."

I did as she asked.

"It's not here."

I peered over her shoulder. "Are you sure?"

She pointed to the screen, which read ITEM NOT FOUND.

The three of us stared morosely at the computer. Our scavenger hunt was over before it started.

"We could ask the reference librarian," Lucas suggested.

"No." I clutched the letter to my chest. Maybe it was the fact that my entire family was mad at me, but I was feeling possessive all of a sudden. Three of us trying to solve the mystery was enough.

"Nobody has to actually see it, Truly," said Cha Cha, passing me a pencil and a piece of paper. "Just write down the call number."

I relented. As I started to write, the lights overhead flicked on and off.

"The library is now closing," announced a voice over the loudspeaker, and the people around us started gathering up their things.

Cha Cha grabbed the piece of paper from me and dashed across the room to the reference desk. Lucas and I followed.

"Sorry, kids, we're closed now," said the woman behind the counter.

"Please?" begged Cha Cha.

The woman shook her head. "I just shut the computer down," she explained. "Can you come back tomorrow?"

Lucas tugged on Cha Cha's sleeve. "Let's go find Mr.

Henry," he whispered, and Cha Cha dashed off again.

"Who's Mr. Henry?" I asked Lucas as we jogged after her.

"The children's librarian," he told me.

We found him upstairs by Charlotte's Corner, sorting picture books. I couldn't help staring. Except for his dreadlocks and the fact that he was African American, Mr. Henry was a dead ringer for *Where's Waldo?* He was wearing hipster glasses, jeans, a red-and-white striped shirt, and red sneakers.

"School project, huh?" he said, when Cha Cha gave him the slip of paper.

"Um, not—" Lucas started to reply. I stepped on his foot. Not correcting someone isn't exactly the same as telling a lie, right?

"It's really important," I said.

Mr. Henry smiled. "Such eagerness! Such zeal!" He rose to his feet. "Who can resist young minds intent on edification? Certainly not Henry Butterworth!"

"Thanks," said Cha Cha.

"Anything for the sister of the most awesome Baxter Abramowitz," he replied with a bow. He crossed to the computer at his desk and typed in the numbers. "Shakespeare, huh? Looks like we don't have the volume you're looking for here on our shelves, I'm afraid. But perhaps I can get it for you through interlibrary loan." He fired off a longer something on his keyboard, peering over his glasses at the screen. "Lovejoy College has a copy." He swiveled around to face us. "Shall I request it for you? It shouldn't take more than a few days, a week at most, for them to send it over."

"Thanks anyway," said Cha Cha at the same time that I said, "Yes, please."

The librarian looked from one of us to the other, bemused. "Which shall it be?"

Cha Cha elbowed me sharply. "It's a no, Mr. Henry. But thanks for your help."

"That's what I'm here for. You kids come back anytime."

"What was that all about?" I asked, once we were back outside again. My question rose like a smoke signal in the frosty air.

"That was all about the fact that I have a better idea," Cha Cha replied. "Why wait a whole week when we can just go over there ourselves?"

"How are we supposed to do that?" I protested. "They won't let middle schoolers in—you have to have a college ID and everything." I'd seen my mother's.

"They'll let us in," Cha Cha told me. "But there's a catch." She paused. "We're going to have to talk to Calhoun."

# CHAPTER 14

"Can you keep the kids out of my hair this afternoon, Truly?" my mother asked. It was Saturday afternoon, and Pippa had a playdate scheduled with Baxter Abramowitz, who was due to arrive any second. Annie Freeman was already here with Lauren. "I have a pile of homework to finish before my shift at the Starlite."

I promised her I would.

"Pippa's upstairs in her room," I told Baxter a few minutes later, when I interrupted my piano practice to answer the doorbell. He and Cha Cha were waiting on the doorstep, their cheeks rosy from the cold. Cha Cha had offered to walk her brother over so that the two of us could hang out. Lucas was on his way to join us.

They came inside, and Cha Cha helped her little brother out of his jacket. He sat down and pulled his boots off impatiently, then scampered upstairs.

"Who are all these people?" asked Cha Cha, staring at the portraits on the wall as we followed him.

"Lovejoys," I told her. "That's the original Truly."

She paused. "You look a bit like her."

"You think?"

She nodded. "Yeah. Same eyes and nose."

This was good news. If I had the original Truly's nose, that meant I wasn't doomed to inherit the dreaded Nathaniel Daniel Lovejoy proboscis.

I led Cha Cha down the hall to my room. She looked around in approval. "Nice," she said. "But what's with all the owls?"

I shrugged. "I just like them, that's all."

Cha Cha plunked herself down on the braided rug in front of my bookshelf. "You have a lot of bird books."

This was an understatement.

She ran her finger across the row of titles. "Have you read all these?"

I nodded.

"Wow. So you must know a lot about birds, huh?"

I glanced at her out of the corner of my eye, trying to tell if she was really interested or just being polite. Or worse, if she was asking me out of pity. Did she think I was a bird nerd?

Well, I sort of am.

"Yeah, I guess I do," I replied, deciding she was sincere. "Would you like to see my life list?"

She nodded and I pulled a dog-eared leather notebook

from the shelf. Gramps gave it to me back when I was Lauren's age. The front was stamped with gold silhouettes of birds, but the gold had mostly worn away.

I opened it to the first page. "All real birders keep a life list," I explained. "You add to it every time you spot a new bird. See? This one here at the top, the northern cardinal? That was the very first bird I saw after I got this notebook."

I looked at my round and careful nine-year-old handwriting, remembering how thrilled I was when Gramps taught me the Latin name—*Cardinalis cardinalis*—and made me write it down. It was like a secret handshake, something that let me into his club.

I scanned a few of the pages, thinking about all the walks we'd taken together here in Pumpkin Falls, and all the birds we'd seen—from the barn swallows that came back every year to nest in the eaves over Lola's studio to the purple finch (*Carpodacus purpureus*), New Hampshire's state bird. Gramps had told me that his birding hero, Roger Tory Peterson, a naturalist who wrote a bunch of field guides, once described the purple finch as "a sparrow dipped in raspberry juice." He laughed about it, but the description stuck in my head, and I've never had any trouble spotting a purple finch since.

No owls, though. I still didn't have one of those on my life list.

Cha Cha's gaze wandered down to the bottom shelf. "Whose yearbooks are those?"

"My aunt's," I told her. "This used to be her room."

Cha Cha pulled one from the shelf at random and flipped it open. "West Hartfield Pep Squad," she read aloud. "Whoa, check out these hairstyles!"

I knelt down beside her and peered over her shoulder. "My aunt should be in there someplace," I told her. "I think this one's from the year she graduated."

Cha Cha flipped to the back to check out the senior portraits.

"Wait, you passed it," I said, and Cha Cha turned the pages until we found Aunt True. Instead of the typical headshot, my aunt had chosen a candid pose that showed her perched on the railing of the covered bridge, with the waterfall sparkling in the sunshine behind her.

"She's really pretty," said Cha Cha. "Even with the big hair."

I nodded. Looking at the picture, I realized that I had stood in the exact same spot just a few days ago on our science class field trip. I could tell because the camera had caught some of the same graffiti that Lucas had sketched: SAM LOVES BETTY; JOJO AND CARL; and that lopsided heart with E & T FOREVER inside. Things didn't change much over the years in Pumpkin Falls.

I read the list of activities beneath my aunt's picture. She'd been on the debate team, which explained how she could win so many arguments with my father, and she'd also been captain of the tennis team, editor of the school newspaper, and a member of the Thespian Club, whatever that was.

"Sweet," said Cha Cha. "She was voted 'Most Likely to See the World.'"

"They sure got that right," I replied. "Aunt True's been everywhere."

We looked for my father next, and found him lined up with the other wrestlers for the team photo. I noticed that he was already wrestling varsity, even though he was only a sophomore that year.

"He looks a little like Hatcher," said Cha Cha.

"Wait until you meet my brother Danny," I told her. "He and my dad could practically be twins." I stared at the picture. My father stared back, his jaw set and determined even then. It was weird to think he hadn't met Mom when that picture was taken, or known that he was going to join the army and have five kids.

My gaze strayed to his arms. Both of them. He certainly hadn't known about Black Monday.

"Principal Burnside was a wrestler too," said Cha Cha, pointing to a vaguely familiar face in the lineup. It was perched atop a long, skinny, flamingo neck. Our principal was a sophomore then too, just like my father, only he looked about twelve.

"Guess he hadn't hit his growth spurt yet," I remarked, and Cha Cha snickered.

She turned the page. "Check it out, Belinda Winchester used to be a lunch lady!"

"She looks exactly the same," I noted in surprise. "Well,

except for the hairnet and uniform. And her hair wasn't white back then either."

Cha Cha nodded. "I'll bet she's got kittens in her pockets, though," she said, and we both snickered this time.

I read the caption under the photo: *West Hartfield High welcomed Down-Easter Belinda Winchester to the cafeteria staff this year. Everyone's hoping she'll add lobster to the menu!*

We flipped around in the yearbook a bit more, poking fun at the stupid hairstyles and clothes.

"Hey, there's the guy from the stamp store," I said, pointing to another senior portrait. "See? Earl 'Bud' Jefferson Jr."

"Nice mullet, Bud," said Cha Cha.

"Business in the front, party in the back," I intoned, and she grinned.

"Not a good look," she scolded, wagging her finger at the picture. "Especially for a 'Future Business Leader of America.'" She turned the page again.

"Who names their kid Erastus?" I said, pointing to a photo of a boy with bushy dark hair and glasses. "Sheesh."

Cha Cha gave me a sly look. "Um, pot calling the kettle black much?"

My mouth fell open. I swatted her on the shoulder with the mystery envelope. "You're one to talk, *Cha Cha*."

Her dimple flashed again, and I had to laugh. It felt good to be joking around. I hadn't done much of that since leaving Austin, and Mackenzie.

I looked back at the yearbook. Erastus Peckinpaugh had been on the National Honor Society and was voted "Most Likely to Get a PhD." He also proudly listed his membership in "The Fighting Fifth"—a living history group that portrayed the Fifth New Hampshire Regiment Volunteers.

"Civil War reenactors," I told Cha Cha. My father had lots of army buddies who did that for a hobby. "In other words, total geek."

Cha Cha turned the page. "Hey, there's Calhoun's parents." I leaned in for a closer look. James Calhoun had been class president, captain of the soccer team, and, like Aunt True, a member of the yearbook staff and the Thespian Club. He had the same sandy hair and dark eyes as his son but he looked a whole lot friendlier. Mostly because he was smiling. I didn't think I'd seen Calhoun smile yet. A real smile, that was, not just a stupid smirk.

"That's Calhoun's mom," said Cha Cha, pointing to a picture of a pretty brunette on the opposite page. Jennifer Upton had played in the school orchestra, was president of the National Honor Society, and had starred in a whole bunch of plays while she was at West Hartfield.

"I overheard Ella Bellow and Lou talking about them once at the diner," Cha Cha said. "Calhoun's parents were high school sweethearts. Everybody figured they'd be famous one day, because they were really awesome actors."

"So what happened?"

"They got married after college and moved to New York."

"To be actors?"

She nodded. "After their parents retired and moved away, though, they stopped coming to Pumpkin Falls. And then one day out of the blue last year, the *Patriot-Bugle* announces that Dr. Calhoun has been hired as president of Lovejoy College, and he turns up with Calhoun and his sister, but no Mrs. Calhoun. I guess they got divorced right before the move."

As I was digesting this information, there was a knock on my door. Hatcher poked his head in. "Drooly?" he said. "Your friend Lucas is here."

*"Hatcher!"* My face flamed. The last thing I needed was for that stupid nickname to get out. I could only imagine what would happen if Scooter and Calhoun got ahold of it.

"Drooly, huh?" boomed Cha Cha, and my brother looked a bit taken aback. I was used to it by now, but Cha Cha's deep voice seemed to surprise people the first time they heard it. "You and Erastus are definitely tied, Truly."

"Shut up!" I swatted her with the envelope again.

Cha Cha laughed. "Don't worry—your secret's safe with us. Right, Lucas?"

Lucas stood in the doorway, looking like he might bolt at any second. His face was even redder than mine. He'd probably never been in a girl's room before.

"It's okay, Lucas," I told him. "You can come in. We won't bite."

Behind him, Hatcher bared his teeth and pretended to chomp down on the top of Lucas's head. I ignored him, but Cha Cha let out a raspy giggle.

Lucas shuffled timidly forward. He gazed around my room. "Nice owl," he said, spotting the woodcut over my bed.

"Thanks."

"What are you guys up to, anyway?" asked Hatcher, lounging against the doorjamb.

I hesitated, tempted to tell him about the mystery we were trying to solve. Between school, tutoring sessions, and his endless wrestling practices, I felt like I'd hardly seen him since we'd moved to Pumpkin Falls. I was used to not seeing much of Danny—he was three years older and busy with high school—but I really missed spending time with Hatcher.

"Homework," Cha Cha told him before I could open my mouth.

My brother made a face. "Too bad. Danny and I are heading to the General Store. Tell Mom we'll be home in time for dinner, okay?"

He'd barely left before Lauren and Annie Freeman wandered in with Miss Marple. Annie had quickly established herself as Lauren's new best friend.

"Want to meet my turtle?" Lauren asked. She loves showing off her pets.

"Sure," said Cha Cha, taking it gingerly from her. "What's his name?"

"Methuselah," Lauren replied.

"I can spell that," Annie told us, and promptly did. "Methuselah lived to be nine hundred and sixty-nine years old. Do you think your turtle will live to be that old, Lauren? I'll bet your hamster won't. I had a hamster named Nantucket, because that's where we got her. We called her Nan for short. She was only two when she died."

Lauren shot me a worried look. Nibbles had turned two just before we left Austin. We'd had a birthday party for him and everything.

"You have pets, don't you, Cha Cha?" I said hastily, and she nodded. "Tell Lauren about them."

"We have two cats—Fred and Ginger. They're named after Fred Astaire and Ginger Rogers."

Seeing our blank looks, Cha Cha added, "Guess you guys don't watch old movies. They were famous dancers. My father thought it would be funny, since we own the Starlite and everything."

She passed Methuselah back to Lauren, who offered to let Lucas hold him too.

"No, thanks," he said, taking a step back.

"He doesn't bite," Lauren assured him. "Don't you have any pets?"

Lucas shook his head. Big surprise there. His helicopter mom was probably too worried he'd get fleas.

Pippa and Baxter must have heard us all talking, because

they barged into my room next. Baxter ran over to Cha Cha and gave her a big hug.

"I can tap danth," my little sister announced. Without waiting for a response, she launched into a shuffle-step routine. When she was done, she went over and plunked herself down next to Baxter and Cha Cha. I rolled my eyes, and Cha Cha grinned.

"Ooh!" said Annie, pouncing on a brochure I'd left on my desk. On the cover, beneath the words PUMPKIN FALLS COTILLION!, was a picture of Mr. and Mrs. Abramowitz and a bunch of kids, twirling across a dance floor with huge smiles on their faces. Annie sighed. "I can't wait until I'm in middle school. My sister Sarah says Cotillion is totally awesome. You should have seen her at the Winter Festival the year she was in it. She had on this really pretty dress with sparkles and everything. There was a live band and decorations and snacks too. Everybody said she was the best dancer."

Did Annie ever shut up?

"Go find something else to do," I told my sisters and their friends, shooing them out of my room. I shut the door firmly behind them.

They left, but just barely. I could hear whispering out in the hall. The four of them were trying to spy on us.

"Baxter does the same thing when I have friends over," Cha Cha assured me.

I racked my brain, trying to think of someplace more

private that we could go. Danny and Hatcher were gone, but if we went up to the third floor the younger kids would simply follow us. And the basement—which my brothers had dubbed "The Spider Farm"—was too creepy.

Then I had a bright idea. But I was going to have to be sly.

"Snack time!" I announced loudly, shoving the envelope in my backpack. I shouldered it and crossed the room, motioning for Cha Cha and Lucas to follow me. Lauren and Annie and Pippa and Baxter fell in behind us as we headed down the hall. Miss Marple took up the rear.

Downstairs, my mother was still sitting at the dining room table, her homework spread out in front of her.

"Can we make popcorn?" I asked.

"Sure," she replied absently. "Bring me some, would you?"

"I want popcorn too," Pippa whined.

"You bet, Pipster," I told her. "Why don't you and Bax go help Lauren and Annie pick out a movie to watch while I make it."

The four of them vanished through the door to the ell. Most really old houses in New England have an "ell," a room that used to connect the house to the barn. That way the farmers and their families could easily get from one to the other without having to go outside in the cold. Back when Dad and Aunt True were teenagers, Gramps and Lola had turned their ell into a family room.

"Thanks, honey," my mother said a few minutes later, when I brought her a bowl of popcorn. "I'm so glad to see you having fun with your new friends."

I was a little surprised to realize that I was having fun. Maybe not quite Mackenzie-level fun, but still, fun.

Cha Cha and Lucas and I lingered for a few minutes, waiting until the younger kids were engrossed in the movie. Then I picked up our popcorn bowl and motioned to my friends to follow me as I slipped through the door to the garage. We tiptoed up the stairs to Lola's art studio. Nobody would think to look for us there.

Fortunately, the key was still by the door, tucked behind my grandmother's painting of Lovejoy Mountain. I slipped it from its hook, unlocked the door, and led Cha Cha and Lucas inside.

Shivering, I switched on the heat and crossed the room to the sofa. Afternoon sun flooded through the wall of windows behind it. Technically, we probably weren't supposed to be up here, but nobody had exactly told me that it was off-limits, and there wasn't anyplace else I could think of for us to go.

"The first meeting of the Pumpkin Falls Private Eyes is called to order," I said, taking a seat.

"Seriously?" Cha Cha's dimple flashed.

"What's wrong with that?" I replied, stung.

Cha Cha wrinkled her nose. "It's kind of dorky."

"You come up with something better, then."

She shook her head. "No, that's okay. You can call us the Pumpkin Falls Private Eyes if you want to."

"I don't have to," I said stiffly.

"No, really. It's fine."

Somewhat mollified, I pulled the envelope out of my backpack, along with a pad of yellow lined paper and a pen, and placed them on the coffee table.

Lucas circled the spacious room, looking at Lola's paintings. My grandmother loved flowers, and a bright spill of them lit up the canvases on the walls.

"These are really good," he said.

"I know," I told him. "Can you pay attention, please? Our top order of business today—review the evidence." Drawing a line down the center of the yellow lined pad, I wrote two categories across the top: *What We Know* and *What We Don't Know*.

"So, what do we know?" I asked, scooping up a handful of popcorn.

Cha Cha took the letter out of the envelope and looked at it again. "We know it's from B to B."

I wrote that down.

Lucas raised his hand.

"Spit it out, Lucas," I told him. "It's just us, not school."

"We know the stamp is twenty years old," he said.

I wrote that down too. "And thanks to you," I told him, "we know that the numbers at the bottom of the letter aren't code, but call numbers for a book. Anything else?"

"The letter is part of a scavenger hunt, we think," said Cha Cha, reaching for more popcorn.

I wrote down *scavenger hunt.*

"We don't know who B and B are," said Lucas.

I wrote down *Who are B and B?* in the *What We Don't Know* column, then tapped my pencil on the notepad. "Let's make a list of everyone we know whose names have a *B* in them," I said, flipping over to the next page. "Like Principal Burnside."

"And Mr. Bigelow, our science teacher," said Lucas.

"Right." I jotted down both of their names.

"How about Mr. Jefferson?" said Cha Cha. "He told us that everyone calls him Bud, and it said so in the yearbook, too."

"What yearbook?" asked Lucas.

"The one back in Truly's room," Cha Cha told him. "It belonged to her aunt."

"Good catch," I said. "Oh, and we can't forget Belinda Winchester. Don't you think she looks like exactly the kind of person who would stick a letter in a book and forget about it?"

"Maybe," said Cha Cha. "But it seems like kind of a strange letter for a lunch lady to write."

"She was a lunch lady?" said Lucas, surprised.

"Yeah," I told him, adding Belinda Winchester to the list anyway.

"How about Ella Bellow?" said Cha Cha.

"Got it," I said, jotting her name down. "And there's Mr. Henry, too."

"That's an *H*," Cha Cha objected.

"He introduced himself as Henry *Butter*worth," I reminded her. "He's definitely a *B*." I shot her a mischievous look. "And of course we can't forget Baxter."

"He wasn't even born back then!"

"I'm *joking*, Cha Cha. Anyway, there are way too many *B*s in this town." I threw down my pen. We were getting nowhere. "So what's the deal with Calhoun?" I asked. "Did you talk to him about getting us into the library?"

"Not yet," Cha Cha replied. "I want to catch him at just the right moment. I think I have an angle, though." She gave us a sly smile. "I've seen the Cotillion list. We might have an in with his dance partner."

# CHAPTER 15

"Places, everyone!" Ms. Ivey clapped her hands.

Reluctantly, I took a step closer to Scooter Sanchez, who was trying his best to ignore me. It was Monday afternoon and we were in the Daniel Webster School gym with the rest of our classmates, gearing up for our first ballroom dance practice.

I still couldn't believe I'd gotten stuck with Scooter as my partner. I thought it was a joke at first, when Cha Cha told me. I know Ms. Ivey only did it because we're both tall. It's not fun being a seventh grader and my height, since most guys my age come up to my armpit, but Scooter Sanchez? I'd rather dance with Lucas Winthrop's mother.

Who'd managed to humiliate Lucas yet again about ten minutes ago, when she showed up with a video camera. Ms. Ivey had to ask her to leave.

"I promise there'll be plenty of photo opportunities later

on, Amelia, after the kids are feeling more confident," Ms. Ivey told her as she escorted her out.

Scooter was all over that, of course. "Smile for the camera, Pookey!" he warbled, doing a little leap in front of Lucas. "Mommy wants a picture for your baby book!"

"That's enough, Scooter," said Ms. Ivey wearily, closing the door behind Mrs. Winthrop. I figured she must get really tired of saying that. Scooter only picks on Lucas about a hundred times a day.

Ms. Ivey introduced Cha Cha's parents, and we all clapped politely when she asked us to thank them for contributing their time. Well, all of us except Scooter.

"This is stupid," he muttered.

I looked at him, startled. "Mr. and Mrs. Abramowitz?"

"No, dork—Cotillion."

Privately, I agreed with him. Dancing is so not my thing. Especially not dancing with Scooter Sanchez.

Ms. Ivey had paired Cha Cha with Lucas, probably because they were the two shortest kids in the class. Jasmine had asked to be partners with Franklin, of course—she's as obsessed with him as Mackenzie is with Mr. Perfect Cameron McAllister—but Ms. Ivey had put him with Amy Nguyen and assigned Jasmine to Calhoun instead.

Which Cha Cha and Lucas and I are hoping will work in our favor.

Cha Cha's plan meant telling Jasmine about the mystery

letter, so now a total of four people know about it. Five, counting Mackenzie.

Ms. Ivey clapped her hands again. She was wearing white gloves, which were identical to mine. I'd picked them up at the General Store—naturally, they carried them—just like the brochure had instructed me to.

"How come you have to wear glovth?" Pippa had asked this morning, when she saw me putting them in my backpack. "Becauth of cootieth?"

I had to smile at that logic. I'd forgotten what a big deal cooties are when you're in kindergarten.

On the other hand, now that I was actually here in the gym, I was grateful for the gloves. I definitely didn't want Scooter cooties.

*Scooties?* The word popped into my mind, and I stifled a giggle.

He shot me a look. "What?"

"Nothing."

The music started, and Mr. and Mrs. Abramowitz demonstrated how we should position ourselves properly. Scooter watched, then reached into his back pocket and pulled something out. A moment later, he plopped a hand covered with a giant ski glove on my shoulder. I gave him a withering look. He was trying to get a laugh from his buddies, as usual.

It worked. A ripple of laughter flowed across the gym.

"Really, Mr. Sanchez?" said Mr. Abramowitz, when he

spotted the source of the hilarity. He crossed the gym and held out his hand. Scooter grinned and dropped the ski glove in it. He was unrepentant, however, and still on the hunt for laughs. We were supposed to be learning how to fox-trot ("Slow, slow, quick, quick," Mr. Abramowitz called out over and over again, as he and Cha Cha's mother led us through the steps), but Scooter turned it into a Truly-trot instead. He spent most of his time "accidentally" stepping on my feet. By the time Mr. Abramowitz caught on and told him to knock it off, my toes were numb.

Things went downhill from there. Next, Scooter thought it would be fun to sing "Truly Gigantic" under his breath in time to the music and steer me around the cafeteria like a bumper car.

"Oops!" he said, as we crashed into Cha Cha and Lucas, sending Lucas sprawling onto the floor. "Pardon me!"

Ms. Ivey clapped her hands once more, signaling a break, and I limped over to one of the chairs that lined the wall to sit down. After helping Lucas to his feet, Cha Cha joined me.

"Having fun yet?" I asked sourly.

She smiled. "You'll get the hang of it."

"Easy for you to say," I grumbled. "You're not stuck with Scooter." Plus, Cha Cha was an old hand at this. She was even managing to make a pipsqueak like Lucas, who'd probably never danced a step in his life, look like a pro. I, on the other hand—well, let's just say that I was not looking forward to making a fool of myself in front of the entire town.

Jasmine flopped onto a seat beside us. "This would be *so* much more fun if Ms. Ivey had let me dance with Franklin," she said with a sigh. "Calhoun never even cracks a smile."

"It's probably because you have cooties," I told her.

She laughed. "Or because he has two left feet."

That was an understatement. Calhoun was an even worse dancer than Scooter, as it turned out. He went left when he was supposed to go right, and right when he was supposed to go left, and he tripped over Jasmine's feet as well as his own. I looked across the room to where he was lounging against the wall, scowling.

"I think he's gotten worse since last year," Jasmine said.

"That's what I'm counting on," said Cha Cha. "That and the fact that he hates to lose. Especially to Scooter."

The music started again and Scooter and I stumbled and bumbled our way—slow, slow, quick, quick—across the floor. My big feet just weren't meant for this. My whole self just wasn't meant for this. Sometimes I wonder if I'm even meant to be a land animal. Life would be a lot easier if I were a bird—especially an owl, swooping silently through the sky. A fish would be good too.

Thinking of fish made me think of swim team tryouts. They were still a couple of weeks away, but I hadn't made any headway with my father.

At least my family was talking to me again. The whole "cross my heart and hope to fly" mess seemed to have blown over. There hadn't even been a big showdown that night when I'd gotten home from the library. My father had still been at the bookstore, finishing up inventory with Aunt True, and my mother was on the couch in the family room nodding off over her homework, too tired to do more than simply remind me of my promise to be more thoughtful of Dad.

"This move has been good for him," she'd said to me. "I see it already, even if he doesn't. But he still has a long road to recovery, sweetheart. Physically and mentally. And anything we can do as a family to help smooth that road will really help him. Even the little things that might not seem important, okay?"

I nodded. "I know, Mom. I'm really, really sorry. I didn't do it on purpose."

"I know you didn't, Little O."

I hadn't heard that nickname in a long time. It was short for "Little Owl," which seems kind of silly now that I tower over my mother by nearly a foot. She's called me that ever since I was a baby and refused to sleep through the night. There's even a picture of us wearing matching sweaters that she knitted with owls on the front and the initials "L. O." for me and "M. O."—that stands for Mama Owl—for her on the back.

The thing is, there are advantages to being a night owl. With five of us kids to take care of and Dad deployed most of the time, there hadn't always been enough of my mother to go around. And ever since I could remember, when I'd wake up in the middle of the night and go to get a drink of water or whatever, she'd still be awake. Sometimes she'd be waiting for a call from Dad—when your husband is stationed halfway around the world, you can't be picky about when to schedule a call—and sometimes she'd be reading or knitting or watching a movie, or just drinking tea and staring into the dark. It was the perfect opportunity to get some alone time with her.

I loved those nighttime visits. Sometimes my mother would make me tea or cocoa too, and sometimes we'd talk or she'd read aloud to me, but mostly I'd just curl up beside her on the sofa, content to be breathing the same air.

Since Black Monday, though, the initials in my nickname might as well have stood for "Largely Overlooked." Between the move, worries over my father and the bookstore, going back to college, and now a part-time job, my mother had reformed her night-owl ways. These days, she was in bed, sound asleep, well before I was.

"Ouch!" Scooter squawked, springing back indignantly. "Quit daydreaming! You stepped on my foot!"

"Like you haven't stepped on mine a million times already!" I retorted.

The music came to a stop, and Ms. Ivey clapped her hands one last time. "Excellent work, everyone!"

"Before you go," added Mr. Abramowitz, "we have an announcement to make."

Cha Cha and I exchanged a glance. This was it—the worm we were hoping would bait the hook for Calhoun.

"This year, for the very first time, the Starlite Dance Studio will be offering cash prizes at Cotillion!"

There was an audible buzz of excitement in the gym at this news. Scooter brightened, and I glanced over at Calhoun to see if it had piqued his interest too, but the expression on his face was unreadable.

"They'll be awarded in a number of categories, including best dance partners, of course, but also best dressed and most improved." Mr. Abramowitz slipped an arm around Cha Cha's mother's waist. "Mrs. Abramowitz and I are hoping that this will give you all an incentive to work especially hard this year, since it's the one hundredth anniversary of our town's Winter Festival. We're expecting media coverage!"

Media other than the *Pumpkin Falls Patriot-Bugle*? Fat chance.

"Remember," added Cha Cha's mother, "you all need to sign up for two complimentary practice sessions at the Starlite."

"Attendance will be taken!" noted Ms. Ivey. "Be sure and show up on time, and bring your best Pumpkin Falls manners!"

I smothered a grin. I'd have to add "Pumpkin Falls manners" to my list of things to tell Mackenzie next time we talked. My cousin is completely fascinated with my new hometown.

"It's like you stepped through a wormhole or something,"

she told me the other night. Mackenzie is a big fan of sci-fi movies. "*Pumpkin Falls: The Town That Time Forgot!*" she added in a fake radio announcer's voice. "I can't believe there's a place that has a dance for the entire town."

"Tell me about it."

"Earth to Truly!" said Cha Cha, yanking me back to reality. "Come on—we're going to be late for math."

# CHAPTER 16

"So, did you talk to him?" Cha Cha asked Jasmine, as the three of us headed back upstairs to our classroom. Lucas trailed a few feet behind.

"Franklin?" said Jasmine dreamily.

"No! Calhoun, duh," said Cha Cha. She looked over at me and rolled her eyes. Jasmine's case of Franklin-on-the-brain was starting to drive us both nuts.

"Oh, right," Jasmine replied, tucking a strand of her dark hair behind an ear. "Yeah."

"So what did he say?"

"He's interested. Especially when I told him that my brother was sure to try for one of the prizes too."

Jasmine had told us that even though they're best friends, her brother and Calhoun are super competitive.

"The worm is on the hook!" crowed Cha Cha.

Now all we had to do was get the worm to the bookstore,

where we'd unleash the second part of our plan.

The four of us were hoping to cut a deal with Calhoun. Private dance lessons with Cha Cha—and a shot at winning one of the prizes—in exchange for getting us into the college library.

Would he go for it? Would he even stay put long enough to listen to our offer? Calhoun was bound to be mad when he found out we'd tricked him.

Lucas had bravely volunteered as bait for our trap. Jasmine's job was to cut Calhoun out of the herd after school, which mostly meant separating him from Scooter. Cha Cha and Lucas and I would run on ahead to Main Street, where I'd make sure the coast was clear at the bookstore while Cha Cha covered the door. Lucas would wait outside, hiding behind the mailbox in front of Lou's Diner with an arsenal of snowballs. Calhoun always walked down Main Street to get home, and we figured once Lucas stepped out and fired off a snowball at him, Calhoun wouldn't be able to resist chasing him down.

It was like dangling a red scarf in front of a bull.

At least we hoped so.

If everything went as planned, Lucas would duck inside the bookstore, Calhoun would come after him just like he and Scooter did before, and bingo, we'd have him cornered. Easy peasy lemon squeezie, right? Of course, there was the risk that Calhoun would break Lucas into tiny pieces when he found out we'd tricked him, but probably not with Aunt True onsite as backup.

First, though, I had to get through math.

"Pop quiz!" Ms. Ivey announced as we took our seats, and everybody groaned.

I glanced down at the sheet of paper she set in front of me. Word problems! My nemesis.

"When you're finished, I'd like you to swap your test with the person next to you, and then we'll all grade them together," said Ms. Ivey.

Ten minutes later, our time was up. I handed my quiz to Cha Cha and she gave me hers. Our teacher put the answer to the first problem on the board. Dang! Cha Cha had gotten it right, but I hadn't. A lot of my other answers were correct, though, which gave me hope that the end result would be enough to convince my father to let me try out for swim team.

Final score: 76 percent.

"Much better, Truly," said Ms. Ivey, patting me on the shoulder as she came by to collect our papers. "Looks like that tutoring is paying off."

I smiled at her. Out of the corner of my eye, I saw Scooter slouched down in his seat at the back of the room. He didn't look so happy with his grade. *That's what you get for stomping on your dancing partner's feet*, I thought smugly.

After class, as I went to my locker to get my jacket, I texted the quiz results to my father.

ONLY 24% MORE TO 100%! he texted back.

I looked at his message, deflated. Lieutenant Colonel Jericho T. Lovejoy was not easy to please.

"Are you ready?" Cha Cha whispered, nodding toward Jasmine and Scooter, who were over by their lockers arguing.

"Mom didn't say anything this morning about another orthodontist appointment!" Scooter protested.

"You weren't listening, that's all," Jasmine told him. "She's meeting you in the parking lot in ten minutes. She won't be happy if you're a no-show."

Scooter's shoulders slumped. "Sorry, dude," he muttered to Calhoun, who was waiting for him. "Maybe we can hang out later."

Jasmine slipped a hand behind her back. She made a shooing motion at Cha Cha and Lucas and me, and the three of us hurried past her. Mrs. Sanchez was nowhere near School Street, but Scooter didn't know that, and by the time he found out, we'd be long gone.

Outside, it was snowing yet again. My friends and I jogged through the flurries toward town, and five minutes later we were in place.

"Don't let your mother see you," I warned Lucas, who was crouched down between the mailbox and the curb outside the diner. "Cha Cha is right over there by the door, in case anything goes wrong. She's got your six."

"My what?"

"Sorry—military-speak. Your back." I trotted over to Cha Cha. "Any sign of Calhoun?"

"Nope."

"Okay. Keep your eyes peeled."

I doubled back and made a brief stop at the diner, then ducked into the bookstore. Now that inventory was finished, Lovejoy's Books was officially open again, but business wasn't exactly bustling. The only one inside the bookshop was Aunt True.

"Truly! What are you doing here?" she said, looking at me in surprise. "You're early for tutoring. Your dad's not back from his physical therapy session yet."

"I know. I brought you a Winter Elixir." My aunt's eyes lit up, and I felt a pang of guilt. The steaming cup came with a side of ulterior motive. I was buttering Aunt True up.

"How thoughtful of you," she said. "Thanks."

"You're welcome."

Aunt True had gotten hooked on Lou's Winter Elixirs. They're the diner's most popular seasonal drink, a piping-hot blend of ginger tea, apple cider, and cranberry juice. I waited until she took a sip, then said, "Remember Lucas and Cha Cha?"

She nodded.

"They're here again today."

She looked around, frowning. "Where?"

"Outside," I replied. "Waiting."

"Waiting for what?"

I had to get this next bit just right. "Um, for a boy."

"Ohhhhhhh," said Aunt True, her eyebrows arching skyward. "A *boy*." She said the word like it had half a dozen syllables.

"You know the Winter Festival dance? Well, Cha Cha wants to—"

Aunt True held up her hand. "Say no more! I've got the picture. I'll make myself scarce when they come in, shall I?"

I nodded. "Thanks, Aunt True."

She was quickly becoming my favorite aunt.

Two minutes later, the front door flew open and Cha Cha and Lucas ran in. Our plan had gone off like clockwork, and Calhoun was right on their heels with a snowball.

"Excuse me, young man," called Aunt True. "This is a snowball-free zone."

Calhoun froze.

"Don't make me sic Miss Marple on you!"

Over on her dog bed, Miss Marple heard her name. The snoring whuffled to a stop and she cracked open an eye, sizing up the situation. Fortunately, Calhoun wasn't familiar with my aunt's sense of humor or with Miss Marple. He eyed the dog warily, then dropped his arm.

"That's more like it," said Aunt True briskly. She held out her hand for the snowball. Calhoun gave it to her, and she opened the door and tossed it in the gutter. Closing the door again, my aunt regarded us thoughtfully. "If I leave the four of you alone while I go rustle up some snacks, will you promise not to kill each other?"

Cha Cha and Lucas and I nodded. Calhoun hesitated, then he shrugged and nodded too.

"Good," said Aunt True, and she disappeared into the office.

We stood there awkwardly for a couple of moments. Then the bell over the door jangled and Jasmine came in, breathless from running. She broke into a big grin when she saw Calhoun. "Hey, it really worked!"

"What worked?" Calhoun glanced from her over to Cha Cha and Lucas and me. His eyes narrowed. "Wait a minute, you did this on *purpose*?"

Jasmine crossed her arms over her chest. "You're the world's worst dance partner," she told him. "People are making fun of us behind our backs."

Calhoun's face went from angry red to embarrassed red.

"But we can fix that for you," Cha Cha added. "And we can make it so you have a shot at beating Scooter for a prize."

Calhoun snorted.

"Really, we can." Cha Cha explained what we wanted from him.

Calhoun looked baffled. "You want me to get you into the college *library*?"

We all nodded.

"What's the catch?"

"There isn't one," I told him.

"So what's so important about the library?"

"None of your business," said Cha Cha. "Are you in?"

He hesitated. "I'll think about it."

Aunt True returned just then with a tray of pumpkin whoopie pies. "You've multiplied!" she said, looking over at Jasmine.

"Oh hey, Aunt True, this is my friend Jasmine Sanchez," I told her. "And you've already met Calhoun."

"Greetings and salutations!" said Aunt True. "Welcome one and all to Lovejoy's Books. Would you like one of our signature treats?" She held out the tray and we each took one of the silver-dollar-size whoopie pies.

"Take more than that," she urged. "Please. Unless we get a rush of customers"—she looked around at the empty store and sighed—"these will just go to waste."

"I'm going to walk my friends down to Lou's," I told her. "If Dad gets here before I get back, tell him I'll only be a minute, okay?"

"You bet." She winked at me as I walked past her. "Cute guy," she whispered.

My mouth fell open.

Aunt True was supposed to think that *Cha Cha* had a crush on Calhoun, not me!

# CHAPTER 17

"So," said my mother, cutting up Pippa's sausages. Wednesday was breakfast-for-dinner night, everybody's favorite. "Do you think you'll be able to join us at the meet tonight?" Her tone was neutral, and she gave my father the briefest of glances.

"Let him find his way back into the family again in his own way and his own time," the therapists at the military hospital in Maryland had counseled my mother. She'd shared their advice with Danny and Hatcher and me, and we were all trying to help her follow it. It wasn't easy, though, especially since progress seemed glacial.

Before, whenever he was home on leave, Dad had always come to as many of our practices and meets as he could, but now, even though he's technically around, we hardly see him outside of the bookstore.

My father chewed his waffle, swallowed, then washed it

down with a sip of coffee. "Maybe," he said, and my mother left it at that.

I glanced at the clock on the wall. "I'm due at the library in five minutes," I said. Calhoun had thought our offer over and said yes, and my classmates and I were scheduled to meet him tonight at six. "If it's okay with you, ma'am," I finished politely.

"Sure, honey," she replied. "Just be back by seven, okay? I don't want to be late for Danny's first meet."

I practically sprinted down Hill Street into town, the freshly fallen snow crunching under my feet at every step. Passing under Lovejoy College's arched iron gates, I jogged on toward the library.

I'd been to the campus plenty of times before. My brothers and I used to play hide-and-seek here in the summertime when we'd visit Gramps and Lola. I'd never seen it in winter, though, and I looked around with curiosity as I crossed the quad. The old buildings and tall, sturdy trees were shawled in white, and the snow falling in the soft glow of the old-fashioned streetlights lining the paths was like something out of a postcard. In fact, I was fairly sure I'd seen this very scene on a postcard at the General Store. Students scurried along, bundled up in hats and mittens and scarves, and out in the middle of the quad, a group of them was building a snowman. I didn't linger to watch, though. It was too cold, and I didn't want to be late.

Calhoun was the only one on the library steps so far.

"Um, hi," I said.

He grunted a hello back. I stood beside him, squirming a little inside when I recalled how Aunt True thought I had a crush on him. Crushes are right up there on the list of things I'm not good at. The last time I'd had one I was Pippa's age. Growing up with two older brothers didn't leave much room for crushes—in my experience, boys were mostly loud, smelly creatures who liked to tease me and make Toot Soup noises and play practical jokes. I liked boys just fine—but as friends and brothers, not crushes.

Mom and I had talked about it once last summer, after we'd moved into our Austin house and Mackenzie started talking nonstop about Mr. Perfect Cameron McAllister, the guy on our swim team.

"I just don't get it, Mom," I'd said. "He's not that interesting. Or cute, whatever that means. Really, he's not."

She'd laughed. "You'll get it one of these days, honey. No rush, though. And I know exactly how you feel—you think you've got it bad with two brothers? I have six of them!"

My mother told me she didn't date much at all until she got to college, and I guess I just figure it'll be the same for me.

My feet were cold, and I stamped them, wishing Cha Cha and Jasmine and Lucas would hurry up.

A few minutes later they finally showed, and Calhoun led us inside. "Hey, Chester," he said, waving to the security guard.

"Calhoun, my man! What's up?"

"Is it okay if I show my friends around?"

The guard looked past him at Cha Cha and Jasmine and me and grinned. "Way to impress the ladies, dude!"

Calhoun blushed to the roots of his sandy hair. The security guard laughed. "I'm just pulling your leg. Sure, go on in, buddy. Anybody asks, you tell them Chester okayed it." He waved us through the metal detector.

From the outside, the library looked like just another traditional New England building, all white clapboard and sashed windows. Inside, however, was another story. I couldn't help gawking as we entered the soaring lobby. To the right a broad marble staircase curved toward the upper stories. Overhead were rows and rows of skylights, and straight ahead the lobby opened onto a huge glassed-in courtyard.

"Wow," I said. "It's like being inside a snow globe."

Calhoun gave a half smile. It made him look almost human. "Yeah, it's pretty cool," he replied. Then the smile vanished, and the gruff mask slid back into place. "For a library, I mean."

As we started to pass a bronze statue in the middle of the lobby, I did a double take. I'd recognize that nose anywhere! I drew closer and read the plaque on it—sure enough, it was Nathaniel Daniel himself. FOUNDER OF LOVEJOY COLLEGE AND FRIEND TO ALL, the plaque proclaimed.

"Hey, that's the guy in the picture over your fireplace," Cha Cha said, and I nodded.

"How come his nose is so shiny, compared to the rest of him?" I asked Calhoun.

"Chester says students rub it for good luck at exam time," he told me.

I gave it a swipe too. It felt a little weird, rubbing my ancestor's nose, but the Pumpkin Falls Private Eyes could use all the luck they could get.

"So how do we find what we're looking for?" asked Cha Cha.

Calhoun led us over to a bank of computers. I pulled the envelope from my backpack, took the letter out, and read the call number aloud.

He typed it in, then gave me a funny look. "You didn't tell me you were looking for a Shakespeare book," he said as the search results flashed onscreen.

"You didn't need to know," I replied.

"It's upstairs," he said, and led us to an elevator behind the marble staircase. We emerged on the fourth floor.

"How come he knows so much about this place?" I whispered to my friends as we followed Calhoun down a long central aisle.

"Scooter says he spends a lot of time here," Jasmine whispered back. "His father's office is in the building next door."

Calhoun stopped and pointed down one of the rows of bookcases. "It should be on one of those shelves at the end."

"We can take it from here," I told him.

Calhoun turned to Cha Cha. "What time is our first practice?"

"Saturday at eleven," she replied. "See you there."

He nodded and left.

The four of us walked slowly down the row, scanning the stickers on the books.

"Got it!" I said, plucking a thin volume from between two larger ones on one of the bottom shelves. I read the title aloud: "*Much Ado About Nothing* by William Shakespeare."

"Careful, it looks old," said Cha Cha.

"Is there another letter inside?" Jasmine asked eagerly, craning to see over my shoulder.

I riffled through the brittle, mottled brown pages. "Doesn't look like it," I replied. I went through the book again, then turned it upside down and gave it a gentle shake. "Nothing."

We looked at each other. Was this another dead end?

"There has to be something!" said Cha Cha.

"There isn't." I couldn't hide my disappointment.

"Check the book pocket," said Lucas.

"Huh?"

He tugged the book from my hand. Turning to the very back, he pointed to the cardboard pocket still glued in place. "Lots of old books have them," he explained. "Mr. Henry showed me. Before computers, it's where they used to put the book card that kept track of borrowers and due dates. It would make a good hiding place."

"Lucas! You're a genius!" I poked a finger inside, and sure enough, there was something there. I fished it out. It was a piece of paper with two words written on it: *Check shelf.*

We did, dropping to our knees and searching thoroughly. Nothing but books and more books.

"If I were an envelope, where would I be?" mused Jasmine.

"Hang on a sec," I said. "I've got an idea. Move over, you guys."

Lying down on the floor, I inspected the underside of the shelf directly above where we'd found the book. Sure enough, something was stuck to it: an envelope. "Got it!" I said triumphantly, peeling off the duct tape that held it in place.

I scrambled back to my feet. Like the other envelope, this one simply had the letter *B* written on the outside. Unlike the other envelope, though, there was no stamp.

"Open it," urged Jasmine, and as I did, my friends crowded around to read over my shoulder.

Just as before, this letter also contained a quote:

*I see, lady, the gentleman is not in your books.*

It, too, was signed simply with a *B*. I read what was written below: "Wednesday the third, B-4."

"So who do you think the *B*s are?" asked Jasmine. "And what the heck does that quote mean?"

I shook my head. "I have absolutely no idea."

"I do," said Calhoun from the other side of the stacks. He smirked at us through a gap in the books. "But it's going to cost you."

# CHAPTER 18

"It's a quote from *Much Ado About Nothing*," Calhoun told us, after we'd coughed up all the money we had in our wallets.

"Well, duh," snapped Jasmine. "We didn't need to pay you almost twenty bucks for that."

Calhoun smirked again. "Not my fault you don't know your Shakespeare," he said. "The main characters in the play are Beatrice and Benedick." He pointed to the initials on the envelope and the letter. "There's your B and B."

I stared at him. "How'd you figure that out so fast?"

Calhoun shrugged. "My father is a Shakespeare scholar," he told us. "He teaches classes on the Bard."

"Who's the Bard?" asked Jasmine.

"Well, duh," said Calhoun softly, repeating Jasmine's earlier words. "Shakespeare, of course. Everybody knows that."

Jasmine flushed.

"This quote here," Calhoun continued, tapping a finger

against the letter, "'I see, lady, the gentleman is not in your books'? That means Benedick is on Beatrice's blacklist—he's not in her 'good books.' Get it? She's mad at him." Looking around at our stunned expressions, he grabbed the book away from Cha Cha. "Here, check it out, Act I, Scene 1: 'There is a kind of merry war betwixt Signior Benedick and her: they never meet but there's a skirmish of wit between them.'"

"And that is supposed to mean what, exactly?" I asked.

Calhoun sighed, clearly disgusted by my ignorance. "The two of them spend most of the play bickering with each other. They argue all the time, but it turns out that they're really in love."

My mouth fell open. "Are you telling us that this is a *love letter*?"

"Duh," Calhoun said again.

I gave him the stink eye.

Calhoun was smart. Why did he take such pains to hide it, I wondered? I looked over at Cha Cha. "Should we show him the other letter too?"

She shrugged. "Might as well."

"Sorry, kids, I'd like to stay and play but I have to go," Calhoun told us, before I could fish it out and hand it over. "My sister's cheering for some wrestling meet tonight, and my father wants me to go along and watch."

"Shoot," I said, glancing at my cell phone. "My family's going too. I was supposed to be home five minutes ago,"

"Me too," said Cha Cha. Her cousin Noah is on Danny's team.

"How about you all come over to my house tomorrow after school?" I suggested. "You're invited too," I told Calhoun.

I could tell he was curious. "We'll see" was all he said, though, playing it cool.

I ran all the way home. Fortunately, my family was running late, so nobody noticed I'd blown my deadline. Dad had gone back to the bookstore, and my mother tried not to sound disappointed as we all piled into the car.

"Danny's first meet of the season!" she said in an overly enthusiastic tone. "Won't this be fun?"

I was surprised at how full the gym was at West Hartfield High. I guess there aren't a whole heck of a lot of other things to do in the heart of maple syrup country on a weeknight in the dead of winter. I spotted Belinda Winchester up in the stands, and Ella Bellow was there too, talking to Bud Jefferson from the stamp store.

"Truly! Up here!" Cha Cha called. She and her mother and Baxter were saving seats for us.

Pippa and Baxter were so excited to see each other they nearly fell off the bleachers and had to be corralled into a coloring project. Lauren made a beeline for Belinda Winchester, who was sitting a couple of rows in front of us. Belinda reached into her pocket and handed Lauren something—a kitten, most likely. The two of them have bonded over their mutual love of animals. Mom was a little worried at first, since Belinda is, well, kind of odd. In fact, odd is putting it mildly if you ask me, which nobody ever does.

"She's nuts, but not *nuts* nuts, you know?" Aunt True assured my mother, after Belinda invited Lauren over to view the latest litter. Lauren's dying to have a kitten, but my mother says she has enough pets. "Unless you consider someone who doesn't own a TV and doesn't read the newspaper nuts, Belinda's just your garden-variety cat lady. I've spent a lot of time with her over the past few weeks—she's practically a fixture at the bookshop these days. Lauren will be perfectly safe."

"Lauren!" my mother called a few minutes later, motioning her back. "Honey, you've got homework to do. You can visit after you're done."

Lauren slumped down on the bench beside me with a sigh of resignation. Reaching into her backpack, she pulled out her book report on *Charlotte's Web*.

"Will you read what I've written so far?" she asked me.

"Sure."

"Aunt True says that if the first edition hasn't sold by the time I give my report, she'll bring it to school so I can show everybody," Lauren told me.

"Cool." I started to read.

*Elwyn Brooks White, known to his friends as Andy, was born on July 11, 1899, in Mount Vernon, New York.*

I only got as far as the part where Mr. White and his wife bought a saltwater farm in Maine, when the lights in the gym dimmed and loud rock music blared. A moment later, Danny and his team came running out in their maroon-and-white warm-up suits. The West Hartfield fans clapped and cheered.

Of all of us, my brother Danny is the most like our father. Same strong jaw, same wiry build. When he's in his wrestling singlet, he looks almost exactly the way Dad did in his yearbook pictures.

I waved to Hatcher, who was standing on the sidelines. Scooter Sanchez was there too, along with several other guys I recognized from school. In Pumpkin Falls, the middle school wrestlers attend all the high school meets and tournaments. They help set up and tear down the mats, warm up the team, and watch and learn.

Danny and Cha Cha's cousin Noah both wrestle in the 152-pound weight class, so they wouldn't be up for a while. As Cha Cha and I settled in for the long wait, I noticed that our mothers had somehow gotten onto the topic of how they met their husbands.

"Harry and I were rivals in a dance competition," Mrs. Abramowitz said as the music faded and two guys even skinnier than Lucas Winthrop stepped onto the mat for the first match. Watching 106-pounders wrestle always makes me anxious. Their twiggy arms and legs look like rubber bands that might snap at any moment as they flail around trying to pin each other. "I lost the competition but gained a husband."

My mother laughed. "J. T. and I sat next to each other in freshman English at the University of Texas," she said. "When he told me he was from a place called Pumpkin Falls, New Hampshire. I thought he was making it up!"

"Wasn't he there on a wrestling scholarship?" asked Cha Cha's mother. "I seem to remember Ella Bellow saying something about that."

"I'll bet she did," my mother replied, and she and Mrs. Abramowitz exchanged wry smiles. It's no secret that our postmistress loves to gossip.

"So wrestling runs in the family, then?" said Cha Cha's mother.

Mom nodded. "My family too. J. T. was the first guy I dated who was willing to take on my brothers." My mother loves telling this story, and we all love hearing it. It's practically a legend in our family.

"I have six of them," she continued, her Texas twang deepening as she warmed to her tale.

"You have *six* brothers?" said Mrs. Abramowitz. Her eyes, which were the same green as Cha Cha's and Baxter's, widened.

My mother smiled her sunflower smile. "A boy for every day of the week and a girl for Sunday, my grandmother used to say. Anyway, my brothers made J. T. arm wrestle each one of them before he was allowed to take me out on a date."

Cha Cha's mother laughed.

"I'm serious!" said my mother, grinning. "He must have really wanted to ask me out, because he beat every single one of them."

"That's quite an accomplishment," said Mrs. Abramowitz, glancing over my mother's shoulder. I looked up and saw my father making his way through the crowded bleachers toward us. Aunt True was with him, bundled up in a sheepskin jacket and another hat from her seemingly bottomless collection of embarrassments—a rainbow knitted number this time, with a spray of tassels on top that looked kind of like Annie Freeman's braids.

My mother gave my knee a squeeze, which I knew meant, *Don't make a big deal about your father coming along; just act normal.*

"J. T., True, this is Rachel Abramowitz," she said. "My boss at the Starlite."

"And more importantly, Cha Cha and Baxter's mother," said Mrs. Abramowitz. She smiled up at my father. "I hear you're quite the arm wrestler, J. T. Dinah was just telling me about your exploits back in college."

He gave her a brief, polite nod. "Yes, ma'am."

We all fell silent as he took his seat. I couldn't help but notice as Cha Cha's mother's gaze wandered to the hook at the end of his shirtsleeve.

My father's arm-wrestling days were over.

# CHAPTER 19

"I can't believe Hatcher did that to you!" Mackenzie's shocked face looked out at me from my laptop screen.

Disaster had struck after the wrestling meet.

As we were heading to the lobby, Hatcher came bounding over and slung a sweaty arm around my shoulders. He knows I hate this, which of course makes him do it even more.

"Eew, get off!" I cried, shoving him away. "Go take a shower!"

"What's the matter?" he teased. "Just trying to share the love." He hoisted his elbow in the air and fanned his armpit in my direction.

"Mom, make him stop!" I protested.

My mother shot him a look.

Hatcher dropped his arm. "Jeez, Drooly, can't you take a joke?"

I froze. Scooter Sanchez was standing directly behind

him. At first I thought maybe I was in the clear, but then I saw a slow smile slide across Scooter's face, and I knew he'd heard my brother, and that I'd be hearing about it too, for as long as I lived in Pumpkin Falls.

I ran up to my room when we got home and slammed the door. Miss Marple whined to be let in, but I ignored her. Flinging myself on the bed, I shoved my head under my pillow to muffle the noise as I let out a howl of rage and humiliation. Angry tears spilled over, and I let them.

"Go away!" I hollered a little while later when someone knocked on my door. It was probably Hatcher. He'd tried to apologize in the car on the way home, but I wouldn't listen. I didn't plan on ever speaking to him again. Scooter would never let this go.

"I don't know what to do," I wailed to Mackenzie.

"Maybe your parents will let you come live here with us," she replied. "You know, like the witness protection program or something."

"Fat chance."

"Well, you're going to have to deal with it, then."

She was right. I needed a plan. The problem was, I couldn't think of one.

The next day at school I tried to keep my distance from Scooter, but, of course, that didn't work. Somehow he managed to pop up at every turn, with the same stupid grin on his face that had been there at the gym last night.

"Truly Drooly," he sang to me softly in math class.

"Could you pass me that beaker, Truly Drooly?" he asked in science class.

"Pardon me, Truly Drooly," he said when he bumped into me on purpose in the lunch line.

Things took a turn for the worse during our ballroom dance class, when he started calling me "Drooly Gigantic."

I stomped on his foot then, hard. Unfortunately, Cha Cha's father saw me. He frowned. "Miss Lovejoy? Pumpkin Falls manners, please."

*The heck with Pumpkin Falls manners*, I thought bitterly and stomped again the second Mr. Abramowitz's back was turned.

"What's your problem?" Scooter whispered angrily.

"You know exactly what my problem is!" I whispered back.

Somehow, I managed to make it through the day. At least I had the Pumpkin Falls Private Eyes to look forward to.

Nearly twenty-four hours had passed since we'd all met at the college library. My parents had left for Boston early this morning, so my tutoring sessions had been canceled for the rest of the week. My father was finally ready to get fitted for a more permanent prosthetic arm, and Aunt True was going to look after my brothers and sisters and me while he and my mother were away.

Dad would actually be coming home with two new prostheses: a flesh-colored silicone one that's strictly for show, and a high-tech one made of black titanium and polymer that's controlled by electrical impulses sent from his brain. It's the latest technology, and unlike the one he's been wearing, there's no harness; it's held on by suction and is supposed to be much more comfortable. Mom showed us a video of it online, and it looked pretty awesome. Hatcher and Danny have already dubbed it "The Terminator."

Ever since that day in the bookshop, all of us had been calling his temporary prosthesis "Captain Hook." Dad rolls his eyes when we do, but Pippa thinks it's funny, so he puts up with it. We can tell he's relieved he doesn't have to hide it in a gym bag anymore.

I had the house to myself until dinnertime. Hatcher and Danny were at their wrestling practices, Lauren had gone up the street to visit Belinda Winchester and her menagerie, and Pippa had a playdate with Baxter over at the Abramowitzes'.

Even so, my friends and I still wound up in Lola's art studio. It was beginning to feel like a clubhouse of sorts. Calhoun came too, tagging along behind us on the walk home from school. Even though curiosity won out in the end, he was careful not to get too close so people wouldn't think we were together. He wanted to make it clear that we were the dorks and he was still the cool one.

"You are not seriously calling yourselves the Pumpkin Falls Private Eyes, are you?" Calhoun said when I called the meeting to order.

I could feel my face flush. Calhoun was almost as infuriating as Scooter Sanchez. "So do you want to see the first letter we found or not?" I snapped.

"You don't have to bite my head off," he said. "And, yeah, I do. I wouldn't have come otherwise."

I passed the envelope to him, explaining how I had found it at the bookstore.

He scanned the letter. "This is from *Much Ado* too," he told us. "'February face'—cold and stormy, get it? Whoever is writing the letters is trying to get someone not to be mad at them. They're trying to say they're sorry."

My friends and I looked at each other. Who was this guy, and what had he done with Calhoun?

"So why make up some elaborate scavenger hunt? Why not just pick up the phone and call, or send flowers?" asked Cha Cha.

Calhoun shrugged. "Don't look at me. I didn't write the letters."

"Um, so B and B are nicknames, then, right?" said Lucas, who was sitting scrunched up on the floor, as far away as possible from Calhoun.

We all nodded.

"That means they could be just about anybody."

My friends and I looked at each other. Lucas was right. Making a list of people with B names hadn't narrowed down the field at all.

"We don't stand a chance of solving this," I said glumly.

"Don't give up yet," said Cha Cha. "We still know what year the stamp was issued. That makes a difference, doesn't it?"

"And figuring out this clue's gotta help too," added Jasmine. "What did it say again?"

I recited it from memory. "'Wednesday the third, B-4.' Anybody have any ideas?" I glanced around the room. Nobody raised a hand, not even Calhoun this time.

So much for the Pumpkin Falls Private Eyes. We were back to square one: completely clueless.

# CHAPTER 20

"Hatcher Lovejoy, that's your fifth piece of pizza!" exclaimed Aunt True, looking at my brother in disbelief.

He grinned at her.

"Sixth for me," said Danny smugly, taking a big bite out of the slice he was holding. Danny loves Friday nights. Pizza is his favorite food, and Friday nights have always been pizza night in our family.

My aunt shook her head. "I don't know how your parents do it—it's like raising goats."

Lauren and Pippa thought this was hilarious, especially when Hatcher and Danny stuck their forefingers up on top of their heads like horns and started bleating.

No one seemed to notice that I was on my fifth piece too. Invisible as usual—that's me.

Someone kicked me under the table. I looked up. Hatcher

passed me another piece of pizza, then held up six fingers. I smiled. Not so invisible after all.

My brother and I were speaking again. He'd barged into my room before school this morning to apologize. Well, sort of.

"I hate it when you're mad at me," he'd said, standing in the doorway in his bathrobe with his arms crossed.

"Like it's my fault!" I'd retorted, sitting up in bed.

"You know I didn't mean for it to slip out."

"Yeah, well, it's a little late for that!"

"C'mon, Drooly—please?"

"Don't call me that anymore," I'd snapped, but Hatcher looked so droopy and hangdog that after a minute I added, "Fine. Whatever."

"I'll tell Scooter to keep it quiet, okay?"

I'd nodded, knowing it wouldn't do any good. And it didn't. A nickname like mine was far too irresistible for someone like Scooter.

I was doomed to be Truly Drooly forever.

I sighed and took a bite of pizza. We were at Aunt True's apartment. It was a pretty cool place, I thought, looking around. She'd painted the dining area and living room a warm color she described as "halfway between Golden Retriever and sunset," and the walls were crowded with interesting stuff from her travels: wooden masks, tribal rugs, sculptures, bright beadwork, and art from just about every-place imaginable, plus photographs. Tons of photographs—Aunt True teaching school in Kenya; Aunt True in a dugout canoe in the Amazon rain forest; Aunt True beside a reindeer in Lapland and planting trees in Nepal and standing in front of the Taj Mahal in India. She had stories to go along with every picture too.

Glancing at the mantel, I noticed that she'd framed our family Christmas card. This year's was particularly awkward. It wasn't just the matching sweaters my mother always forces us to wear—a Gifford tradition we keep begging her to ditch—it was me. I was smack-dab in the middle of the lineup as usual, only this year I towered over everyone else.

"I thought we'd go downstairs to the bookstore after dessert," Aunt True said, pulling my attention back to the table. "I need your help with something."

"Can we have dethert now?" asked Pippa, eyeing the cupcakes on the sideboard. No Tibetan spices or yak milk lurking in those puppies—they were in a box that said LOU'S on it. Memphis was seated beside it, a great big black lump of furry fury. His tail lashed back and forth as he glared down at Miss Marple. Memphis didn't think much of the fact that a dog had been invited home for dinner.

"Of course," said Aunt True. She reached for the box and passed it around the table. We each took a cupcake. As Danny started to take another, Aunt True snatched them out of his reach. "Not so fast!" she said. "Follow me if you want seconds."

We trailed downstairs after her, Miss Marple bringing up the rear. A circle of folding chairs was waiting for us and we each took a seat, along with another cupcake. Miss Marple settled onto the floor nearby, keeping a hopeful eye on us, and our dessert.

"Here's the thing," said Aunt True, wiping some pink frosting from her lips. It matched her outfit, which Pippa had helped her choose this morning—pink leggings, a pink-and-white striped sweater, and pink clogs. "Two weeks ago, your father set a six-week deadline for turning this business around before we throw in the towel."

This was news to my siblings, and while it sailed right over Pippa's and Lauren's heads—especially Lauren, who was surreptitiously reading *A Little Princess*—my brothers looked shocked.

"I posted an ad for the first edition of *Charlotte's Web* on our website," Aunt True continued, "and we've had some nibbles, which could make all the difference in being able to pay back the bank loan. Meanwhile, though, I think there's more we can do to make this next month count."

Hatcher and I exchanged a glance. Aunt True had something up her sleeve.

"What I'm talking about"—she paused dramatically—"is a makeover!"

We looked at her blankly. Aunt True didn't wear makeup. Was she planning to start? I didn't see how that was going to boost sales. But it turned out she had something much bigger in mind.

"This is where you all come in," she explained. "You know how your father always says that Lovejoys can do anything? I want us to prove that to him this weekend! He won't recognize this place by the time we're done with it."

She was talking about a *bookshop* makeover.

"This is a family business, and the only way it's going to work is if the whole family is involved," she continued, pacing back and forth in front of us. "First, I think we should list the store's strengths and weaknesses. You kids have a different perspective, you might zero in on things I've missed." She paused and looked at us expectantly.

"Um, I'm not sure what you mean?" said Danny.

"You know, like for instance the fact that the store has great windows," she explained, with a sweeping gesture toward the front of the store. We all swiveled around and stared. The display windows looked pretty ordinary, if you asked me, which nobody ever did. "What other things does it have going for it?"

We glanced around, then looked at each other, then shrugged.

"There'th a lot of bookth," offered Pippa, and Danny snorted.

Aunt True ignored him. "Excellent observation, Miss Pippa."

"The ceilings are really high," said Hatcher, craning his head back. "Maybe you could use the wall space above the bookshelves for artwork and stuff." He was thinking of her apartment, I suspected, nearly every inch of which was covered with something.

"Interesting," said Aunt True. "I hadn't thought of that. See what I mean about a different perspective?"

I raised my hand.

"Truly?"

"This isn't a strength, Aunt True," I said, "but it's dark in here."

"That's because it's nighttime, you moron!" scoffed Danny.

"Daniel," Aunt True chided. "I've noticed the same thing, Truly. The place needs brightening up." She stared thoughtfully at the ceiling. "We should probably invest in better light fixtures eventually, but these still work, and they have a nice retro flair. We can certainly wash the glass globes on them for starters."

Crossing to one of the windows, she grabbed a handful of the dark green material that was hanging beside it and gave it a shake. A big cloud of dust flew up. "These drapes have got to go, don't you think?" she said, as we all started waving our arms and coughing. "Your father claims they protect the merchandise from fading, but I say they block the light. The more we can open this place up, the better. Who votes for taking them down?"

I raised my hand. So did Hatcher and Pippa. Danny and Lauren looked uncertain.

"Can Mith Marple vote?" asked Pippa, slipping the dog a bite of cupcake.

"Technically, she's family, so yes, she gets a vote," said Aunt True, and my little sister hoisted Miss Marple's paw into the air.

"So that makes four in favor—five if we count Miss Marple—and two against," my aunt continued. "Or maybe more on the fence than against. The ayes have it!"

"Um, Aunt True," Danny began, "don't you think you should wait and ask—"

Aunt True flapped a hand dismissively. "Don't worry. Your father and I don't always see eye to eye on everything, but he'll love it. So, any other comments?"

"The walls could probably use a new coat of paint," said Hatcher.

"Can we paint it pink?" Pippa looked hopeful.

"No way!" Danny and Hatcher burst out simultaneously. I shook my head too.

"Pink's probably not going to work, Pip," Aunt True told her. "But the walls definitely need painting, and they definitely need to be a cheerful color. You can help me pick one out, okay? Now, what else?"

"How about this?" said Hatcher, scuffing his foot against the carpet on the floor. "It's gross." He was right. The carpet was dark green like the drapes, and had been there for as long as I could remember.

My aunt made a face. "Hideous, isn't it? Replacing it isn't in my tiny remodeling budget, though."

I poked my toe under a loose corner by the nearest bookcase. "Do we have to have carpet? Maybe we could just get rid of it instead of replacing it."

Aunt True came over to where I was sitting and knelt down. Peeling back the loose corner, she inspected the floor underneath. "You may be on to something, Truly," she said, her voice rising in excitement. "This is wide-plank pine, if I'm not mistaken, and it looks to be in pretty good shape." She stood up again, brushing off her pink leggings. "I doubt it's something the six of us could tackle this weekend, though. It's a big demolition job. "

My brothers perked up at this. "Demolition" is one of their favorite words.

"I thought you said Lovejoys could do anything," Danny reminded her.

"Point taken," said Aunt True.

My brother grinned. "What if we got some of our wrestling buddies to help?"

"Do you think they would?"

Danny and Hatcher both nodded.

"Well, then, why not? Let's take the plunge!" Aunt True put her hands on her hips and looked around. "I think that about covers it, although I'd also like to make better use of our existing space. Rearrange some of the bookcases, freshen the children's room, add a display table or two for new arrivals and sidelines—"

"What are thidelineth?" asked Pippa.

"All the stuff we sell that isn't books, honey," Aunt True told her.

Aunt True might call them "sidelines," but my father calls them a word I could get into big trouble for repeating.

"I want a gift-wrapping station behind the counter too," my aunt continued, "and maybe we could bring in some armchairs and lamps and set up a few cozy reading nooks."

Hearing this, Lauren looked up from her book. "I like that idea."

"You can be the reading-nook consultant, then." Aunt True smiled at us. "It's going to look like a brand-new store by the time we're done!"

Her enthusiasm was contagious. I liked the idea of surprising our parents, and I could tell that my brothers and sisters did too.

"Do you really think we can pull this off?" I asked.

"We're going to need some help," Aunt True admitted.

"But if there's one good thing about small towns, it's the fact that word travels fast on the grapevine. It's time to activate my secret weapon."

"You have a thecret weapon?" Pippa's eyes widened behind her sparkly pink glasses.

Aunt True put her finger to her lips. "I certainly do. And her name is Ella Bellow."

# CHAPTER 21

Score one for the town's biggest gossip.

Ella Bellow totally came through. By nine o'clock the next morning, there were two dozen people waiting for us on the bookshop doorstep.

Not only that, there was a news truck too. And not just any news truck, but the one from Channel 5 in Boston.

"Are you the owner of Lovejoy's Books?" someone called out, shouldering his way through the crowd. I recognized the questioner's face—well, his smile at least. Half the people on the planet knew that smile. A video of it flying across a room on its own and landing on a plate of cream puffs had been leaked onto the Internet a few years ago, and made him, his dentures, and his morning news show, *Hello, Boston!* famous.

Carson Dawson was smaller than he looked on TV—way shorter than me—and a lot wrinklier underneath his fake tan. In one leather-gloved hand he clutched a cup of coffee from

Lou's. In the other he held a microphone, which he thrust into Aunt True's face. *Peacock*, I thought instantly. Showy and loud.

"Co-owner," my aunt replied, unlocking the door.

"Is it true that your brother is a wounded warrior, Ms. Lovejoy? And that the two of you are struggling to turn around an ailing family business?"

Aunt True shot a sour look at Ella Bellow, who seemed to be fascinated by one of the buttons on her black coat all of a sudden. Our postmistress had been oversharing again. "Yes, it's true," my aunt admitted.

"I'd love to interview you!" gushed Mr. Dawson. "We're in town to film the famous waterfall, and when we saw the crowd, we came over to find out what all the commotion was about. This would make a wonderful companion piece. You know, 'small town pitches in to help wounded veteran.' Our viewers love local color."

Hatcher looked over at me and rolled his eyes.

"I'll agree to do an interview on one condition," Aunt True replied. Raising her voice to make sure everyone gathered on the sidewalk could hear her, she continued, "What we're doing this weekend is a surprise for my brother and his wife. They won't be home until Monday, and I don't want the story getting out beforehand." She leveled a stern gaze at Carson Dawson.

He nodded, chuckling. "Got it. Mum's the word."

Aunt True asked Hatcher and me to hold the door open for everyone, then taped a piece of paper to the window. I inspected it as the waiting crowd streamed past. My aunt had posted a wish list—furniture, mostly, and other items for the reading nooks she was hoping to set up.

Lou was first in line, carrying a stack of boxes filled with donuts. He winked at me as he passed. "Gotta keep everyone's strength up."

Mrs. Winthrop was right behind him with a big coffee urn. Lucas was next. Annie Freeman, who'd come with her brother Franklin and their parents, was talking his ear off.

"Hey, Truly," said Cha Cha as she trailed in behind the Freemans.

"Hey." I waggled my fingers at Baxter, who was with her. He smiled shyly.

"My parents can't come until after lunch," Cha Cha told me. "They've got Cotillion practice sessions all morning."

I was not looking forward to mine, but I didn't tell her that. "No problem" was all I said.

The Nguyens filed in, along with the Mahoneys from the antiques store next door, Bud Jefferson from Earl's Coins and Stamps across the street, and Reverend Quinn, the minister at Gramps and Lola's church. Mr. Henry the librarian smiled at me as he passed, and so did Ms. Ivey and Mr. Bigelow. Mr. Burnside, our principal, had brought his whole family, and there were a bunch of other people I didn't recognize.

"So happy to help Walt and Lola's family," said Mrs. Farnsworth, who ran the General Store with her husband.

Augustus Wilde swooped in after her, his silver hair brushed back from his forehead like the crest of a wave, and his trademark black cape fluttering in the chilly breeze. Hatcher looked over at me and grinned.

"We're saved! Captain Romance is here!" he whispered, and I smothered a laugh.

Augustus was Pumpkin Falls's resident celebrity. He wrote romance novels under the alias "Augusta Savage." His books fill up an entire shelf in the romance section, or as Hatcher calls it, the shirtless-men-kissing-beautiful-women section. Augustus drops by at least once a week. He sneaks over to the shelf that holds his books and turns them face out when he thinks no one is looking.

"Guerrilla marketing," he'd confided to me when I'd caught him at it. "We authors have to do what we can."

Danny and Hatcher's wrestling buddies swarmed in last, decked out in their team sweatshirts. Scooter Sanchez grinned at me as he sauntered past. I skewered him with a look that could have stopped an elephant.

"I didn't say anything!" he protested.

He didn't have to. I knew exactly what he was thinking.

Belinda Winchester was the final one through the door. I caught the faint strains of "My Girl" from her ever-present earbuds as she craned to see over my shoulder.

"Where's Miss Marple?" she demanded.

I pointed to the office, where Aunt True had corralled her for the day. Belinda marched over and clipped a leash to the dog's collar. "Too much excitement in here for this old girl," she announced, heading right out again. "I'm taking her for a walk."

Carson Dawson and his crew trotted around behind Aunt True as she gave them a tour of the bookshop. She unlocked the rare book cabinet and showed off the first edition of *Charlotte's Web*, which it turned out was Mr. Henry's favorite book.

"Mine, too!" exclaimed my aunt. "It's the perfect novel, isn't it?"

"Sublime," he replied as she passed it to him.

"I'm rather fond of it myself," the TV host admitted.

Mr. Henry held the book reverently. "I'd give anything for an autographed copy!" he said, and Carson Dawson got some footage of him talking with Aunt True about E. B. White, and the author's farm in Maine, where he'd raised actual pigs and observed actual spiders, and how he'd called the book his "hymn to the barn."

"Fun fact," said Mr. Henry. "Did you know that E. B. White did the narration for the audiobook? And that it took him seventeen takes to get through the passage about Charlotte's death without crying?"

"I can never get through it without crying, either," said Aunt True, and Mr. Henry nodded sympathetically.

I couldn't help noticing that Scooter had managed to wedge himself in front of the camera. I also couldn't help noticing Calhoun when he showed up a few minutes later, after the *Charlotte's Web* lovefest was over. This was mostly because my aunt made such a big deal out of it.

"Truly!" she called from across the store, with one of those big "your secret is safe with me" smiles. "Your friend is here!"

My face flamed. Scooter gave me an odd look. Calhoun didn't even glance my way, just went over and joined the wrestlers, who had formed a human chain and were ferrying boxes to the basement.

"Keep the books in the exact same order you find them, please," Aunt True instructed them, then crossed the store to organize the group in charge of rearranging the bookshelves.

Lucas and Franklin and Amy Nguyen were put to work dusting, and Cha Cha and Jasmine and I were assigned two jobs: keeping the little kids out of everyone's hair, and washing the glass globes on all the light fixtures.

"You can set up headquarters in my apartment," said Aunt True. "Don't let Memphis out, okay? There are board games in the trunk in the living room, and you'll find rubber gloves and dish soap and whatever other cleaning products you need under the kitchen sink."

"I have a practice session at the Starlite at eleven thirty," I told her.

"That's fine. Just see if someone can cover for you with the little ones while you're gone."

"I can do that no problem, Ms. Lovejoy," Jasmine told her.

While Jasmine rounded up the younger kids, Cha Cha and I went to join Mr. Jefferson and Mr. Freeman, who had brought a ladder up from the basement. The two men started dismantling the light fixtures, handing the white glass globes down to Cha Cha and me.

"Wow," said Cha Cha, as we carried the first two up to Aunt True's apartment. She looked around in amazement. "Your aunt's been everywhere."

"I know, right?"

"Can I show Annie Aunt True's scrapbooks?" begged Lauren, who had plunked herself down on the floor by the coffee table.

"I guess so," I told her. "Be careful with them, though."

In the kitchen, Jasmine was setting up a game of Candy Land for Pippa and Baxter. While Cha Cha returned downstairs for more glass globes, I rummaged under the sink for the rubber gloves and dish soap, and a few minutes later was up to my elbows in scummy water.

"This is disgusting," I said, holding up a sponge that had quickly turned black with grime. "You think dissecting a frog was bad, Jazz, you'd faint if you saw all the dead bugs floating around in here."

I rinsed the globe and handed it to her. She dried it carefully and set it on the countertop.

"One down, eleven more to go," she said.

It took us a while to clean them all. When we were done. Cha Cha and I began carrying the now-sparkling results back downstairs. I paused in the bookshop doorway and looked around. The last time I'd seen so many people working together on a project was when all my Texas uncles showed up to build a deck for our new house in Austin. The one we sold. The one I'd still move back to in a heartbeat.

"Gotta go," said Cha Cha, grabbing her jacket off the bench by the door. "I'm due over at the Starlite."

"Oh, yeah," I replied. "Calhoun's first practice session, right?"

She nodded. "Wish me luck."

"Truly! Could you bring your sisters down here for a minute?" called my aunt, who was standing by the sales counter with Carson Dawson. "Channel 5 wants a family shot to go with the interview."

I nodded and trotted back upstairs.

"Hey, Truly, have you seen your aunt's prom picture?" said Annie, holding up one of the scrapbooks. "Check out her B-O-U-F-F-A-N-T!"

She and Lauren dissolved into giggles.

"Very funny," I said, glancing at it. Then I looked a little closer. What caught my eye wasn't so much the picture of my aunt in her prom dress and huge hair—almost as huge as the hair on the guy she was with, whose picture I was pretty sure I'd seen somewhere before—but rather the program on the opposite page. It was for a West Hartfield High School drama production of *Much Ado About Nothing*, starring none other than Calhoun's parents.

As I hustled my sisters back downstairs to the waiting camera crew, my brain shifted into sudoku mode, puzzling over this new piece of information.

"Smile, everyone!" said Carson Dawson, baring his own toothsome grin as he bounded out in front of the camera.

*"Hellooooooooo, Boston!"* he announced, launching into his show's trademark opening cry. Work in the bookshop ceased as our friends and neighbors crowded around to watch. "Greetings from beautiful Pumpkin Falls, New Hampshire! I'm here today at Lovejoy Books, where an entire town is banding together to give a wounded warrior a helping hand."

Hatcher pinched me, and I pinched him back. Could this possibly be more embarrassing?

Mr. Dawson quickly zeroed in on Pippa. "What's your name, sweetheart?" he asked, crouching down and holding out the microphone.

"Pippa Lovejoy," my little sister replied, twisting one of her strawberry blond ringlets around a forefinger.

"And is this your family?"

She nodded, her sparkly pink glasses flashing in the bright spotlights.

"You have a big family!" the TV host exclaimed.

Pippa nodded again. "Theven."

"What?"

"There are theven of uth," Pippa repeated, holding up seven fingers.

"Ohhhhhh," chuckled Carson Dawson. "Theven of you!" He winked at the camera. "Isn't she just the cutest, folks?"

"Get me out of here," muttered Danny under his breath.

Carson Dawson straightened up and turned to face the rest of us.

"Whoa, tall timber!" he said when he spotted me. Chuckling, he made a show of craning his neck to look up into my face. Which was in the process of turning bright red. "What's your name, young lady?"

"*Drooly Gigantic*," said Scooter in a stage whisper from somewhere in the crowd.

My face went from red to five-alarm fire. I gritted my teeth and promised myself that I would flatten Scooter Sanchez the minute I had the chance.

"My name is Truly," I managed to tell the TV host.

"You grow *truly* tall timber up here in the Granite State, don't you?" Carson Dawson quipped, looking over at my aunt. Sizing her up, he added, "but then, I can see that your niece here is a chip off the old block."

I winced.

"Uh-oh," muttered Hatcher. "Incoming!"

Aunt True gave Carson Dawson a withering look. Stepping forward, she put her arm around my shoulder. "Ayuh," she replied in a broad, fake New Hampshire accent, "but then we Granite Staters always have preferred tall timber to *splinters*." She looked down from her considerable height at the TV host and sniffed.

His smile faltered. He turned to the cameraman and whispered, "Remind me to edit this bit later."

Smiling his big fake smile again, Mr. Dawson blathered on about our family, and the bookstore, and Dad's injury, and what we were doing this weekend to surprise him. "It's a veritable 'Bookshop Blitz,' folks! I'm told we won't recognize the place when they're done with it tomorrow."

The lights were hot, so was my face, and my cheeks hurt from smiling. Would this ever be over?

"Good one, Aunt True," whispered Danny, as the camera finally stopped rolling and the news crew began packing up. "Way to put that twerp in his place."

"I have no idea what you're talking about," Aunt True replied, the picture of innocence.

Carson Dawson promised to return the following afternoon for some "after" footage of the remodeled bookshop. On his way out, he and his news crew posed for the photographer from the *Pumpkin Falls Patriot-Bugle*, who'd been prowling around snapping pictures for the past hour.

"Never apologize for being 'tall timber,'" Aunt True told me, slipping her arm around my waist. "You and I were born to stand out in a crowd, Truly, and there's nothing wrong with that."

I gave her a rueful smile. That was the difference between an owl and a parrot. I didn't want to stand out in a crowd—I much preferred stealth mode. But I thanked her anyway.

"This is great!" the photographer said happily to my aunt as the Channel 5 crew left. "Definitely A-section material. I'm going to push for front-page placement in this week's issue."

The minute she said that, something clicked. I knew where the next clue was!

But first, I had an appointment at the Starlite Dance Studio.

# CHAPTER 22

At least my practice session was Scooter-free.

We'd been told to come solo to our first private appointment at the Starlite, so that Cha Cha's parents could assess our abilities. Which were pretty much zero in my case.

It was a little weird dancing with Cha Cha's father. He wasn't that much taller than Cha Cha, so I towered over him, for one thing. He was really nice, though, and didn't make me feel at all awkward about it. Plus, even when I made mistakes he didn't act like I had two left feet.

"Slow, slow, quick quick," he said, moving me around the dance floor as easily as Pippa and Baxter had moved their game pieces around the Candy Land board. "That's it, you're getting the hang of it!"

I surveyed the spacious studio over his shoulder. It had hardwood floors and cushioned benches lining the mirrored walls. Potted trees twined with twinkle lights stood in all four corners of the room, and chandeliers blazed overhead. Maybe ballroom dancing wasn't so bad after all.

"Oops, sorry," I said as I stepped on Mr. Abramowitz's foot again.

"Not to worry," he replied quickly, smiling up at me. "That's why I get hazardous-duty pay." The smile vanished as he realized what he'd just said. Hazardous-duty pay is extra money soldiers receive for really dangerous jobs. Like flying a helicopter in a war zone. Flustered, Mr. Abramowitz stopped dancing. "I am so sorry, Truly. That was a thoughtless remark, considering all that your father has been through."

I shook my head. "It's okay, really."

"I hope your family knows how proud we all are of his service," Cha Cha's father continued. "And I think it's very brave of him, moving all the way across the country to take over the store from your grandparents. It can't be easy, having to suddenly shift gears like that."

"Um, yeah, I guess," I said.

I was quiet as we started to dance again. I'd never really thought about it that way. Was Mr. Abramowitz right? Had my dad done a brave thing, moving to Pumpkin Falls?

Cha Cha's father hummed along to the music, and I felt myself starting to relax. There was a flow to dancing that was not unlike swimming. Maybe I really was getting the hang of it.

Or maybe not.

"Oops," I said again, and Mr. Abramowitz winced.

"I think that's enough for today." He gave my arm a consoling pat. "Perhaps you and your partner could schedule a practice slot together before our next session at school? We'll be reviewing fox-trot this week, then moving on to the waltz."

*Fat chance*, I thought. I wasn't planning on spending any more time with Scooter than I absolutely truly had to. But, remembering my Pumpkin Falls manners, I thanked Mr. Abramowitz politely, then went to get my jacket.

Hearing music from the other, slightly smaller dance studio off the lobby, I peered through the window. Cha Cha and Calhoun were practicing the fox-trot. This must be where Pippa and Lauren took their lessons, I thought, noting the ballet barres in front of the mirrors.

Calhoun looked up just then and spotted me. He stopped dancing and scowled.

Cha Cha scurried over and popped her head out. "Hang on a sec, okay? We're almost done."

"Sure," I replied, and wandered over to the bulletin board to read the notices: upcoming classes (*learn to tango!*), local events (*bean supper at the church!*), and items for sale, including a tractor, a rooster, and a snowplow. Life sure was exciting in Pumpkin Falls.

A few minutes later, the music stopped and my classmates emerged. Calhoun brushed past me without a word.

"Pumpkin Falls manners!" I called after him, and Cha Cha grinned at me. "Not going so well, I take it?"

"He's not entirely hopeless," she replied.

As we crossed the street a few minutes later, I spotted the man in the green jacket who I'd seen before hanging around outside Lovejoy's Books. He reminded me of a stork, with his long, skinny legs and the way he was craning to peer through the window again. He wasn't wearing his hood this time, and I watched as he ran a hand through his bushy dark hair. I nudged Cha Cha. "Do you know that guy?"

She shook her head. "Nope. Why?"

I shrugged. "No reason." It was probably nothing—just somebody looking at a book. That's why we put them in the window, after all.

"Where's Calhoun going?" said Cha Cha, gazing down the block.

I turned to see our classmate heading into the offices of the *Pumpkin Falls Patriot-Bugle*. Suddenly, every nerve in my body went on full alert.

"Get Jasmine and Lucas and meet me there!" I told Cha Cha as I took off down the street. "I think Calhoun's trying to double-cross us."

# CHAPTER 23

"What is this, kiddie day?" said the *Patriot-Bugle*'s receptionist, looking up from her magazine and snapping her gum.

"Um, we'd like to look at old issues of the paper," I said.

"Funny, young Clark Kent just said the same thing." She pointed a scarlet-tipped nail toward the door at the end of the hall. "Archives are downstairs to the left. Know how to use a microfiche machine?"

Cha Cha and Lucas and I hesitated.

"I do," said Jasmine.

"Good. Be sure and turn it off when you leave." She went back to her magazine.

"Since when do you know how to use a microfiche machine?" asked Cha Cha as the four of us headed down the hall.

"Since my parents are lawyers, duh," Jasmine replied. "They're always looking stuff up. Why are we here, anyway?"

"The next clue," I told her. "I overheard the photographer talk about putting our story in the paper. She said it was 'A-section material,' so it hit me that B-4 might be a section of the newspaper too."

Cha Cha snapped her fingers. "Truly Lovejoy, private eye, strikes again!"

"Yeah, only not soon enough. Calhoun's trying to beat us to it."

"Why?" asked Jasmine.

"I'm not sure."

The lights were on downstairs, and Calhoun was deeply engrossed in the microfiche screen across the room.

"What are you doing?" boomed Cha Cha.

He jumped, then glanced back over his shoulder at us. "None of your business."

"It is our business," I replied as we went over to join him. "It looks to me like a rat trying to steal the cheese."

His face flushed. "I would have told you if I found anything."

"Yeah, right," said Jasmine. "For a price."

I looked over his shoulder. "So what is B-4, anyway?"

"Classified ads."

Of course! The classifieds were the perfect place to leave a message for someone. "How far have you gotten?"

"I've checked through January, February, and March of the year the stamp was issued. Nothing so far."

The four of us crowded around him as he continued to scroll through the back issues. There was lots of news that year, some of it involving people we knew: My dad's wrestling team won the state tournament. The covered bridge was scheduled to be repainted. Ella Bellow and her husband visited the Grand Canyon and gave a slideshow afterward at the library. The destination for the senior class trip was announced: Montreal! Reverend Quinn of First Parish Church lectured at Lovejoy College on the Paul Revere bell; Aunt True was interviewed about the gap year she was planning to take in Patagonia; Belinda Winchester went home to Maine to visit her sister. Also, Calhoun's father was accepted to Dartmouth, and Bud Jefferson was headed to UNH.

We finally found what we were looking for, on Wednesday the third in the first week of June.

"There it is!" said Lucas, pointing to a boxed item. *For B* was at the top, and below it was another quote:

> *When you depart from me, sorrow abides and*
> *happiness takes his leave.*

Calhoun nodded. "Shakespeare," he said, sounding pleased.

I looked at him. Something was up.

Beneath the quote was another capital *B*, of course, just like before, but no numbers this time, only words. Exactly two of them: *HIGH NOON.*

The five of us stared at the screen. Seconds ticked by.

"I've got nothing," I said. "You guys?"

My friends shook their heads. So did Calhoun.

"You'd tell us if you did, right?" I asked him, and he nodded.

"'When you depart from me'—it kind of sounds like the writer is talking about somebody taking a trip," mused Cha Cha.

"There were a lot of people going places that year," said Jasmine. "Ella Bellow. Belinda Winchester. The entire senior class."

"I suppose Belinda could be one of our Bs," I said doubtfully. It was still hard to imagine anyone writing a love letter to the former lunch lady, though.

My friends and I pondered this idea, then we all burst out laughing.

"Yeah, that's what I thought," I said. My stomach rumbled. "We'd better get back. My aunt is counting on us, plus Lou's is catering lunch."

Jasmine went directly upstairs to Aunt True's apartment, where she'd left Lauren and Annie temporarily in charge. The rest of us filed back into the bookshop.

During the hour that we'd been gone, the space had been transformed. The carpet had vanished; all the books had been boxed up and taken to the basement; and dropcloths had been spread over the floor to protect the newly exposed hardwood, which would be washed and waxed tomorrow once the volunteer paint crew was finished. They were already hard at work, spreading the yellow paint that Aunt True and Pippa had picked out on the walls.

"Wow," I said.

"No kidding," echoed Cha Cha.

"Check out the office," said Hatcher, who was behind the sales counter handing out sandwiches and sodas.

I poked my head in to see Aunt True's entire wish list— armchairs, lamps, rugs, tables, and a bunch of other furniture— piled in the middle of the room. Belinda Winchester had brought Miss Marple back, and the dog was curled up on one of the donated chairs.

"People just keep dropping stuff off," my brother told me, shaking his head.

"Wow," I said again. Maybe there really was something to small-town living. "Where is Aunt True, anyway?"

My brother jerked his chin toward the back of the store. "In the children's section."

As I rounded the sales counter to go find her, something caught my eye. I froze in my tracks.

"Aunt True!" I shrieked.

She came running. So did everyone else within earshot, including Miss Marple, who started barking furiously.

I pointed to the rare books cabinet. It was unlocked, and the glass door was standing wide open. The autographed first edition of *Charlotte's Web* was gone!

# CHAPTER 24

By the time Carson Dawson and his camera crew returned on Sunday afternoon, the bookstore shone. Its freshly painted walls glowed a sunny yellow, the washed and waxed hardwood floors gleamed, the windows and light fixtures sparkled, and the books were all neatly arranged on the newly repositioned shelves.

On the walls above them, just like Hatcher had suggested, Aunt True had hung colorful book posters, maps, and even some of Lola's artwork. Aunt True's vision of comfortable reading nooks scattered around the store was a reality now too. The donated rugs and armchairs and tables and lamps had been set up in several corners, and there was even a makeshift window seat in the children's room created from a blanket chest flanked by a pair of bookcases. Lauren had installed herself there among a pile of plump throw pillows, deep into a copy of *The Wolves of Willoughby Chase*.

There was only one thing missing: *Charlotte's Web*. The book had disappeared, and our excitement about what Carson Dawson was calling "the Bookshop Blitz" had evaporated along with it.

"This looks like a whole new store!" gushed the TV host. Pausing to face the camera, he added, "Folks, you couldn't ask for a cozier bookshop in all of New England!"

"Books bring people together, and people bring communities together," said Aunt True with a stoic smile.

"Great quote," said Carson Dawson. "I like that." He quickly replaced his big grin with a concerned expression, though, when Aunt True went on to tell him about the missing copy of *Charlotte's Web*.

"Looks like there's trouble," he intoned to the camera, "right here in River City—I mean Pumpkin Falls. Anyone having information about this crime should contact the local authorities."

The police—actually, Pumpkin Falls only had one policeman—interviewed Aunt True and dusted the cabinet for fingerprints, but with so many people coming and going all day, there were too many of them and they were too jumbled and smeared to be of any help.

"What about video footage from the security cameras?" asked Carson Dawson.

Aunt True snorted. "I don't think there is such a thing in Pumpkin Falls. We certainly don't have one."

The TV host's eyebrows shot up. "Well, then perhaps the dog saw something?" He winked at the camera, which promptly panned over to Miss Marple. But if she knew who took *Charlotte's Web*, she wasn't telling.

"Not much of a watchdog, I take it," chuckled the TV host.

"It's not Miss Marple's fault," said Lauren, rushing over to put her arms around the dog's neck.

"I never said it was," said Carson Dawson hastily. He turned to face the camera again. "That's it for this weekend's update, folks! From frozen waterfalls to a literary makeover, Pumpkin Falls is a happening place. And don't forget to check out next month's Winter Festival! It's the celebration's one hundredth anniversary, and I hear there's lots of fun in store. Until next time, this is Carson Dawson signing off for *Hello, Boston!*"

"Good-bye and good riddance," said Aunt True after he and his camera crew left. "What a phony."

She was even madder at him later that evening, though, when we turned on the TV at dinner and discovered that while Mr. Dawson had technically kept his promise—he hadn't leaked any footage of our remodeling project—somehow word had gotten out to the local news affiliate about the missing copy of *Charlotte's Web*.

The result was that Dad knew all about it by the time he got home.

"I never should have left you in charge!" he hollered at

Aunt True, thirty seconds after he came through the front door.

I understood why he was upset, of course—he was counting on the money from the sale of the book to help pay off the bank loan. Everybody was. But blaming it on Aunt True wasn't fair.

And if any of us had thought that a new high-tech bionic arm would magically transform Silent Man into the father we knew and missed, we were wrong. Way wrong.

"Can we see it?" begged Danny as we all crowded around, dying of curiosity.

"Later," Dad said shortly. "Right now I need to talk to your grandparents. They're in for an unpleasant surprise."

And before he even took off his jacket, he steered Aunt True to the living room, where he set up a videoconference under the watchful eyes of Nathaniel Daniel and his wife Prudence.

Dad was the one who ended up being surprised, though.

"We don't have an autographed first edition of *Charlotte's Web*," Lola said after he'd finished talking.

"Of course you do, Mom," Aunt True told her. "I saw it with my own eyes. Truly did too, right?"

I nodded.

My grandmother shrugged. "Well, I certainly don't remember it."

"Me neither," said Gramps. "And trust me, we'd remember something like that."

As for the rare books cabinet, it turned out that there was a key stashed on a hook behind it. A key everybody in town knew about it. It was there just in case any customers wanted to take a closer look at something in the cabinet and nobody was around to show it to them. Like the "mystery swap," the rest of Lovejoy's Books operated on the honor system too.

My father shook his head in disgust. "Great," he said. "That means anybody could have taken it."

He got up and stalked out of the room. Mom hurried after him. The rest of us crowded around the computer, eager to talk to our grandparents. They gave us a quick tour of their house—more of a concrete hut, really—in Namibia, told us a bit about the classes they were teaching and the library they were helping to build at the local school, then asked for all the news from Pumpkin Falls.

"Ella Bellow ith a bithybody," Pippa informed them, which made everybody laugh.

"You're a smart cookie, to figure that out so fast," said Gramps.

"Truly told me," Pippa replied, and my family laughed again.

"Has the January thaw finally arrived?" asked Lola.

"Nope," said Danny. "Everything's still frozen solid."

"A TV news crew came up from Boston over the weekend to film the falls," Hatcher told them. "They filmed us at the bookstore too."

"Really?" Lola looked surprised to hear this. "Why?"

Keeping her voice low and checking over her shoulder to make sure our parents were out of earshot, Aunt True filled Gramps and Lola in on the bookshop makeover.

"Well done!" said Lola, when she finished. "Our instincts were right to hand over the reins. We knew you and your brother would do wonders with the business."

Gramps looked out at me from the computer screen and smiled. "So, have you added anything to your life list, Truly?"

"Not much," I told him. "It's been too cold and snowy. There've been lots of cardinals and jays and chickadees around the feeders, of course, and I spotted a woodpecker the other day."

"Downy or pileated?" asked Gramps.

"Downy."

"My favorite!"

I shrugged. "Yeah, but they're nothing special."

"Every bird is special, Truly," Gramps said. "Backyard magic, remember?" He smiled at me again. "Be patient and keep your eyes peeled, and Pumpkin Falls might surprise you."

It already had. But I couldn't tell him that, of course.

# CHAPTER 25

The third clue was much harder than the first two.

It took us nearly two weeks to figure out. And, surprisingly, a lot can happen in Pumpkin Falls in two weeks.

Like Math Boot Camp.

After I got an 83 percent on the next algebra test (or "17 percent more to 100 percent," as Lieutenant Colonel Jericho T. Lovejoy was quick to point out), Ms. Ivey sat up and took notice.

"Do you think your father would be interested in tutoring other students?" she asked me.

I shrugged. "Um, maybe?"

"He could charge a fee, of course. I think I'll stop by the bookshop this afternoon and ask him."

She walked me there after school and explained her idea to Aunt True.

"Of course he'll do it," said my aunt, who was dressed all

in black and wearing a Sherlock Holmes–style hat she called a "deerstalker." She was setting up chairs for the Mystery Mavens book club meeting,

Lovejoy's Books had four different book clubs gathering regularly now, thanks to the ad that Aunt True placed in the *Pumpkin Falls Patriot-Bugle*, and the blurb in our new book-shop newsletter. In addition to the Mystery Mavens, there were the Heart Throbs, who read romance novels (Aunt True wears flowery skirts and dresses for that one and serves high tea), the Highbrows, who like what Aunt True calls "literary fiction," and the Reel Readers, who read books that have been turned into movies and spend most of their meetings arguing about which version is better.

"We offer a wide range of services for our community here at Lovejoy's Books, including Math Boot Camp," Aunt True told Ms. Ivey, roping off the corner where the Mystery Mavens would meet with yellow "crime scene" tape.

I stared at her, openmouthed. Since when?

"Wonderful!" said Ms. Ivey. "I'll definitely be sending some students your way."

Afterward, when Aunt True told my father what she'd signed him up for, he protested, of course.

"It's extra money," she reminded him. "You're the one who keeps talking about the need for additional income streams."

My father continued to grumble for a while, but he

eventually agreed to do it. And that's how come I'm now sharing my tutor with Lucas (which really means Lucas and his mother, since, naturally, Mrs. Winthrop feels it's important to sit in on the sessions), Scooter Sanchez, and Annie Freeman, who may be the Grafton County Junior Spelling Champion but whose multiplication and division skills are sorely lacking.

Dad, of course, runs it like a military operation. The one time Mrs. Winthrop couldn't come, Scooter took advantage of her absence and started teasing Lucas. Dad caught him at it and told him to drop and give him twenty.

"Twenty what?" asked Scooter, mystified.

"Twenty what, *sir*," my father corrected him sternly. "And that would be push-ups, young man."

Scooter hasn't picked on Lucas since. At least not at Math Boot Camp.

The other thing that happened is that I went to the movies with Calhoun.

Well, not exactly. Cha Cha and Jasmine and Lucas were there too.

The way it happened was that I saw a flyer on the bulletin board at the General Store. I swear, every store in Pumpkin Falls has a bulletin board. Anyway, this particular flyer was squeezed in between a three-by-five card advertising free kittens (courtesy of Belinda Winchester, naturally) and another ad for a snow-shoveling service. The flyer caught my eye because it was bright yellow. CLASSIC WESTERN FILM SERIES was printed in large letters across the top, along with a picture of a cowboy on a horse. The first movie listed in the lineup? *High Noon.*

We had to investigate. The film was showing at Lovejoy College, and Calhoun made us bribe him again (dessert at Lou's afterward) in exchange for getting us tickets.

They'd scheduled it on a Friday at noon—I guess whoever organized the film festival thought this was funny—and on Wednesday at dinner I asked my mother if I could go.

"Friday's a no-school day because of parent-teacher conferences," I reminded her.

"It's also the day of Hatcher's first wrestling tournament," she replied. "We're all going, remember?" Her eyes slid over to Dad, who was focused on eating his pork chop. The fingers of his new bionic hand were gripping the fork while he sawed away with the knife in his left hand. So far, the new prosthesis seemed to be working well.

"Please, Mom?" I begged.

"Well, I suppose I could ask True if she'd be willing to stay with you. We won't be back until late."

"Mo-om! I don't need a babysitter!"

My father glanced up from his pork chop. "Truly," he warned. Talking back is one of Lieutenant Jericho T. Lovejoy's pet peeves.

"True isn't a babysitter; she's your aunt," my mother told me.

"Wait, you're going to miss my tournament?" said Hatcher.

"Sorry," I told him, not sorry at all. Wrestling tournaments are about as exciting as watching paint dry. You sit in the bleachers in a gym somewhere with a zillion other families, watching a zillion other wrestlers from a zillion other schools. It takes forever. The only time it's even remotely interesting is during the few minutes when somebody you know is out on the floor for their match. Maybe people feel the same way about swim meets, but I'm not stuck in the bleachers for those, I'm in the water.

"There'll be other tournaments," my mother told Hatcher. She turned to me and smiled. "I'm glad you're making friends, Little O. I really like the Abramowitzes' daughter."

"You mean the kazoo?" said Hatcher with a sly smile. That's what he calls Cha Cha behind her back. He thinks her deep voice is hilarious.

"Shut up, Hatcher," I said.

"Don't say 'shut up,'" my mother chided as my father looked up at me again and frowned. It was another of his pet peeves, of course.

"Yes, ma'am," I replied meekly, kicking my brother under the table instead.

On Friday, when I stopped by Lucas's house to pick him up, Mrs. Winthrop met me at the door. She was grinning from ear to ear, as excited as if Lucas and I were going on a date or something. Which we absolutely truly weren't. I was worried for a minute there that she was going to take a picture of the two of us.

"You'll drop him off at Lou's afterward, right?" she asked about fifty times, fluttering around nervously as she made sure Lucas had money, hat, mittens, an extra scarf, and anything else she could think of. Poor Lucas looked like he wished the floor would open up and swallow him.

I reassured her that I'd return him in one piece, and finally managed to pry him away. It was snowing again outside, and Lucas was quiet as we scuffed our way down Hill Street to the rendezvous point at Calhoun's house.

"Sorry about that," he said finally.

"Hey, you have to put up with my father," I told him.

He glanced over at me. "Your father's really nice."

I snorted. "Used to be. He's pretty cranky these days."

"Yeah, but I was kind of glad the day he got cranky with Scooter." Lucas smiled at me, and I smiled back.

A few minutes later we arrived at the ornate iron gate in front of the college president's house.

"Fancy schmancy," I said.

A freshly shoveled brick path led to the front door, which was flanked by twin urns containing small fir trees. They stood at attention like a pair of evergreen sentries. I resisted the urge to salute, and lifted the heavy brass knocker instead.

"Hello, Lucas," said the tall, sandy-haired man who

answered a moment later. "How nice to see you again. And you must be the Lovejoy girl that my son has been talking about." He smiled, and I gave him a tentative smile back. Calhoun had been talking about me?

"Make yourselves at home," said Dr. Calhoun, ushering us into the living room. "R. J. will be right down."

Lucas and I sat on the sofa. I surveyed the room. It was twice as big as my grandparents' living room, and decorated with all sorts of medieval-looking stuff. There was an actual suit of armor in the far corner, tapestries hanging on the walls, and a portrait of Shakespeare over the mantel. On either side of the fireplace were floor-to-ceiling built-in bookcases filled with books by and about Shakespeare.

"No wonder Calhoun knows so much," whispered Lucas.

The coffee table in front of us was piled with more books and magazines, most of them about Shakespeare too, and in the middle was a replica of a roofless building shaped like a circle.

"That's the Globe Theatre," said Dr. Calhoun, noticing my interest. He took a seat across from us, his dark eyes alight with enthusiasm. "The open-air theater in London where Shakespeare's plays were performed. The one that's there now is a reconstruction, of course."

"Cool," I said politely.

He smiled. "I like to think so. This room is my tribute to the Bard. His works are my great passion in life. Do you like Shakespeare?"

Before I could answer, the doorbell rang and he went to answer it, reappearing a moment later with Cha Cha and Jasmine. We all made polite conversation—mostly about Shakespeare—until Calhoun finally appeared.

"Have a wonderful time," said his father as we got up to leave. "I spoke with the film department and they've reserved a whole row of seats for you. I think you'll enjoy the movie; it's one of my favorites. Grace Kelly is at her most incandescent!"

I wasn't sure what that meant, but from the expression on Dr. Calhoun's face, I figured it must be something good.

My friends and I were by far the youngest people at the movie. Most of the audience were college students, but there were a few older people too, including Belinda Winchester. She was sitting in the back row, plugged into her music as usual and eating yogurt out of a cup. Spooning it into her pocket, actually. Or at least that's what it looked like at first, until I saw a furry little head pop out. She was feeding yogurt to a kitten.

Belinda waved her spoon at me. I waved feebly back.

"Friend of yours?" whispered Calhoun, giving me a sidelong glance.

"Uh, customer from the bookstore," I whispered back.

Black-and-white movies aren't my favorite, although I've seen a lot of them over the years, thanks to all the night-owl visits with my mother. She's a big fan. This one grabbed me right away, though. It started out with Gary Cooper, who played a marshal in the Wild West, getting married to a Quaker lady—that was Grace Kelly. "Incandescent" must mean really pretty, because she was gorgeous. Anyway, after the wedding, Gary Cooper turns in his badge so he can retire and go be a shopkeeper, but then he finds out this outlaw is coming to town on the noon train. The outlaw wants revenge on the marshal for putting him in jail. Being a Quaker and all, the marshal's new wife is against violence, so the newlyweds start to leave town. But then the marshal's conscience bothers him, because he feels like it's his duty to defend the place, so they turn back. This doesn't go over too well with his bride.

Things quickly go from bad to worse. The townspeople are too afraid to help, and as the countdown continues to the arrival of the train—clocks are constantly ticking onscreen, and people keep looking at their pocket watches—the marshal frantically tries to round up some deputies. Meanwhile, his wife is still mad at him for going back on his promise to quit being a marshal, and she tells him she's leaving on the same train. Time is running out for everyone and everything.

Halfway through the movie, I was pretty sure I knew where the next clue was.

"What are we waiting for?" said Calhoun after I whispered my theory to him and the others. He started to stand up. I grabbed his sleeve and pulled him back into his seat.

"Hang on, I want to see how it ends!" I protested.

"Shhhh!" Belinda Winchester hushed us sternly from the back row. "Pipe down!"

We did.

After the movie was over, we left in a hurry. "It's got to be the clock in the steeple," I told my classmates. "There was so much stuff about time and everything—and all those images of clocks! What else could it be?"

Cha Cha gave me an admiring glance. "Truly brilliant."

Calhoun snorted. "Maybe, if she's right. That's a big 'if,' though."

"So, we owe you dessert at Lou's, right?" Jasmine said to him as we made our way across the quad.

Calhoun looked a little embarrassed. "Actually, my father wanted me to invite you all back to our house for dessert. He made cupcakes."

I tried to imagine Lieutenant Colonel Jericho T. Lovejoy making cupcakes for my friends. Nope. No way. Not even before Black Monday.

"If the clue is somewhere in the steeple clock, how are we going to get up there to look for it?" I said a few minutes later, pulling a stool up to the island in Calhoun's kitchen. I selected a vanilla cupcake piled high with chocolate frosting.

"It's a church, duh," said Jasmine. "It's open to the public."

"I know *that*," I replied, stung. My grandparents were members of Pumpkin Falls First Parish Church, and we always went with them when we visited. "What I meant was how are we going to get into the *steeple*?"

"Don't look at me," said Cha Cha, whose family was Jewish. "We go to the synagogue in West Hartfield."

"Maybe we can ask for a tour?" Jasmine suggested.

"Reverend Quinn is really nice," said Lucas. "I'll bet he'd take us up there."

"It's settled, then," I told my friends. "We'll meet at the church on Sunday."

Lucas shook his head. "Reverend Quinn won't be there. He had dinner at Lou's last night and I heard him tell my mother that he was going away this weekend to some conference."

"Well then, that gives us a week to make plans," I said. "We can schedule another meeting of the, uh, Pumpkin Falls Private Eyes." My cheeks grew pink as I said this, knowing it would prompt a smirk from Calhoun. Which it did.

"Hey, bro!" A dark-haired girl poked her head into the kitchen. She was dressed in a cheerleader's uniform, and I recognized her from Danny's last wrestling meet.

"Hey, Jules," Calhoun replied.

"Make sure you and your friends clean up when you're done," she told him. "You know how Dad is about the kitchen being messy." She turned to walk away, and I noticed her name emblazoned on the back of her uniform: Juliet Calhoun.

Not Jules—*Juliet*. I didn't know much about Shakespeare,

but even I knew the title of his most famous play. I glanced across the kitchen island at Calhoun, who was absorbed in chocolate frosting.

No way.

No one would do that to their kid! Not unless they were nuts about Shakespeare.

Calhoun's father was nuts about Shakespeare.

I'd just figured out Calhoun's first name.

# CHAPTER 26

I heard it before I saw it—a soft fluttering in the pine tree branches overhead. I held my breath and waited, arm extended, palm up, standing absolutely still.

Was I finally going to witness some backyard magic?

It was just barely light out. The rest of my family was still asleep, including my father, which was highly unusual. Lieutenant Colonel Jericho T. Lovejoy doesn't do sleeping in. But for once, he'd taken a day off from the bookshop and gone along to Hatcher's wrestling tournament yesterday. It was way upstate in Lancaster, and what with the snow and everything, my family hadn't gotten home until nearly midnight.

After the movie, I had spent the remainder of the afternoon at the bookstore with Aunt True. She'd unofficially hired me to be her Story Hour helper, and we worked on organizing craft supplies and making treats—little bullfrogs made out of kiwis, with grapes for eyes, since she was planning on reading *Frog and Toad Are Friends* at this morning's event.

"Right now it's just for glory, but we should be able to pay you soon," Aunt True told me. "Business has picked up a bit, thanks to the *Hello, Boston!* feature."

Even though *Charlotte's Web* was still missing and we only had a few weeks to go until Dad's deadline, Aunt True was thinking positively. I liked that about her.

Ella Bellow had come in as we were setting out cushions on the children's room floor.

"Brought your mail," she said, which I learned was code for *I've got some hot gossip.*

"Thanks, Ella," Aunt True replied. "Just set it on the counter."

"Did you hear about the Mahoneys next door?" the post-mistress said, unwinding her black scarf. "They got picked to be on that TV show about antiques. *Attic Treasures*, or some such."

My aunt and I exchanged a glance. Ella was so predictable.

"By the way, I saw Bud Jefferson at the Savings and Loan yesterday morning," she continued, not even waiting for a reply. "He seemed worried. He headed straight for the loan department."

"Is that right?" murmured Aunt True, not paying the slightest bit of attention.

Ella's eyes glinted behind her black-rimmed glasses. "How's business for you folks?"

Aunt True's face flushed. She really hates having to fend off Ella's nosy questions. "Fine," she said shortly, and changed the subject. "By the way, any word on when we can expect that January thaw?"

"Nope. Longest I've ever had to wait for it, with February just around the corner." The postmistress shivered, rubbing her arms. "This cold is seeping into my bones."

Aunt True sprang into action. "I have just the book for that!" she said, suddenly all smiles. She handed Ella a copy of *Retirement in the Sunshine State*. "It just came in, and it's selling like hotcakes."

This was an overstatement. We'd sold exactly two copies.

Ella's mouth pruned up as she leafed through it. "Florida does sound tempting this time of year."

"It's always good to keep one's options open," Aunt True agreed, nodding sagely. She looked over at me and winked.

I smothered a smile. Word around town had it that our postmistress was thinking about retiring—maybe Aunt True was hoping to help spur it on.

Ella bought the book, which I took as a hopeful sign.

Later, after we closed up shop, Aunt True had come over to the house to stay with me.

She'd made us blueberry pancakes for dinner, with maple syrup from Annie and Franklin's family farm, and then she'd taught me how to play cribbage. While we played, we talked. We talked about swim team tryouts, which were on Monday, and which Dad still hadn't made up his mind about, except to tell me to quit bugging him, and we talked about the movie. It turned out that *High Noon* was one of Aunt True's all-time favorites.

"If you liked Grace Kelly, you should watch *To Catch a Thief*," she'd said. "Trade Gary Cooper for Cary Grant, the Wild West for the French Riviera, add in Alfred Hitchcock's trademark suspense, and—well, I won't spoil it for you."

I'd promised her I'd watch it.

My aunt told me about growing up in Pumpkin Falls, and stuff that she and my father had done when they were my age. It was a great place to be a kid, she'd said, but just like Dad she couldn't wait to go experience more of the world.

"I left the day after high school graduation, and I've only been back for brief visits in the years since," she'd told me. "This is the longest stretch of time I've spent here since I was a teenager, in fact."

"Are you planning to leave again?" I'd asked, surprised at how anxious that thought made me feel.

She'd hesitated. "Not any time soon. I'm actually having fun running the bookstore. I'd forgotten how much time I spent there when I was your age. It used to be my job to tidy up every night before closing. Plus," she added, "I know it's helping your father."

She and my mother kept saying that, so I figured they must be right, even though I hadn't seen much sign of it.

"Cha Cha's father said that Dad was really brave for moving here. Do you think that's true?"

Aunt True considered this. "There are all different sizes of brave, Truly. There's warrior brave, of course, and there's everyday brave, and everything in between. I happen to think Mr. Abramowitz is right. Your father is one of the bravest people I know. And not just because of what happened in Afghanistan. It's not easy to completely change course in life the way he has—especially when it wasn't his choice. I'm very proud of him."

I thought this over for a moment. "What about the bookstore—do you think it's going to make it?" Again, I was surprised at how anxious the thought of it failing made me feel. I'd spent a lot of time at the shop this past month, and most of it had actually been fun.

Aunt True hesitated again. "Well, I won't lie to you, we were really counting on selling *Charlotte's Web*. But Lovejoys can do anything, right?" She smiled. "We'll pull through somehow."

And if we didn't? I had wondered later, upstairs in bed. There was only one way to make sure we did, and that was to get *Charlotte's Web* back. It was time to catch a thief. The Pumpkin Falls Private Eyes already had one mystery to solve, though, so I decided to tackle this one on my own.

Which was why I'd gotten up early this morning. I had some work to do.

My grandfather's hat slipped forward, slightly obscuring my view. I was tempted to reach up and adjust it, but I knew I'd ruin everything if I did. So I continued to stand in the middle of the backyard and wait, the only movement the rise and fall of my chest and the steady puffs of my frosty breaths.

And then it happened. Backyard magic. There was another flutter of wings followed by the very lightest touch as a chickadee landed on the palm of my hand. It cocked its head and regarded me for a couple of seconds with a bright black eye—probably wondering who the stranger was wearing Gramps's hat—then it plucked a sunflower seed from my mitten and flew off.

A huge smile spread over my face. I wanted to laugh out loud, but I resisted the urge, hardly daring to breathe now for fear of scaring away the winged visitors that began darting toward me in a steady stream.

I glanced over at the house and spotted a face in one of the upstairs windows. It was my father. His eyes met mine and he smiled. A flutter of a smile, like bird wings. Then, swift as flight, it was gone and so was he.

I fed the birds until my toes were numb. Then I went back inside to have my own breakfast, get ready for Story Hour, and figure out how I was going to catch that thief.

# CHAPTER 27

"His name is *Romeo*?" Mackenzie gaped at me from my laptop screen, incredulous. The two of us were talking while I got ready to go to the bookstore. "Are you sure?"

I nodded. "Pretty sure." What I wasn't so sure of was whether I was going to say anything to Calhoun. It was obvious that he didn't want anyone to know. I wouldn't either, if my name was Romeo. That was even worse than Truly.

"I guess it's kind of romantic, if you think about it. Tell me more about him," Mackenzie coaxed. "What does he look like?"

I sat down on the edge of the bed to pull on my socks, and frowned. "Why?"

"Is he cute?"

"I don't know! He's—Calhoun."

"What color is his hair?" she asked, as I started to brush my own.

"Kind of blondish-brownish, I guess."

My cousin heaved a sigh. "You're impossible!"

I grinned at her. Not only could Mackenzie describe the exact shade of Mr. Perfect Cameron McAllister's hair, she could probably tell you the exact number of hairs on his head. The difference was, she had a crush and I didn't. Absolutely truly not.

She tried one last stab at it. "Is he short? Tall?"

"Tallish," I told her.

"Ish? What's ish? Is he as tall as you?"

I grinned again. "Nobody's as tall as me, Mackenzie."

Walking downtown a little while later, my thoughts turned from Romeo Calhoun to the missing copy of *Charlotte's Web*. The more I thought about it, the more I realized how many people might have had a motive for taking the book.

For starters, there was Mr. Henry, the children's librarian. He'd flat-out said he would give anything for an autographed copy. Carson Dawson seemed pretty interested in it too. So was Aunt True, but she didn't count, of course. The Mahoneys could have taken it, I supposed, to show off on the TV show Ella told us about yesterday. And then there was the tidbit she'd shared about seeing Bud Jefferson at the bank looking worried. Was she right about him talking to a loan officer? Maybe he was in trouble and needed money. It would have been an easy thing to slip a book into his jacket pocket. Which reminded me, what about the man in the green jacket who was always hanging around outside the bookshop like he was casing the joint?

I sighed. Catching the thief wasn't going to be easy. There'd been so many people in the store during the Bookshop Blitz!

There was a big crowd at the bookstore this morning too, waiting for Story Hour to start. Aunt True had been talking it up on the bookstore's website and she'd even convinced the *Patriot-Bugle* to run a feature story about it. Attendance had doubled since the makeover.

After my dad had cooled off about the missing *Charlotte's Web* that day, we'd all taken him down to the store to show off our handiwork.

He didn't say much at first, just walked around inspecting everything. "You all did this?" he'd said, finally, and we nodded.

"Me too!" Pippa did a pirouette. She loved doing pirouettes on the bookstore's newly polished wooden floors.

My father had turned abruptly to Aunt True. "I owe you an apology," he said stiffly. The stiff part was because apologies aren't easy for Lieutenant Colonel Jericho T. Lovejoy.

"For what?"

"For what I said earlier. You were *exactly* the right person to leave in charge."

My father had been especially thrilled when he learned that she'd managed to do everything on a shoestring, and we all had basked in the glow of his approval. Especially Aunt

True. Unfortunately, it didn't last long, and the two of them soon returned to their bickering.

Which was what they were doing this morning.

"J. T., can you take Memphis upstairs?" Aunt True asked, thrusting her cat at him. "He's hissing at the toddlers again."

Memphis did not like toddlers. Or Story Hour.

"Blasted cat," grumbled my father, as Memphis hissed at him, too. Memphis didn't like the bionic arm either. "Can't Truly do it?"

"She's got her hands full," Aunt True told him, pointing to the tray loaded with little kiwi-grape bullfrogs that I was carrying to the children's room.

"Like I even have two hands to be full," my father muttered. Aunt True shot him a look. He heaved a sigh, somehow managing to corral Memphis, and the two of them disappeared upstairs.

Story Hour was a big hit, but what happened afterward was even better. Some fairy dust from this morning's backyard magic must have settled on me, because my father finally agreed to let me try out for swim team.

I brought the subject up as I was putting away the craft supplies in the office storage closet. "Please, Dad?" I begged. "Tryouts are Monday. You saw that last test—my grade has come way up!"

"Yes, it's come up, but there's still room for improvement," he insisted.

Aunt True came in just then. Hearing this exchange, she put her hands on her hips and glowered at my father. "Jericho Lovejoy, wake up and smell the coffee!" she said. "Look at how hard your daughter is working! She's done exactly as you've requested: She's been here every day for tutoring after school, right on time and without complaining. And she's gone above and beyond to help us here in the store—including working on weekends. Don't you think you could cut her a little slack?"

"I'll thank you not to tell me how to raise my own child," my father replied.

"Haven't you heard?" countered Aunt True. "It takes a village to raise a child—which is an actual fact, by the way, because I've been in many villages in many countries—"

"I don't need a travelogue, True."

My aunt grabbed him by his good arm and towed him out into the store. I followed at a safe distance—I didn't want to get caught in the brother-sister cross fire.

"Have you seen our front window this week?" said Aunt True. "It's all Truly's doing." She gestured at the sign I'd made that read WELCOME TO WINTER . . . BIRDING. I'd found a little fake evergreen Christmas tree downstairs in the storage room and placed it on the display table, which I'd covered with a white cloth, and hung some of Gramps's carved wooden birds from the tree's branches. Then I'd scattered birdseed underneath it, and propped a pair of binoculars alongside a stack of field guides from the shop's birding section, a couple of life-list journals, and a copy of *Owl Moon*, of course.

"It's brilliant!" Aunt True continued. "She's a born book-seller. I've sold out of the journals, and I've had five orders for *Owl Moon* this week alone. Five!"

The muscles in my father's jaw worked. Lieutenant Colonel Jericho T. Lovejoy doesn't like being told what to do. Especially not by his big sister. Aunt True must have been a star debater in high school, though, because in the end she managed to broker a deal.

"How about you let her try out for swim team, but she continues with the tutoring until you're satisfied with her grade?" she said.

*Please oh please oh please oh please*, I thought as my father pondered her suggestion.

"I suppose that could work," he said finally, and I started jumping up and down and squealing.

A nearly six-foot-tall person with size-ten-and-a-half shoes makes a whole lot of noise when she's jumping up and down. Especially on wooden floors. And that's not even counting the squealing.

"Enough!" said my father. "There's a condition, Truly."

"Anything," I promised.

"No backsliding. If your math grade slips, you're off the team."

I nodded. I could live with that. I could live with any-thing, as long as it meant getting back in the water.

# CHAPTER 28

Water is my natural element.

At least that's what my father always says. He says that I was swimming practically before I learned to walk. Mom says I did a cannonball in the baptismal font, which I know is a Texas tall tale, but I'm never quite sure about the one she tells about bathtime. She says I used to get so excited splashing around in the tub that she had to put floaties on my arms.

What I know for sure is that I've always loved the feeling of being in the water. Plus, it doesn't matter where you live or how often you move, there's always a pool and the water is always the same. Water doesn't care how tall you are either.

Right now, I couldn't wait to dive back in.

"Swimmers on the block!" shouted the coach, and my toes curled automatically over the edge of the starting block. The 50 Freestyle was the first of several hurdles here at tryouts that would determine whether I'd become a member of the Pumpkin

Falls Youth Swim Team. I just hoped I wasn't too out of shape from not having been in the water for several weeks.

"Take your mark!"

I moved into the track start position, placing one foot behind me and grabbing the block on either side of my forward leg, focused like a hawk on its prey as I waited. At the sound of the buzzer, I arced forward, launching myself into the air. For a brief moment I heard the shouts and cheers of the onlookers from the bleachers, and then the water closed over my head and the world fell away.

A current of pure joy coursed through my body. Swimming is probably as close as I'll ever get to flying.

As for being out of shape, I needn't have worried. It was like I'd never been away. I quickly fell into the familiar rhythm as my arms and legs sliced through the water, and I hit my pace after just a few strokes. A quick flip-turn at the end of the lane, push off and glide, and I was in the home stretch. I cranked up the tempo, pouring it on until I practically flew the last few yards. I slapped the edge of the pool and glanced up at the clock.

Not my best time, but not bad, either. Especially if you considered the fact that I hadn't been in the water since we moved to New Hampshire. Plus, I was the first one at the wall by a long shot.

The coach looked at me in surprise over the top of his clipboard. "I wasn't expecting that."

I smiled. No one ever is.

The thing is, I don't necessarily look like a jock. Most people figure girls my age who are as tall as I am and have feet as big as mine (helpful brother that he is, Hatcher calls them "flippers") are uncoordinated, like maybe we've sprouted too fast or something. Although I'm not always supergraceful—especially not on the dance floor—I'm not a total klutz, either. But put me in the water and it's like my body has found its reason for existence.

"You've got mermaid DNA," Dad used to tell me.

I glanced over at the bleachers and waved to him. He gave me a brief two-finger salute in return. Aunt True was next to him with Pippa and Lauren. She'd sprung them from after-school daycare so they could come watch. Well, Pippa was watching. Lauren had her nose in a book, as usual.

Cha Cha and Jasmine had come to cheer Lucas and me on, and my mother was going to try and make it for the last bit too. She had a late-afternoon history class with Professor Rusty. Danny and Hatcher were both at wrestling practice.

"Go, Truly!" my aunt shouted.

I grinned at her and hauled myself out of the pool. Grabbing my towel from the nearby bench, I looked over to where the next batch of hopefuls was lining up. Lucas Winthrop was among them. Lucas in a swimsuit was not a sight for sore eyes. Skinny as a whistle and pale as milk, he was easily the sorriest excuse for a seventh grader I'd ever seen. He had determination, though. When the coach blew his whistle, Lucas was the first one in the water, and if he churned his way across the pool with more grit than grace, he still ended up with a respectable time.

"Way to go, Winthrop!" I called, and he looked over, startled, then smiled shyly.

Behind me, some of the moms were talking in the bleachers.

"Swimming is the perfect sport for Lucas," I heard Mrs. Winthrop say. "My son was delicate when he was younger, you know, and contact sports are far too dangerous. Plus, he comes home from the pool so wonderfully clean."

Glancing over my shoulder, I saw the other mothers exchange amused looks. Mrs. Winthrop rattled on, oblivious.

Maybe Lucas and I had more in common than I thought. The pool was probably the one place he could go to get away from his mother. It's always been my refuge too. Being underwater is the ultimate form of stealth mode.

A little while later I was on deck again for the 100 Individual Medley. My mother waved to me from the stands. I was glad she'd made it in time, because the medley has always been my favorite race—twenty-five yards each of butterfly, backstroke, breaststroke, and freestyle.

"Let's see what you can do," said Coach Maynard.

At the sound of the bell I dove in, launching myself a few inches below the surface of the water into a streamline propelled by a mighty dolphin kick. Every muscle in my body zinged as I surged forward. The butterfly is my favorite stroke. I love that split second when I lunge out of the water and am almost airborne. It's like flying.

Thinking about flying made me think of my father. Would he be able to pilot a helicopter or plane again someday? Not commercially—he'd explained to us why that was out—but just for fun? I knew how much he hated being grounded. It was probably the same for him as not swimming was for me. I couldn't imagine not ever being able to swim again.

I would feel like a bird without wings.

I finished the medley not too far off my own personal best time. When I got out of the pool, Coach Maynard shook my hand.

"Welcome to the team, Truly," he said. "I don't need to see any more. Stick around for the rest of the tryouts if you want, but I'll expect you here starting tomorrow afternoon. We practice every day from four until six."

I nodded happily. Glancing up in the stands again, I gave my family and friends an exuberant thumbs-up. Then I headed to the dressing room to shower and change.

"Congratulations, honey," my mother said a little while later when I emerged. She gave me a big hug. "Not that I had any doubt."

"Thanks, Mom."

My father gave me an awkward squeeze. "I expected no

less from a Lovejoy," he said. This was high praise coming from Silent Man, and I practically floated to the parking lot.

Outside, snow was falling thick and fast.

"Can you believe this?" Aunt True marveled. "It's like something out of a Russian novel! I swear I don't ever remember a winter like this when we were growing up, do you, J. T.?"

My father shook his head.

Mom turned her face up to the sky and closed her eyes. "Do you remember the part in *Anna Karenina*—"

"You mean when—" Aunt True began.

"Yes! Wasn't that incredibly—"

"Totally!"

"Tolstoy is the best!"

Aunt True and Mom are soul mates when it comes to books. They speak in this weird literary shorthand that none of the rest of us can understand at all.

"Would you guys mind if I walk home?" I asked, spotting Cha Cha and Jasmine emerge from the swim center. The Pumpkin Falls Private Eyes needed to talk.

"Not at all," said my mother, sliding into the driver's seat of our minivan. My sisters climbed in the back. "Are you coming, J. T., or are you heading back to the bookshop?"

"I should head back to the shop," he told her. "The accountant is dropping by in a bit to go over the end-of-the-month financials."

"I'll keep you company," said Aunt True, linking her arm

through his good one. "And just because you're my favorite brother, I'll even make you dinner."

My mother laughed. "Now, there's an offer you can't refuse. I'll see y'all later, then." She waved at us and drove off.

I said good-bye to my father and my aunt, then headed over to find Cha Cha and Jasmine, who had disappeared around the corner of the swim center. I followed and quickly came upon Calhoun stuffing snow down the neck of Lucas Winthrop's jacket again, while Cha Cha and Jasmine tried to stop him.

I ran over to help. "Knock it off, Romeo!" I hollered.

Calhoun froze.

I did too. I hadn't meant to drop the R-bomb that way. Once again, I'd put my big foot in my mouth.

Cha Cha and Jasmine and Lucas gaped at us.

"Romeo?" said Cha Cha. "Who's Romeo?"

I pointed wordlessly at Calhoun.

"Your name is *Romeo*?"

Calhoun's face flamed.

"I always wondered what the *R* in 'R. J.' stood for," said Jasmine. "I figured the *J* was for 'James,' like your dad, but I never would have guessed 'Romeo' for the *R*."

Calhoun abruptly let go of Lucas's jacket. "I'm outta here," he muttered.

Thinking quickly, I realized that I could use this to my advantage. "No, actually, you're not," I told him. "I've had to put up with 'Truly Gigantic' and 'Truly Drooly' for weeks now. You can deal with Romeo. Which," I added, "we won't tell a soul about, on one condition."

He regarded me warily.

"Quit picking on Lucas. And while you're at it, see if you can get Scooter to stop picking on him too. And on me."

Calhoun lifted a shoulder, then gave a reluctant nod.

"Good. Your secret is safe with us."

"Promise?" he asked, darting a glance at me.

"Cross my heart and hope to . . ." My voice trailed off. "Whatever. Our lips are sealed."

"Sealed," said Cha Cha solemnly, holding up three fingers in the traditional Boy Scout salute. Then her dimple appeared and she grinned broadly. "Scout's honor . . . *Romeo!*"

I grinned back. "Guess what?" I told my friends. "I think I have a plan for getting us into the steeple."

# CHAPTER 29

With two weeks to go until Winter Festival, there was a change in the air in Pumpkin Falls.

It wasn't the January thaw. That still hadn't arrived, even though the calendar now said February. It was more a sense of anticipation, a crackle of excitement you could feel around town, at school, and in the shops as people talked about "the big weekend."

Aunt True says Winter Festival is Pumpkin Falls's answer to homecoming. She says people who grew up here or used to live here often come back for it, although if you ask me, which nobody ever does, I could think of better ways to spend a weekend than stuck in freezing-cold Pumpkin Falls, New Hampshire.

My math grade crept up a few notches, which pleased my father and made me feel a little more secure about my spot on the swim team. At practice, I did planks and push-ups and sit-ups and swam endless laps in preparation for our first race. The Pumpkin Falls Youth Swim Team always kicked off its season with a face-off against Thornton during Winter Festival.

Everywhere I've ever lived, there's always an archrival, and for Pumpkin Falls, Thornton is it. And everywhere I've ever lived, it's always the coach's job to get his or her team whipped into a frenzy over this rival. Coach Maynard droned on every day at practice about how we need to do our best and believe in ourselves and get out there and show Thornton what we're made of, blah blah blah. I'd heard it all before.

Casting a shadow over all of this, at least for me, was the bookshop's make-or-break deadline. I wished I could be more like Aunt True, who sailed ahead thinking positively and planning for the future, but the spike in sales after Carson Dawson's TV feature on Pumpkin Falls had leveled off, and with no *Charlotte's Web* in sight, I didn't see how we were going to make it. I saw all the long hours my father still spent behind closed doors with the accountant, and how he worried constantly over things called "profit margin" and "overhead" and "cash flow."

The other shadow was Cotillion. I was so not looking forward to the exhibition dance, even though Scooter and I were doing marginally better in class. This was mostly because Scooter had stopped goofing off. He'd caught wind of Calhoun's extra practice sessions—which he thought Calhoun was paying for—and that had lit a fire under his competitive streak.

"Oh good, the kittens are here," said Jasmine as she and Cha Cha and I took off our jackets and piled them on the bench by the bookshop door.

Ever since the remodel, Lovejoy's Books had become Belinda Winchester's home away from home. She and at least one kitten showed up pretty much every afternoon now, right around the time that Aunt True took her mini pumpkin whoopie pies out of the oven. When Saturday rolled around, though, the treats—and Belinda—arrived earlier, for Story Hour.

Cha Cha and Jasmine had volunteered to help Aunt True and me on this particular Saturday. Plus, my friends were eager to check out the new shipment of jewelry. They really liked all the new stuff that Aunt True had started to stock as part of her scheme to add more income streams.

The three of us helped ourselves to some of the whoopie pies that were waiting on the sales counter. My father emerged from the office to grab one too. He still complains about the expense, but I've noticed he's first in line when Aunt True brings them down from her apartment.

"She never leaves," he grumbled, casting a baleful eye on Belinda Winchester, who had settled into an armchair over by the front window with her latest paperback from the mystery swap. "And she never buys anything either."

"So? It's her happy place," my aunt replied from her perch on a stepladder behind the counter. She fiddled with the clothesline she was anchoring to the ceiling. "Pass me a thumbtack, would you please, Truly?"

Cha Cha and Jasmine and I poked around in the pile of literary T-shirts (EAT SLEEP READ! LITGEEK! I ♥ MR. DARCY!) that were heaped by the cash register, waiting to be strung up. The T-shirts were one of the new sidelines Aunt True had decided we should stock.

"You're turning us into the General Store," my father said, picking one up and grimacing at its slogan (SO MANY BOOKS, SO LITTLE TIME!).

"If it brings in customers, why not?" Aunt True replied cheerfully.

Mom and I think the sidelines have really livened things up. Cha Cha and Jasmine agree. They drop in often after school now to check out the new stuff on display, from cool little notepads and pens and tote bags to stationery, mugs, jewelry, and locally made soaps and candles. We've started stocking maple syrup and maple candy from the Freemans' farm too.

"Have you girls seen Truly's new Valentine's Day window?" Aunt True asked.

"It's not mine, exactly," I said. My aunt and I had worked on it together last night after dinner.

"You did the lion's share of the work," Aunt True replied.

I followed Cha Cha and Jasmine as they went over to the front of the store to check it out.

"Sweet!" said Cha Cha.

Across the top of the window was a banner with WE ♥ HAPPY ENDINGS on it, and I'd taped red construction-paper hearts and Cupids on the glass. The display table was covered in a floor-length red tablecloth and piled high with things that my aunt and I had gathered from the far-flung corners of the store: Valentine's Day cards; a red leather-bound copy of Shakespeare's sonnets; heart-shaped chocolates and soaps; a pink mug with white hearts on it, pink notebooks, pink sticky notes, pink pens—everything we could think of that celebrated love and romance. There were piles of books too: *Pride and Prejudice*, *Cinderella*, *Jane Eyre*, and a whole bunch more.

"I love happy endings too," sighed Jasmine. "They're so romantic."

Cha Cha and I looked at each other and grinned.

"Here are the new necklaces I was telling you about," I told my friends. "The ones made of Scrabble tiles. See? There's a letter on one side, and a design on the other."

"Cute!" said Cha Cha.

"I have a ballerina on mine," said Pippa, emerging from her favorite hideout under the table. "And a *P* for 'Pippa.' Aunt True gave it to me."

Jasmine and Cha Cha fussed over her necklace, of course,

and Pippa let them each take a turn wearing it. Then she disappeared back under the table again.

"Ooh, look at this one!" Jasmine held up a tile with a picture of a bear on it reading a book.

Aunt True was wearing one just like it in honor of Story Hour.

"So, all systems go for tomorrow?" I asked my friends, and they nodded.

"I'm sleeping over at Jazz's tonight," Cha Cha told me. "And my parents said I could go to church with her tomorrow."

"Perfect. We'll all be there—Calhoun's coming too."

Jasmine looked over at Cha Cha. "How are his private lessons going?"

"He's making progress, but he's not exactly Romeo on the dance floor," Cha Cha replied, and the three of us giggled. It was going to be hard to keep the lid on Calhoun's real name.

The bell over the door jangled, and Mrs. Abramowitz came in with Baxter. I pointed to where Pippa was hiding and he dove under the table to join her. Mrs. Abramowitz took off her coat. She looked like she'd just breezed in from a dance competition. She often looks that way. She has thick, curly dark hair like Cha Cha's, but Mrs. Abramowitz's is always swept into an elegant updo, and unlike my mother, who dresses mostly in jeans these days now that she's a college student again, or Aunt True, who dresses like, well, a parrot, sequins are a staple in Cha Cha's mother's wardrobe. Even her snow boots have high heels.

"I don't know about you girls, but I am ready for spring," she said, unwinding her scarf. "Where is that January thaw when you need it?" She glanced around the store. "Is your mother here, Truly?"

I shook my head. "She's coming in later. We're driving down to Manchester this afternoon."

"Let me guess—dress shopping?" Cha Cha's mother smiled at me. "Your mother told me you've grown another inch since your move to Pumpkin Falls."

There really are no secrets in small towns.

"That's the best part of Cotillion, I think," Cha Cha's mother continued. "It's such fun to have an excuse to get all dressed up."

*Um, not really*, I thought. I don't do dresses. They're way up there on the list of things I'm not good at.

Maybe Mrs. Abramowitz saw the worried look on my face, because she slipped an arm around Cha Cha, and smiled at Jasmine and me. "You girls are all going to shine, no matter what you wear."

Over at the sales counter, Aunt True pinned the last of the T-shirts to the clothesline, then climbed down from the stepladder and picked up the old-fashioned handbell she'd bought next door at Mahoney's Antiques.

"Story Hour!" she called, ringing it loudly.

Pippa and Baxter popped out from under the table and dashed to the children's room. Mrs. Abramowitz and my friends and I followed. So did Belinda Winchester, who was quickly surrounded by an admiring crowd of young kitten-lovers.

"She's like Mary Poppins or Mrs. Piggle-Wiggle or something," Aunt True said, watching her.

Dad looked mystified. "Who?"

Aunt True sighed. "Never mind." My father is so not a bookworm.

Initially, my father had been worried that Belinda might scare kids away, and more important, their parents—who were the paying customers, after all, as he pointed out—but she hadn't. In fact, she's kind of turned into another store mascot.

Of course, it helps that she almost always has a furry creature or two with her. Dad was not thrilled about allowing more pets into the shop, but the kittens have proved to be a huge hit.

"They're free advertising!" Aunt True had argued, and it's true. Some people—especially those with little kids—drop by the store now just to see the kittens, and most of them end up buying something.

"Girls, why don't you go ahead and pass these around," said my aunt, handing us each a plate of mini whoopie pies.

We dutifully distributed the snacks, which disappeared in nothing flat. The silver-dollar-size treats are almost as popular with the Story Hour crowd as the kittens are.

"Are these the same ones you brought in last week?" Aunt True asked Belinda, peering into the basket beside the chair where she was sitting.

"Maybe," Ms. Winchester replied slyly.

Aunt True frowned. "These are orange, though. I thought last week's were gray."

Belinda Winchester drew a large cotton handkerchief from her pocket and blew her nose loudly.

"How many do you have, exactly?"

"Handkerchiefs?"

"Kittens."

A slow smile spread across Mrs. Winchester's face. "Hundreds of cats, thousands of cats—"

"Millions and billions and trillions of cats!" Aunt True finished, laughing. "Perfect choice for today's Story Hour." She winked at me. "Change of plans," she said, then went over to the picture-book section and plucked a slim volume from one of the shelves. Holding it up, she asked, "Who knows the name of this book?"

A flock of little hands flew into the air.

"Baxter?" said Aunt True.

"*Millions of Cats,*" he replied, and she nodded.

"That's right. It's *Millions of Cats,* by Wanda Gág." Aunt

True sat down, and the little kids crowded around her as she started to read.

The bell over the front door rang again. I glanced over to see Ella Bellow come in. My heart sank as I realized that my father had vanished. Again. He had an uncanny way of doing that whenever Ella showed up.

It was up to me to man the sales counter. "Back in a sec," I whispered to my friends, and crossed the store to greet her. "Can I help you?"

"*May* I help you," she corrected.

*Whatever*, I thought, but aloud I replied meekly, "May I help you?" adding, "ma'am" for good measure and plastering a smile on my face. Paying customers are paying customers.

There was a burst of laughter from the children's room, and the postmistress and I looked over to see what the commotion was about. Aunt True and Cha Cha and Jasmine had the kids on their feet now, and they were all singing "Three Black Cats" to the tune of "Three Blind Mice" as they marched around Belinda's chair.

Ella Bellow sniffed. "So unsanitary."

I wasn't sure if she was talking about Story Hour, or Belinda Winchester, or the kittens, or what.

"I'm sure it's a violation of our town's health code to have so many animals on the premises," she said, casting a sour look at Miss Marple, who was sleeping peacefully in her dog bed on the floor below the sales counter.

I didn't reply, grateful that Memphis was upstairs in Aunt True's apartment. Ella Bellow was another item on the list of things my aunt's cat didn't like.

"You left a message that my special order is in." Ella picked up one of the flyers stacked by the cash register and scrutinized it while I retrieved her book from behind the sales counter. I looked at its title: *Second Acts: Starting a New Career in Your Golden Years.* So maybe the rumors really were true! Maybe Ella really *was* thinking about retiring.

"Grand Reopening Celebration, huh?" the postmistress said, peering down her knife blade of a nose at me.

"Yes, ma'am."

She waved the flyer. "You're holding it during Winter Festival?"

I nodded. That was Aunt True's idea, of course. She wanted to do something splashy to spotlight the bookshop's makeover.

"The paper says they're expecting a record crowd, since it's the centennial," Aunt True had told my father, who as usual was skeptical of her plan. Mostly because he didn't want to spend any money. "The bed and breakfast and all the motels up along Route Four are booked solid. What better time to show off our store?"

Ella Bellow frowned as she peered over her black-framed glasses at the schedule of events. In addition to next weekend's Valentine's Day Story Hour, featuring special guest star Mr.

Henry from the local library, there was a love poetry open mic night, prize drawings and giveaways all weekend, special gift bags with all purchases, a cooking demonstration by Franklin and Annie's mother with maple syrup from the Freeman farm, and a reading and book signing by Augusta Savage, aka Augustus Wilde, a.k.a. Captain Romance.

Ella Bellow arched an ink-black eyebrow at me. "Don't you think you might have bitten off more than you can chew? Do you really think that visitors will want to bother with all this?"

I stared at her. This was the real reason that she'd come in! The old crow was in fishing mode, not shopping mode, snooping around for gossip about our family's business as usual. Well, I wasn't about to give her the satisfaction of leaving with any.

"Of course they will!" I gushed in reply. "Business has been fantastic ever since *Hello, Boston!* Thank you so much, by the way, for telling Carson Dawson about us. That was brilliant."

Ella seemed taken aback. "I see. Well, I—that's good news, then," she said, and after paying for her book she beat a hasty retreat to the door.

It was almost as if she was hoping for bad news, I thought. But why? What possible difference could our bookstore's struggles make to a soon-to-be-retired postmistress?

# CHAPTER 30

"Hey, Little O," said my mother.

"Hey, Mama Owl," I replied.

We smiled at each other.

"Can't sleep?" I shook my head and she set her book aside and patted the sofa. "Come sit by me."

I curled up next to her and she rearranged the quilt to cover us both. The remnants of a fire crackled softly in the fireplace. I stared at the glowing embers while my mother sipped her tea.

I'd missed this. We hadn't been Little Owl and Mama Owl for ages, not since before Black Monday. I was probably getting too old for it, but still, it was really nice.

"Seems like old times, doesn't it?" my mother murmured, resting her chin on my head. "So, are you happy with your dress?"

I nodded. The two of us had actually had a lot of fun

shopping earlier. And the dress we'd finally settled on was okay, as far as dresses go.

"And are you happy with your new friends? Cha Cha and Jasmine sure seem like great girls," my mother continued. "And that Winthrop boy has taken a shine to you too."

"Yeah," I replied. "They're all really nice. I still miss Mackenzie, though."

"We were going to keep this as a surprise, but your dad and I have been talking. We know this move hasn't been easy for you, and we really appreciate the way you've pitched in to help here at home and at the bookstore. So we're getting you something special for your birthday." My mother smiled at me. "Mackenzie!"

I sat bolt upright. The quilt dropped from my shoulders. "Really?"

She nodded. "Really. I've already checked with Aunt Louise and Uncle Teddy, and they said she can come for spring break. Aunt True donated some frequent-flier miles, and the ticket is booked."

I started to squeal, but my mother quickly put her finger to her lips, so I threw my arms around her instead. "Thank you so much, Mom!" I whispered, doing a quick calculation in my head. Spring break—and my birthday—was in the middle of March. That was only a little over a month away!

"Bedtime for bonzos," my mother announced a few minutes later. She gave the embers a good stir with the poker and secured the fireplace screen. "Come on, I'll walk you upstairs."

The following morning I woke at the crack of dawn. Between the rendezvous with my friends at church in a few hours and the thought of my cousin's upcoming visit, I was too excited to sleep. I glanced at my alarm clock. Still too early in Texas to call Mackenzie. I could text her, though.

Throwing back the covers, I slid my feet into my fuzzy slippers and grabbed my bathrobe from off the bedpost.

*Thump. Thump. Thump.* Miss Marple was awake too, her tail smacking softly against the bedspread as she wagged it.

"Hey, girl," I murmured, giving her a pat. Over the past month I'd had to resign myself to the fact that I was Miss Marple's favorite Lovejoy, at least while Gramps and Lola were away. I'd given up trying to foist her off on Lauren, and totally caved on letting her into my room. Miss Marple even slept in here most nights. She'd start out on the floor, but somehow she always ended up at the foot of my bed by morning.

The house was silent, except for the telltale clank and rattle from the radiators as they roused themselves to their daily business of keeping us warm. I dashed off a quick text to Mackenzie, telling her to call me the minute she woke up, then crossed to the window. It was still dark outside, except for a patch of light on the snow below me. My bedroom was directly over the kitchen, so someone was up. Most likely my father. Lieutenant Colonel Jericho T. Lovejoy is an early bird, up at zero dark thirty every morning for his daily run.

Sure enough, I found him in the kitchen, drinking coffee and reading the paper. The radio on top of the fridge was on low, a melodious male voice letting listeners know that the record-breaking cold that had gripped the valley for weeks now might finally be coming to an end.

"According to the National Weather Service, we can expect a warming trend by the end of the week," the announcer said. "Nothing like the January thaw finally showing up in February!"

"Too bad it's not showing up today," I said, glancing at the thermometer outside and shivering.

"What?" said my father, looking up from his paper. "Oh, right."

"Morning, by the way," I said.

"Morning," he replied.

"Hey!" I blinked in surprise when I spotted the big box of donuts on the counter, along with a pitcher of juice. That's what we always used to have on Sunday mornings, whenever Dad was home on leave. Yet another family tradition that got shelved after Black Monday.

"Hey, what?" Dad asked.

"Um, nothing." I gave him a sidelong glance. Silent Man seemed to have made a donut run. I helped myself to a chocolate-covered old-fashioned with sprinkles, poured myself a glass of juice, and sat down at the table across from him.

He was wearing the Terminator. The new prosthesis had made a lot of things easier for him to do, and I watched as he gripped the newspaper in its high-tech fingers and turned the page.

My father has three prosthetic arms to choose from now: the Terminator, Captain Hook, and the one he's dubbed Ken, which is his least favorite, even though it's the one that looks the most human. Ken is made of this plastic stuff that's matched to Dad's skin color. He named it after Barbie's companion, because all it does is hang around looking pretty.

"It's useless," I heard him tell Mom in disgust. "It doesn't move; I can't pick anything up or do anything with it—what's the point?"

My father had shocked us all at dinner one night recently when he'd made a joke about the "arms race" in his closet. It was a tiny joke, but still, it was a joke. It made me think that maybe Mom and Aunt True are right, maybe Pumpkin Falls has been good for him.

"Dad, what do you know about Ella Bellow?" I asked, taking a bite of my donut.

He peered at me over the top of the paper. "Why do you want to know?"

I shrugged. "Just curious. She's really nosy."

"That she is." He was quiet for so long I figured I'd been

dismissed. Then he said, "I've known Ella all my life. She's a good woman, and she's good at her job, but she's never been good at staying out of other people's business. And it seems to have gotten worse since her husband died a couple of years ago. I hear she's retiring soon—maybe she'll move to Florida and leave Pumpkin Falls in peace."

With that he returned to his paper. Now I was dismissed.

And still left with more questions than answers.

# CHAPTER 31

"You're not planning on wearing that to church, are you?" My mother frowned at Danny, who'd pulled his wrestling sweatshirt on over his freshly washed and pressed button-down shirt and tie.

"Fine," he said and stomped back upstairs to take it off.

This happens to at least one of us every time we go to church. Well, except for Pippa, who adores dressing up. This morning she was wearing her favorite pink velvet dress, and she'd added her pink tutu plus a tiara for good measure.

We don't always make it to church during wrestling and swim season, but on the Sundays that we do, I'm required to wear girl clothes. This morning I had on a turtleneck sweater and a skirt, beneath which I'd added wool tights and my sheepskin-lined boots. No point freezing to death up in the steeple.

Dad came downstairs last. He'd traded the Terminator for Ken, I noticed. Church was almost the only place he ever wore it.

It was too cold to walk, plus we were late, so we all piled into the minivan and headed down the hill toward town. The Paul Revere bell was pealing its Sunday welcome as we pulled into the parking lot. I glanced up and watched it swinging in the steeple. If everything went according to plan, I'd be up there soon too.

Entire books have been written about the Pumpkin Falls First Parish Church steeple, thanks to the Paul Revere bell. The bell is the main reason the church is featured on so many postcards at the General Store, but the other reason is because the steeple is ridiculously picturesque. It looks like a square-tiered wedding cake. The bottom "layer" is the actual bell tower, which has arched openings on all four sides. Above that is the clock tower, which sports a giant round black disk of a clock face with gilt numbers and hands. Both of these layers are decorated within an inch of their lives with ornamental railings and little pillars and curlicues and stuff. Perched on top of the whole thing is the spire, which looks like an upside-down ice-cream cone, and on top of *that* is the weather vane.

Lots of churches have weather vanes. I've seen some decorated with roosters and others with angels, stars, fish, and doves. What does the Pumpkin Falls First Parish Church have on its weather vane? A pumpkin, of course.

The early church leaders clearly had a sense of humor.

I wondered if Nathaniel Daniel was one of the ones

responsible for the choice. From his portrait, he didn't look like all that much fun, but you never know about people, I guess.

Glancing up, I could see a trio of pigeons perched on top of the brass pumpkin weather vane, their feathers fluffed up against the cold. I hoped that was a good omen.

"See you afterward, kids," my mother said, handing Pippa over to me as we went inside. "Behave yourselves."

My brothers and sisters and I trooped downstairs to the Sunday School, where I was relieved to see that all of my friends had made it.

"Um, I sorta kinda had to tell my brother," Jasmine whispered as I slid into the seat next to her.

"You *what*?!" Aghast, I looked across the table at Scooter, who bared his braces at me in a wide grin.

Jasmine raised her hand and asked the teacher if we had time to visit the ladies' room before class started, then grabbed my arm and towed me down the hall.

"He knew something was up," she told me, when we were safely out of earshot. "He saw the five of us heading to the movie a couple of weeks ago, and then he overheard Cha Cha and me talking last night in my room. He wouldn't stop bugging me about it."

"So? You didn't have to tell him anything!" I was furious.

"He said he'd bring my underwear to school and run it up the flagpole if I didn't," Jasmine said miserably.

I sighed. "Brothers," I said in disgust. I'd probably have caved too.

This was not good. Not good at all. No way did I want Scooter Sanchez tagging along. He would totally wreck everything!

I didn't have time to deal with him right now, though. Right now, I had to put our plan into action.

Sunday School couldn't be over soon enough. When class finally finished, I bolted for the fellowship hall. My friends—and Scooter—were right behind me. I spotted Reverend Quinn chatting with Aunt True, and trotted over to join them.

"You've met my niece, haven't you?" my aunt said to the minister.

"Certainly," Reverend Quinn replied warmly. "How is Pumpkin Falls treating you these days, young Truly?"

"Fine," I replied. "Except for one thing."

"And what is that?"

"I've never seen the Paul Revere bell." I tried to look super disappointed.

"We need to remedy that, don't we?" said the minister, and Cha Cha gave me a discreet thumbs-up. Then he added, "Tours of the steeple are given every weekend throughout the warmer months."

"I have to wait until spring?" I didn't have to fake my disappointment now.

"Isn't there a way we could see it before that?" said Cha Cha. "I've never been up to the steeple either."

Jasmine and Lucas and Calhoun all nodded in agreement.

"You kids can't be serious!" said Reverend Quinn. "I know for a fact that every student at Daniel Webster School is given a tour."

"Yeah, but that was way back in kindergarten!" Lucas trotted out his most pathetic expression.

Scooter, who was clearly enjoying this exchange, flashed his braces at me again. I tried to ignore him.

"Looks like you have a captive audience," said Aunt True.

"Really? You all want to see the bell? In this weather?" Reverend Quinn frowned. "It's terribly cold up there—there's no insulation in the steeple, and the bell tower itself is completely open to the elements."

"We'll put our jackets on," I told him. "Please?"

He sighed. "I'll get my coat." He turned to my aunt. "Would you like to come along, True?"

I held my breath. Having my aunt along was a complication I hadn't counted on.

"Tempting," she said. "I haven't been up there since high school. But I think I'll wait for warmer weather."

We grabbed our jackets and followed Reverend Quinn upstairs. Lucas was careful to avoid his mother, which was smart of him. She'd hyperventilate if she heard he was planning on going up into the steeple.

Our destination was a small vestibule just beyond the church's cloakroom. Two ropes hung from the ceiling; one was floor-length, the other dangled just above our heads. Reverend Quinn grabbed the one above our heads and tugged on it, pulling down a set of fold-up stairs.

"What's the other rope for?" Scooter asked.

"Ringing the bell," the minister told him. "Don't touch it." He pulled his wool hat down over his ears and started to climb. "Follow me, and mind your step."

I made the mistake of being first in line after him.

"I see London, I see France," whispered Scooter as I headed up the ladder. "I see Truly's gigantic under—"

"*Scooter!*" I whisper-hollered down at him. At least he couldn't really see my underpants. Which are absolutely truly not gigantic. I'd never been so grateful in my life for my wool tights.

A moment later I emerged in the middle of an atticlike room.

"Step to the wall, please," said Reverend Quinn. "It's going to be a little crowded up here."

I did as he asked, and something crunched beneath my feet. Looking down, I spotted frozen mouse droppings.

"Eew," I said, just as Scooter's head emerged through the opening in the floor.

"What did I do now?" he protested, scrambling to his feet. He looked around. "Cool!"

"Very," quipped Reverend Quinn, the word emerging in a puff of frost. He hadn't been kidding; it was freezing up here. "Let's make this snappy," he said as the rest of my friends joined us. "Built in 1803, the Pumpkin Falls Parish Church steeple is one of the finest examples of Georgian architecture in all of New England."

I could tell that this was a speech he'd given to a zillion tourists over the years.

"Steeples served several purposes for early settlers," he continued. "First and foremost, they generally housed a bell inside. Bells can ring a warning, mark the passing of hours, celebrate, and call the congregation to worship. By pointing heavenward, the steeple also serves as a reminder of loftier things." The minister paused a moment and raised his eyes toward the ceiling for effect. Jasmine stifled a giggle.

Reverend Quinn cleared his throat sheepishly, then checked his watch. "Five minutes is all I can really spare today, kids," he said. "Let's go on up, shall we?"

We followed him up the next ladder and through a trap-door in the ceiling, emerging this time into the bright sunshine. The view from the bell tower was amazing. To the north, I could see the covered bridge. To the east, the village green spread like a carpet—a white one at the moment—toward the college campus; to the south I could just make out the rooftops of the houses up the hill along Maple Street, including Gramps and Lola's, and to the west were the lower slopes of Lovejoy Mountain, bristling with spruces and pines.

"And there it is in all its glory—our famous Paul Revere bell," said Reverend Quinn, directing our attention overhead.

He pointed out the inscription engraved around the top of it, which read REVERE & SON BOSTON 1804, then swung into his canned speech once again. "Cast in Revere's foundry in Boston's North End, this bronze bell has graced our church for more than two hundred years. It weighs over half a ton—one thousand and twelve pounds, to be exact, including the clapper, which weighs thirty-six pounds. Note the headstock—that's the wooden beam or crosspiece, as it's called, from which the bell hangs. And wrapped around that wooden wheel is its pull-rope."

Scooter inspected it closely. "Is that the same rope we saw downstairs?"

Reverend Quinn nodded. "The very same. Pulleys guide it down through the steeple. The rope turns the wheel, which swings the headstock and sets the bell in motion. Most people don't know that it's the bell that swings, hitting the clapper, rather than the other way around."

"How often do you ring it?" I asked, curious.

"At one o'clock every afternoon, before the church service on Sunday, for weddings, and at noon on New Year's Day and the Fourth of July."

"Why not every hour?" asked Jasmine.

"Our bell is in semiretirement," the minister said drily.

"Would you want to work all day if you were over two hundred years old?"

"I'll bet it's loud up here when the bell rings," said Scooter, reaching up to touch it.

"Extremely. You wouldn't want to be in close quarters without earplugs." Reverend Quinn glanced at his watch again. "Okay, kids, feel free to snap some pictures if you'd like—do NOT lean over the railings, young man"—he was talking to Scooter, of course—"and then we'll head back down."

"The envelope is up in the next level, with the clock, right?" whispered Cha Cha as we moved away.

I nodded and took a picture of her and Jasmine with my cell phone. "Almost time," I told them, then zipped the phone back into my jacket pocket.

Reverend Quinn started down the ladder. "Make it snappy, kids. I'll wait for you below."

This was the chance we'd been waiting for.

"Time to distract him," I whispered to my classmates. "I'm going after the clue."

"How come *you* get to go?" asked Scooter.

"Because that's the plan," I told him. "I know what we're looking for." I started toward the wooden slats that were nailed to the wall and served as a crude ladder.

Scooter shouldered past me. "It's an envelope, duh," he said. "Jasmine told me. How hard can that be to find?"

"Get down from there!" I ordered as he stepped up onto the first slat.

"Dude, do what she says," said Calhoun.

I looked over at him, surprised. Then I remembered the pact we'd made. Romeo was holding up his end of the bargain.

"Hurry up now, kids," Reverend Quinn called to us, and Calhoun jerked his thumb at Scooter, who reluctantly hopped down.

"All I need is five minutes," I told my friends and started up for the clock tower as they disappeared through the trapdoor in the floor.

# CHAPTER 32

The platform of the clock tower was just like the one below, covered with frozen mouse droppings—and also pigeon poo. Piles and piles of pigeon poo. I knew this because I'd just stepped into one of them.

Grimacing, I scraped my boot on a clean spot on the floor and looked around. It was darker here than in the bell tower below; there were no arched openings in the walls to let in light. Enough leaked in from the open trapdoor in the floor that I could see fairly well, though.

I could hear fairly well too, and what I heard was a shriek. It sounded like Jasmine. The distraction we'd planned was under way.

I examined the back of the clock—nothing. No hidden compartments, nothing taped to it, just a bunch of gears whirring and clicking away. The rafters above were empty too. I checked the walls, the floor, every inch of the clock tower. No envelope.

I stood there, puzzled. It had to be here! I was certain of it. The second hand ticked loudly in the background as I searched again. I felt like Gary Cooper in *High Noon*. Time was running out. Reverend Quinn was bound to notice my absence soon.

I searched again, but the envelope wasn't here. And I had been so certain that it would be!

The scavenger hunt was over.

Discouraged, I went back over to the ladder. As I placed my foot onto the top slat, I caught a glimpse of something flapping on top of the thick piece of wood below—the one from which the bell hung. What had Reverend Quinn called it? The headstock?

I climbed down closer for a better look. Sure enough, something was stuck to the headstock's flat surface, and a corner of whatever it was had come loose and was flapping in the chilly breeze. It looked like a length of duct tape. Peering closer, I could see that it had been painted over with white to match the rest of the wood. It was nearly invisible, except for the telltale flash of silvery gray beneath the paint on the loose piece.

I stretched out an arm to see if I could reach it. No such luck. I climbed all the way down to the bell platform below and stretched up, but I couldn't reach it from there, either. There was only one option. I'd have to climb back up, scooch my way out onto the rafter directly above the headstock, then see if I could lean down and reach it from there.

It wasn't easy. The rafter was frosted as thickly as one of Dr. Calhoun's cupcakes with everything that was icky in the steeple. Dirt, mouse droppings, and probably two hundred years' worth of pigeon poo.

Pulling off my wool hat, I smacked it against the wood, sending up a cloud of dust and scattering frozen mouse droppings in every direction. Still gross, but better. I hiked my skirt up and straddled the rafter. As I inched forward, I heard something rip. I'd snagged my tights. So much for wearing my Sunday best—I was going to have some explaining to do when I got home.

Using my hat as a makeshift pigeon-poo snowplow, I continued inching my way out until I was directly above the flapping edge of duct tape. Then I leaned forward until I was lying flat on my stomach. Holding tight to the rafter with one arm, I cautiously extended the other. My fingertips grazed the upcurled edge of tape. I strained to grab it, but it was still too far away.

Frustrated, I sat up again. The only way I was going to be able to do this was if I swung my knees over the rafter and lowered myself down backward, the way I used to do on the jungle gym when I was Pippa's age.

There was no other choice. And if I wasn't quick, Reverend Quinn would be back up here looking for me. Before I could talk myself out of it, over I went. And suddenly I was really, really glad Scooter wasn't up here. He'd be singing "I see London" at the top of his lungs, because my skirt had flipped completely over my head. I swatted it away from my face, tucking the front part into the waistband of my tights. A gust of frigid wind found the open gap between my turtleneck sweater and my back as I did so, and I choked back a screech.

I dangled there upside down like a frozen bat, face-to-face with Paul Revere's bell. I was close enough to touch the inscription with my nose if I'd wanted to. Which I absolutely truly did not.

I also didn't want to be spotted. People were starting to leave the church, and I was in full view of anyone who might happen to look up at the steeple from the street. I needed to hurry.

I pulled myself halfway up and grabbed hold of the headstock with one hand, then reached for the loose corner of duct tape with the other. Grasping it, I tugged. And tugged again, harder. *R-i-i-i-i-p!* The duct tape parted ways with the paint and the wood, and sure enough, there was something stuck to the underside. An envelope! Clutching it tightly, I hauled myself back up on top of the rafter.

I lay there for a second or two, panting. Suddenly, the big wooden wheel below me began to move. I scrambled for safety as the bell began to sway back and forth. And a moment later, all I could think about was covering my ears.

# CHAPTER 33

I was partially deaf until Tuesday, thanks to Scooter Sanchez.

Ringing the bell was not part of our plan. Jasmine was the one who was supposed to create a diversion by pretending to fall off the ladder and sprain her ankle. In the end, though, everything worked out okay. In all the fuss over the unauthorized ringing, as Reverend Quinn hauled Scooter off by his ear, I was able to come down from the steeple without being spotted.

"What happened to you?" asked Cha Cha, staring at me wide-eyed as I climbed down the ladder into the vestibule behind the coat room.

"WHAT?" I hollered. I could see her lips moving, but no sound was coming from them. Or if it was, it was drowned out by the ringing in my ears.

Cha Cha's dimple emerged and she started to giggle.

"WHAT'S SO FUNNY?"

She pointed to my hair, my dust-streaked face, my pigeon-poo-smeared clothes, and my torn tights. By now, Jasmine and Lucas and Calhoun were laughing too.

"Did you get the envelope?" Calhoun made an envelope shape in the air with his fingers.

I pulled it out of my jacket pocket. Everybody crowded around, eager to see what was inside. I opened it. There were the usual *B*s at the beginning and end of the letter, along with another single line of text:

> *I do love nothing in the world so well as you—*
> *is not that strange?*

We all looked at Calhoun, who nodded. "*Much Ado,*" he confirmed.

All it said underneath the quote was *our meeting spot.*

"That's not fair!" cried Cha Cha. The ringing in my ears had started to subside, but her voice was still like the faint buzz from a far-off mosquito. "How are we supposed to know where they liked to meet?"

"Total dead end," said Jasmine in dismay.

It certainly seemed like it. I didn't see how we'd ever be able to solve this clue.

"Maybe not," said Calhoun. "My father might be able to help."

Cha Cha swatted at my jacket with the edge of her scarf.

"We have to get Truly cleaned up first," she told him.

She texted her mother and a couple of minutes later it was all settled. We were invited over to the Abramowitzes' for lunch. Somehow, with my friends forming a human shield around me, I managed to make it out of the church unseen.

"Hey, wait up!" called Scooter, who had been released from Reverend Quinn's custody, unfortunately. He caught up as we were halfway across the village green. "Whoa—you are one big Drooly Gigantic Mess," he said when he caught sight of me.

I shoved him into a snowbank.

Cha Cha's mother was much kinder.

"Good heavens, what happened to you, Truly?" she asked as we came through the front door.

"I fell into a snowbank," I replied, shooting Scooter a look.

When I saw myself in the bathroom mirror, I was surprised Mrs. Abramowitz hadn't called an ambulance. I looked like Belinda Winchester on one of her worst days. Soap and water helped, and I managed to get my hair looking more normal, but the tights were a lost cause. I stuffed them into the trash, then opened the door a crack and handed my skirt and turtleneck to Cha Cha. I could only hope that the washing machine wouldn't ruin them. I'd tried dabbing them with a wet washcloth, but that mostly just smeared the pigeon poo around.

"Put these on for now," said Cha Cha, handing me back a pair of her sweatpants and a shirt that belonged to her father.

"You've got to be kidding me," I replied, holding the sweatpants up. They barely reached my knees. I put them on, though—what else was I supposed to do?

Cha Cha started to giggle again as I slouched into her room.

"Shut up," I said, grateful that the boys were downstairs. I knew how ridiculous I looked. Then I started to laugh too. Jasmine joined us, and pretty soon the three of us were howling so hard that we scared Fred and Ginger, the Abramowitzes' cats, who ran under Cha Cha's bed to hide. Our hilarity drew Cha Cha's mother upstairs to check on us.

"Everything okay in here?" she asked. "Lunch is ready."

As I looked around the kitchen table a few minutes later, it occurred to me that six weeks ago I could never have imagined being here. Not just in Pumpkin Falls, but here with these new friends, trying to solve a twenty-year-old mystery. It felt really strange.

And even stranger when we arrived at Calhoun's house to talk to his father.

"Interesting," said Dr. Calhoun, after he scanned the sheet of paper on which Calhoun had written the Shakespeare quotes. "They're definitely all from *Much Ado About Nothing*, just as you said."

"Do they remind you of anything?" Calhoun asked.

His father shook his head. "Should they?"

Calhoun lifted a shoulder. "I dunno. I thought maybe they would. You know, maybe something from a long time ago?" He looked at his father with a hopeful expression.

Suddenly, the pieces fell into place—*snick!*—like a sudoku puzzle. Calhoun thought his *parents* were the B and B in our mystery letters! It made perfect sense, since they'd played Beatrice and Benedick together back in high school. I'd seen it on the theater program in Aunt True's apartment.

Maybe he'd been hoping the mystery letters would get them back together again somehow. I held my breath as Dr. Calhoun frowned at the piece of paper.

But again, he shook his head. "Sorry, son. Doesn't ring a bell."

*Bad choice of words*, I thought, scowling at Scooter. He shot me one of his trademark *Who me? What did I do?* looks back.

"I was just trying to help," he whispered. "You know, with the diversion?"

*Yeah, right*, I thought.

"So is this for a school project or something?" Calhoun's father asked us.

"Or something," Cha Cha told him. "We're just interested, that's all."

"Glad to hear it. Nothing better than being interested in the Bard. It's a lifetime pursuit." Dr. Calhoun checked his watch. "Well, I'd better go. The pipes have frozen in one of the dorms, and I want to check in with the maintenance staff and see how the repairs are coming along. Juliet is upstairs if you need anything. You kids have fun now." He left, closing the door behind him.

"Sorry, Calhoun," I said. "You were hoping it was them—your parents, I mean—weren't you?"

Calhoun looked down at the floor. "Yeah, I guess. My mother loves Shakespeare almost as much as my father does. She was the one who named my sister and me."

"Named you what?" asked Scooter. "R. J.?"

"Never mind," said Cha Cha and Jasmine and Lucas and me, all at the same time.

And we started to laugh.

# CHAPTER 34

On the morning that the Pumpkin Falls Centennial Winter Festival began, I awoke to the sound of dripping.

"Listen, Miss Marple!" I cried, throwing back the covers and leaping out of bed. "Do you hear that?"

The hardwood floor was freezing, and I hopped quickly over to the window, dancing from one foot to the other as I peered outside. Sure enough, the icicles on the eaves were starting to melt.

The January thaw had finally arrived!

"Better late than never," said the weatherman on the kitchen radio a few minutes later. He sounded jubilant. "Looks like the warming trend will linger into early next week, so all you maple farmers out there can take a deep breath and relax—your sap run is safe."

Lauren had beaten me downstairs to breakfast, and hearing this she ran to the closet under the front stairs to call Annie.

Not that the Freemans wouldn't have figured it out for themselves by now. All they had to do was open their front door.

Which is exactly what I did a few minutes later. I stood on the doorstep a moment, inhaling deeply. For once, my nostrils didn't freeze together the way they had ever since I'd arrived in Pumpkin Falls. The air was practically balmy.

Miss Marple dashed past me and scampered down the path, as frisky as a puppy. I was feeling pretty frisky myself, even though I knew it wouldn't last. Dad had explained to us one night at the dinner table recently that New England's famous January thaw is only a sneak preview of warmer months ahead.

"Old Man Winter is a tease," he'd said. "Every January he relents just a bit, and takes pity on us by opening the window a crack and giving us a peek at spring, then he slams it shut again and hammers us with more cold."

"J. T., you have the soul of a poet," Mom had told him, kissing the top of his head. My father had snorted, but he'd looked pleased.

As I stood there, soaking up the sunshine, I didn't care if it was just a sneak preview. I'd take weather like this any day.

Energized, I took a shower and dressed in record time, then walked to school as usual with my brother and sisters. Pumpkin Falls looked anything but usual, however.

Flags were flying everywhere, and there was bunting on the steeple and a big PUMPKIN FALLS CENTENNIAL WINTER

FESTIVAL! banner had been hung across the front of the Town Hall. The streets around the village green were lined with cars, as spectators and the news media crowded around to watch the sculptors at work.

The Pumpkin Falls Winter Festival is famous for its snow-sculpture competition, and people come from all over to enter it and to watch the sculptors at work. Gramps and Lola send us pictures of it every year. Last year there was a fairy-tale theme, which meant the village green was covered with dragons and knights and castles and lots of familiar characters—Snow White and all the dwarves, Jack and the beanstalk, Rapunzel, Cinderella, the three little pigs, that sort of thing. Cinderella won—probably because of the huge pumpkin carriage.

Pippa tugged on my hand. "Look! There'th Nathaniel-Daniel-lookth-like-a-thpaniel!"

I glanced over at the sculptures on the green, and sure enough, there was a larger-than-life snow sculpture of our famous ancestor, big nose and all.

Because it's the centennial, this year's theme celebrates the history of Pumpkin Falls, so in addition to Nathaniel Daniel Lovejoy there was a giant 100! in the center of the green, a big maple leaf, and a nearly life-size replica of the covered bridge complete with frozen waterfall. Plus, there was a huge Paul Revere bell and the façade of the General Store. A long line of people stretched in front of it, waiting to have their pictures taken on the front porch in the giant rocking chair carved out of snow.

"Can I thit in it too?" Pippa begged. "Pleathe?"

"We'll come back later, Pipster, when it's not so crowded," Hatcher promised.

School was mercifully brief. Nobody could concentrate anyway—everyone was too keyed up over the three days of activities ahead, which kicked off right after lunch with the Winter Festival Spelling Bee, for which Annie Freeman had been practicing for weeks. In addition, there were a bunch of sporting events—ski races, figure skating, and speed skating on the rink at the college, and other games and meets, including basketball, hockey, wrestling, and of course our swim team's grudge match against Thornton. Coach Maynard had been firing us up for that all week.

Tomorrow morning was the famous Polar Bear Swim at Lake Lovejoy, which is about the dumbest idea in the history of the world if you ask me, which nobody ever does. Who'd be stupid enough to jump into a frozen lake? A bunch of people, apparently, because the *Patriot-Bugle* was reporting a bumper crop of entrants.

All of the stores in town were offering special sales and promotions for the weekend too. Donuts at Lou's would be three for a nickel, the same price they were one hundred years ago, haircuts at the Kwik Klips were going for "two bits," which my father told us used to mean a quarter, and the

General Store employees were giving out free bags of penny candy with every purchase. The *Patriot-Bugle* had published a special commemorative edition, complete with "Then and Now" photographs of Pumpkin Falls, along with interviews with the town's oldest citizens.

The highlight of the weekend—at least for everybody but me—was the big dance tomorrow night at Town Hall. Of course, since the festival weekend happens to coincide with Valentine's Day this year, they're making an even bigger deal of it than usual. Mrs. Abramowitz is chair of the entertainment and decorating committee, and my mother, who's been helping her out since she's still working as the Starlite's receptionist, says Cha Cha's mom has been in a dither for weeks.

"I've never been involved in so many decisions involving hearts in my entire life," my mother told us at dinner last night. "Paper hearts! Sparkly hearts! Hearts that light up and hearts that spin and hearts that blow bubbles! Did you know that you can even order heart-shaped ice cubes?"

I did not, and I didn't care. I was so not looking forward to Cotillion. I hated the thought of being on display for the whole world to watch and laugh at. I'd probably trip over my own big feet, right in front of everybody.

I pushed the thought away. No point stewing about tomorrow when I had enough to stew about today—mainly our meet against Thornton.

The bleachers at the swim center were packed by the

time I came out of the locker room. I spotted my friends and family—they were all there, even Dad. Only Aunt True was missing. She'd volunteered to stay behind at the bookstore so that my father could come and watch me. She'd sent a text earlier that made me laugh, though. There was just one word in it: VICTORY!

Aunt True is a total Lovejoy when it comes to sports.

I was swimming a trio of races—the 200 Medley Relay, the 50 Freestyle, and last but by far from least, the 100 Individual Medley. Not for a while, though. First up were the younger kids and the newbies, including Lucas.

"That's my boy," I heard Mrs. Winthrop announce proudly to no one in particular, as Lucas stepped up onto the block.

Aunt True says it's positively painful to look at Lucas in a bathing suit, and she's got a point. I've shared the pool with some skinny swimmers before, but Lucas Winthrop takes the cake. From his knobby knees to his protruding ribs and collar-bone, he's practically a walking anatomy lesson.

Mrs. Winthrop stood up, her video camera clutched nervously in her hands. She's still convinced her son is going to drown somehow. When you think about it, it's amazing he's even allowed out of the house.

Whenever I see Mrs. Winthrop, I remind myself to be grateful that I still have a dad, and not just one overprotective parent. Lucas doesn't seem to miss his father too much—at least, he never talks about it—but then again, he was just a baby when his father died, so he's never known any different.

Lucas didn't drown, of course. In fact, not only did he swim his best time ever, he won his first race ever. The Pumpkin Falls half of the bleachers exploded as he churned his way down the home stretch and slapped the wall. Mrs. Winthrop almost dropped her video camera, she was cheering so hard. I was yelling my head off and so was the rest of the team. Lucas looked at the clock in disbelief, then looked over at us with this huge grin on his face. I wanted to jump in the water and hug his little hummingbird self.

As I got ready for my first race, I hoped that Lucas's win was a good omen. And it seemed like it was, because I won the 50 Freestyle handily and our relay team, which had been performing unevenly, posted a faster time than in any of our practices, even though technically we lost to Thornton. I didn't care as much about those races, though—it was the 100 Individual Medley I was most worried about. That one's always been my race.

"Good luck," said one of the Thornton swimmers as we stepped onto the blocks.

I hate it when my opponents are cheerful. It makes them impossible to dislike.

"You too," I told her, trying to mean it.

The bell rang and I arced forward, my dive perfectly aimed to hit the water in the best possible position. *Half a dozen strong dolphin kicks, break the surface, arms spread like wings*, I told myself. I flew down my lane, did a quick double-touch on the gutter, then pushed into backstroke, every breath, every movement exactly as I'd imagined it.

The thing about swimming is, it's all mental. Yes, of course it matters that you've been working hard in practice, but that's all second nature when it comes down to the actual race. The trick is to picture yourself swimming every lap, picture your time, how many breaths you'll take, how far each stroke will take you, all of it. And most of all, you've got to picture yourself winning.

Which I had been doing for days.

I didn't hear the crowd; I didn't hear anything but my own breathing and my own fierce wanting to win. I moved effortlessly from butterfly to backstroke to breaststroke. As I approached the flip turn that would take me into the final free-style stretch, I was neck-and-neck with the swimmer in the lane next to me. I tucked under, certain that my height would give me the advantage in the home stretch.

Or not.

As my legs flew over my head and I corkscrewed into the turn, my left heel slammed against the tiles.

Hard.

Jolted by the pain, I faltered. Only for a split second, but that was long enough to throw me off my rhythm. I scrambled to recover, pouring it on as I powered toward the finish, but it was too late.

I lost by three-tenths of a second.

I looked up at the clock in disbelief. The extra inch I'd grown since moving here had knocked me off balance and cost me the race! I'd been betrayed by my stupid Amazon feet!

Out of the corner of my eye, I could see Hatcher up in the bleachers tapping his fingers under his chin in our chin-up shorthand. I shook my head at him and closed my eyes. Why oh why did I have to be so freakishly tall? I dragged myself out of the pool, not even stopping to congratulate the winner. I didn't care if it was rude; I just wanted the shelter of the locker room.

"Tough luck, sweetheart," my mother said a while later, when I finally emerged. She gave me a hug.

"Way to hang in there," added my father, which is Lovejoy-speak for *Loser*.

Which was exactly how I felt for the rest of the day.

# CHAPTER 35

"This is embarrassing," said Hatcher.

"Tell me about it," I replied.

The two of us were at the bookstore the next morning, helping Dad and Aunt True. I was still trying to blot out yesterday's disastrous swim meet. My family was being supernice to me, which only made me feel worse, of course. I'd tried to be happy for Danny and Hatcher, who were total rock stars at their wrestling meets last night (people around town are starting to refer to them as "The Lovejoy Brothers," like they're a circus act or something), and I tried to be happy for my mother, too. She could hardly contain herself when Dad wandered down to the mats and started talking to the coaches. It was the first real sign of interest he's shown in wrestling since Black Monday.

None of it made any difference to me, though. All I could think about was that stupid mistake I'd made in the final turn at the pool. And now here I was, about to be humiliated again. For some unknown reason, Aunt True had gotten it into her head that we should dress up in honor of Valentine's Day for the bookshop's Grand Reopening events. She'd even persuaded Dad to agree to spring for a pair of costumes.

She waited until this morning, when we were trapped at the store under Dad's watchful eye, to surprise us with them. Danny took one look and quickly played the homework card—*So sorry, big physics test first thing Monday morning, gotta go study, yada yada.*

Dad wouldn't let Hatcher and me off the hook, though. "Your aunt talked me into wasting money on these foolish things—someone is going to wear them!"

And those someones were us, of course.

"Thanks for throwing us under the bus," Hatcher muttered as our older brother made his escape.

Danny grinned and gave us a thumbs-up as he headed out the door. "Lookin' good!"

We didn't, of course—we looked ridiculous. Hatcher was dressed as Cupid, complete with a Roman toga, gold-painted plastic bow and arrow, and gold wings. My outfit was even more horrible. I was stuck with a hooded red unitard, whose matching headband had sparkly red hearts bobbing on a pair of wobbly antennae, and a poufy heart-shaped pillow that strapped over my body like a sandwich board. It was shiny and red, just like my face.

"At least we didn't have to dress up for the walk over here," said Hatcher grimly, tugging at his toga. "It could have been worse, right?"

The two of us had dropped Lauren and Pippa at Belinda Winchester's before heading to the bookstore. Belinda had offered to watch them until Story Hour, since the rest of us had a lot of work to do—setting up chairs for this afternoon's reading, baking piles of mini whoopie pies, and filling the goodie bags we would be giving out with purchases.

Belinda had met us at her back door wearing shorts, sandals with wool socks, a T-shirt, and a straw hat. "Groovin' to the Beach Boys," she said by way of a greeting, pulling out an earbud. She'd gestured at the blue sky and grinned. "Can you believe the weather this weekend? Made to order."

Pippa had given her a swift hug and run past her into the kitchen. Belinda Winchester's house looks pretty much the way you'd think it would, except that it's spotless. Cluttered as all get-out, but absolutely spotless.

"I was expecting *Tales from the Crypt* and instead I found Mrs. Clean," my mother had told my father the first time she stopped by.

"Hi, Fern," Lauren had said, bending down and scooping up the big tabby cat who'd been curled up by the woodstove. Belinda didn't actually have as many cats as people thought—there were just two permanent residents: Fern and Avery. But there were a whole lot of visitors. Word was out in Grafton

County that she'd take good care of strays, so baskets and boxes and even bags were dropped off on her doorstep, filled with felines in need of new homes. And somehow, Belinda always found them one. She had deputies in all the nearby towns scouting for potential kitten adopters, and she even had her own blog where she featured new arrivals.

I'd handed Mrs. Winchester a loaf of my mother's home-made banana bread. "My mom said to tell you thanks, and that she'll see you later this morning."

Belinda had nodded, her earbud already back in, head bobbing to the strains of "Kokomo."

"Here, Truly," said my aunt, thrusting a book at me and pulling my attention back to the task at hand. "Add this to 'Miss Marple's Picks,' would you? It will make Augustus happy when he comes in this afternoon for his reading."

"Miss Marple's Picks" was another one of Aunt True's bright ideas.

"Every bookstore on the planet has a 'Staff Picks' display," she'd said one afternoon as I was finishing up a tutoring session. "I think we should do something different."

"Who's going to care what the dog reads?" grumbled my father, after she explained her plan. Then he slapped his palm against his forehead in mock self-reproach. "Wait, what am I saying—dogs don't read!"

Aunt True laughed. "Everybody will care, J. T.—you'll see."

And she was right. It's been a huge hit with our customers.

"What's Miss Marple reading this week?" they'd ask, making a beeline for the shelf by the front door. Miss Marple has her own page now on the bookstore website (ghostwritten by Aunt True), which gets more hits than all the other pages combined. Just last week, the *Pumpkin Falls Patriot-Bugle* featured Miss Marple in their "Around Town" column, along with a fake interview and a picture of her sitting proudly by her namesake shelf. The story was picked up by the news wires, and we got a flurry of media interest from as far away as Australia. People everywhere love dogs, I guess.

Mom says Aunt True is a marketing genius.

Catching a glimpse of my poufy heart-shaped reflection in the front window, though, I wasn't so sure. I sighed and placed *Summer's Siren Song* by Augusta Savage face out on Miss Marple's shelf. Looking at it more closely, I was tempted to turn it over. Someone should give the women on the covers of romance books turtlenecks to wear. It's embarrassing.

I went back to the counter to continue stuffing gift bags.

"I keep thinking it just got misplaced and someone will find it," Aunt True was saying to a customer. "I still can't believe that someone would actually take it."

She was talking about *Charlotte's Web*, of course.

I'd come up empty-handed in my efforts to catch the thief. The mystery of the missing book was still unsolved.

Two hours later, I'd replenished our supply of gift bags filled with bookmarks, discount coupons, a copy of our newsletter, and chocolate kisses, and I'd helped Aunt True bake several dozen more mini pumpkin whoopie pies. Hatcher, meanwhile, had set up all the chairs for this afternoon's reading, waited on customers, sorted all the special orders, and was just finishing up getting things organized for Story Hour.

"Mr. Henry!" said Aunt True as the bell over the door jangled. "Right on time. I see you're dressed for the occasion."

The children's librarian, who was wearing his trademark red-and-white striped sweater, laughed. "I'm always dressed for the occasion," he replied. "You're looking very Valentine-y yourself."

Aunt True wasn't in a costume, exactly, but she'd decked herself out in red from head to toe—red skirt, red sweater, red tights, and red cowboy boots.

"I'm not sure," my aunt replied, plucking at the strands of silver paper hearts she'd strung around her neck. "I think I kind of look like Mrs. Claus."

"You couldn't look like Mrs. Claus if you tried," said the librarian gallantly.

My mouth fell open. Was Mr. Henry *flirting* with Aunt True?

Mr. Henry looked over at me. His eyebrows shot up as he eyed my costume. "And you're, uh, very fancy."

I made a face.

"The kids will love it," he told me with a wink. "Trust me."

He was right. Hatcher and I might have felt humiliated, but we were the stars of Story Hour. The kids laughed themselves silly as we circled the children's room with our trays of mini whoopie pies and heart-shaped shortbread cookies. Hatcher totally got into it, smiling his sunflower smile as he pretended to shoot his bow and arrow. I just stuck to handing out treats.

Afterward, the kids all ran over and lined up to have their pictures taken with us, and with Miss Marple, who was also dressed for the occasion, thanks to Pippa and Lauren. My sisters had tied a big red bow to her collar and painted her toenails bright pink. With sparkles, of course.

"Whoa," said a voice behind me. I turned around to see Scooter standing there. Calhoun was with him.

I didn't even give Scooter a chance to open his mouth. Looking him straight in the eye, I said, "If you call me 'Truly Gigantic' or 'Truly Drooly' or anything else ever again, I swear I will deck you!"

Scooter looked at the tray in my hand and laughed. "With what, a whoopie pie?"

"Leave her alone, Scooter," said Calhoun, giving the revolving greeting card rack a twirl.

Scooter over at him. He frowned. "What's up with you, dude? You're no fun at all lately."

They didn't stick around for long after that, thank goodness. They'd just come for the free treats anyway. Believe it or not, though, that wasn't the low point of the afternoon. The low point was after lunch, when the *Patriot-Bugle* showed up to cover Augustus Wilde's book signing.

"Ooh, look how cute you are!" said the photographer when she spotted me in my ridiculous costume. "Come on over—we need a shot of you standing next to Augustus."

Reluctantly, I did as she asked.

"This is definitely front-page material," the photographer assured us.

Augustus, of course, was thrilled. I, on the other hand, was not.

*Just what I need to make my day complete*, I thought sourly. Immortalized forever with Captain Romance.

Hatcher, the booger head, was nowhere to be seen during all this, of course.

I stomped off to look for him, fuming.

"What are you doing back here?" my father asked when I poked my head in the office. "Aren't you supposed to be helping man the cash register?"

"Hatcher can help," I said shortly. "Where is he, anyway?"

My father shrugged. "Haven't seen him. Go on back out there now, Truly. You know we're counting on you."

"Yes, sir," I said sullenly. *How come you get to hide back here?* I wanted to ask him, but I gritted my teeth and did as he asked.

The book signing dragged on forever. I stood politely with Aunt True and listened while stupid Augustus in his stupid cape (a red one this time, in honor of Valentine's Day) read from his stupid book. I stacked copies of stupid *Summer's Siren Song* on the table and herded his stupid starstruck fans into line for the signing. I passed out stupid sticky notes so they could write their names down in case Augustus was too stupid to spell them correctly, and even submitted to posing for stupid pictures afterward.

By the time everyone left and it was finally time to close up, I really, really wasn't in the mood to go to the stupid dance.

"Shouldn't you be getting ready?" Mom asked me back at home a while later. I was dawdling at the dinner table, picking at my macaroni and cheese. Hatcher and Danny and my sisters had already gone upstairs to change.

I lifted a shoulder.

"Come on, honey," she coaxed. "It's Winter Festival!"

What it was was a disaster. It had been a terrible, horrible weekend so far, and it was far from over.

"You've got such a pretty dress, and you've been practicing so hard for Cotillion," my mother continued. "Time to strut your stuff."

I dragged my stuff upstairs to the shower. I didn't feel like strutting anything, ever again.

# CHAPTER 36

My spirits lifted slightly when I put on my new dress. Like I said, girl clothes are way up on the list of things I'm not good at, but this dress wasn't so bad. It was close-fitting black satin on top, with spaghetti straps and what Mom called a "sweetheart" neckline, and white poufy material on the bottom. Not poufy like the horrible pillow-shaped heart costume, but poufy like one of those flowy ballerina skirts. For contrast there was a wide red velvet belt, plus the skirt part was sprinkled with red polka dots. It sounds weird, but it wasn't. It was actually okay. And just the right length too.

I slipped into my size-ten-and-a-half black heels—low ones, like Mrs. Abramowitz recommended, so I wouldn't completely tower over my partner—ran a brush through my hair one last time, and grabbed my white gloves. Pausing to look in the mirror, I told myself that I was ready for anything. Even Scooter Sanchez.

"Oh, honey," said Mom as I came downstairs. "You look beautiful! Doesn't she look beautiful, J. T.?"

She nudged my father, who was trying to stuff his Ken hand into the arm of his jacket. He glanced up at me briefly. "Sure."

"Jericho Tobias Lovejoy, look at your eldest daughter!" Mom said sternly.

My father knows an order when he hears one. His eyes widened as he turned to look at me. *Really* look at me.

"How old is she, Dinah?" he asked.

"Twelve, but only for another month," Mom told him. "She's not our little girl anymore."

He shook his head. "I can see that. Our Truly-in-the-Middle is truly growing up." He smiled at me. "Your mother is right—you look beautiful, honey."

"Thanks." A warm feeling flooded through me. I felt bashful all of a sudden, and dropped my gaze toward my toes. My great big Truly Gigantic toes, which had cost me the 100 Individual Medley. The warm feeling evaporated.

"If it's okay with you," my father said to my mother, "I'm going to leave Ken home tonight. The useless thing is more bother than it's worth."

"So will you go with the Terminator, or with Captain Hook?" Mom asked him.

"Not sure yet. The Terminator was acting up a bit this afternoon—I'll go take a look at it." My father started back upstairs.

I had a sudden wild urge to giggle. Did other amputee families talk like this?

Silent Man had seemed a little more relaxed recently, and was even joking around a bit. Maybe my mother and Aunt True were right—maybe there had been a change in my father over the past weeks, a slow and gradual shift, quiet as the swing of a pendulum or the rise of a thermometer. He wasn't back to normal yet by any means, but maybe he was inching in that direction.

"Did you make vomit bars, Mom?" Hatcher asked anxiously as we pulled out of the driveway a few minutes later.

She pointed to a plastic container by Dad's feet on the floor of the van. "Right there," she said. "As requested."

This time I did giggle. Anybody listening to my family's conversations tonight would definitely think we were nuts.

Vomit bars were what my brothers call Mom's special seven-layer cookies. And it's true, with all the nuts and coconut and other stuff in them, from a distance they do kind of look like somebody barfed. They're our favorite dessert, though. Once, when we were little, our Texas cousins came to visit—all seventeen of them—and Hatcher and Danny were so afraid they wouldn't leave any for us, they decided to try and gross them out. That's when they came up with the name "vomit bars." It worked, kind of. At least until the older cousins saw us eating them and realized they'd been tricked.

A few minutes later we pulled up in front of Town Hall.

"Here, Truly," said my mother, passing me the container and giving Hatcher a stern look. "See that these get to the refreshment table safely, okay?"

"Sure, Mom," I replied, taking it from her.

Hatcher grinned.

"Mind the slush!" Mom called, just as Danny stepped out of the car and directly into a puddle.

"Oh, man!" he groaned, and we all laughed.

My sisters were beyond excited—unlike me, they couldn't wait to show off their dance moves for the crowd, plus they had their own party to look forward to in the Town Hall basement afterward. I'd overheard Mrs. Abramowitz tell my mother that a magician had been hired to entertain them.

My brothers, on the other hand, well, they might not have been dreading the whole thing the way I was, but I knew they'd much rather be at home watching hockey on TV. I was pretty sure Dad felt the same way, but he had his Lieutenant Colonel Jericho T. Lovejoy game face on as he escorted us inside.

The hall was jammed. In one corner, a band was tuning up. In another, Annie Freeman's mother was organizing the refreshment table. I delivered the vomit bars, then went to drop my jacket off at the coat check.

People were streaming through the doors, greeting their neighbors and former neighbors and others who were in town for the weekend celebration. Everyone looked happy. Everyone but me, that is.

*Time to put your game face on too*, I told myself, and went off to find my friends. I spotted Lucas first, looking painfully clean and neat. His hair was slicked back with gel, and he was wearing a tuxedo. This seemed like overkill, and was probably his mother's doing, since the Cotillion guidelines only said that boys should wear a dark suit. Lucas looked like a licorice stick.

"Hey," I said.

"Hey," he said back.

"Nice tux."

He blushed. "My mother bought it for me."

*Ha!* I thought. *I knew it.*

Jasmine jumped out from behind a pillar, beaming. "Notice anything different?"

I looked her over. She was wearing a fire-engine-red dress that set off her shiny dark hair. "Your dress is really pretty," I told her. "I like the sparkles."

"No, you dork, my braces! I got them off!" She beamed at me again, and I gave her a high five. So did Lucas. "Scooter still has to keep his on for a few more weeks, though."

That was the best news I'd had all day, and I perked right up.

Cha Cha waved from across the room. "You guys look great!" she called in her deep voice, coming over to join us.

"You too," I replied, admiring her black velvet strapless mini. "You look at least fifteen."

A moment later the lights dimmed and the band struck a chord. Cha Cha's mother tugged her husband into the middle of the dance floor.

"Good evening, everyone," Mr. Abramowitz said into his microphone. His greeting echoed through the crowded room. "And welcome to the one hundredth annual Pumpkin Falls Winter Festival!"

A deafening cheer went up from the crowd.

"As has long been our town's tradition," he continued, "we ask our young people to help kick things off in style."

That brought another cheer.

"And so, without further ado, I present to you the Daniel Webster School square dancers!" He motioned to the orchestra, who struck up "Turkey in the Straw" as the younger kids all marched out in pairs for their square dance.

"Oh, how adorable!" squealed Jasmine, pointing to Pippa and Baxter.

The two of them were holding hands, and they both wore grave expressions. Pippa took her responsibility as the opening act for the big dance very seriously, and she and Baxter had been practicing their steps faithfully.

Cameras flashed and proud parents beamed from the sidelines as Mr. Abramowitz began to call the dance: "The lady goes right, the gent goes left, circle left so lightly . . ."

Pippa and Baxter didn't miss a beat.

"They are so cute together!" whispered Cha Cha.

"I know, right?" I whispered back.

Annie Freeman twirled past, her multiple braids bouncing almost as quickly as her feet. She was busy talking, of course—probably spelling out the moves to her partner. My sister Lauren was right behind her with Amy Nguyen's younger brother. She shot me a look as she danced by, one that clearly said, *I'm so over this dumb kid stuff and ready to tackle ballroom.* Lauren still had stars in her eyes about Cotillion.

They finished a few minutes later amid thunderous applause. And then it was our turn.

"Places, everyone!" whispered Ms. Ivey, frantically trying to line us all up. The sixth, seventh, and eighth graders had all been practicing separately during gym class at school, and this was the first time we'd all be together. I waved to Hatcher, who was standing with his partner on the other side of the dance floor. He smiled his sunflower smile at me. Nothing rattled Hatcher.

When we were all in place, Ms. Ivey gave Mr. Abramowitz a thumbs-up. She looked really pretty tonight in her long white satin sheath and red heels. It occurred to me that I didn't know if there was a Mr. Ivey. If not, maybe Cupid would visit Pumpkin Falls and find her one.

"I still think this is stupid," said Scooter as he took my hand, placing his other on my shoulder.

"Yeah," I agreed. "Totally lame."

"And now, folks, it's time for this evening's Cotillion ballroom showcase!" announced Mr. Abramowitz.

I could feel Scooter's palms sweating right through his cotton gloves. He was as nervous as I was. This was not a good sign.

My parents both waved, and I saw something glint at the end of my father's sleeve—apparently he'd decided to go with Captain Hook tonight. And then the music started and Scooter and I were off and running. Dancing, rather. *Slow, slow, quick, quick.* I concentrated hard on making my feet go where they were supposed to, and Scooter must have too, because somehow we made it through the fox-trot without a misstep.

As the music segued into the waltz—*one, two, three, one, two, three*—I relaxed a little. Mr. Abramowitz had really helped me with this one during our practice sessions. I hummed along to the music and looked over Scooter's shoulder at my classmates.

Cha Cha and Lucas were zipping around the dance floor like old pros. Franklin Freeman was a little robotic, but he and Amy Nguyen were managing to keep the beat too.

The real surprise was Jasmine and Calhoun. Cha Cha had definitely put some polish on him during their secret practice sessions, because not only was Calhoun totally moving in time to the music, he actually looked like he was enjoying himself. He caught me watching him and smiled.

"Oops," I whispered to Scooter as I stumbled. "Sorry."

"Totally my fault," Scooter whispered back. And then he smiled too.

I almost lost my balance again. Smiles from both Scooter and Calhoun? What was going on?

"Very nicely done!" said Mr. Abramowitz as we all twirled to a finish. "Splendid job!"

The band gave a flourish as Mrs. Abramowitz stepped forward. She and Cha Cha's father conferred briefly, then she passed her husband some envelopes. He jotted down something on each of them.

"This year also marks the beginning of a new Pumpkin Falls tradition, one we hope will last for the next hundred years," Mr. Abramowitz told the crowd. "Prizes for our young dancers, who have worked so hard this winter!" A patter of polite applause rippled through the hall.

"The square dancers each received a ribbon and a gift certificate to Lovejoy's Books"—that had been Aunt True's idea—"but for the members of our Cotillion, we have cash prizes. The first category is best dressed."

This ignited a buzz in the room, and even though fashion isn't my thing, my heart beat a little faster too. I couldn't help it; I'm a Lovejoy and I'm competitive. Plus, this was by far the nicest dress I'd ever owned. Was it nice enough for a prize?

"This was a tough one, folks," said Cha Cha's mother, "but the prize goes to—Lucas Winthrop!"

Lucas turned as red as Jasmine's dress. Mrs. Winthrop leaped to her feet and started filming as he scuttled out to claim his prize.

"Oh, man," muttered Scooter. "That's totally unfair! His mother bought that tux for him."

"Shut up and clap, Scooter," I told him.

"Next we have best dance partners," Mr. Abramowitz continued. "There's a prize for each grade level."

I didn't know the sixth-grade winners, but they sure looked happy when they got their envelopes. Then it was time for the seventh grade. No way did Scooter and I even stand a chance for this one.

"Another tough category," said Cha Cha's father, "and in all fairness, Mrs. Abramowitz and I decided we would eliminate our daughter and her partner, because, as most of you know, our wonderful Charlotte, better known as Cha Cha, practically grew up in a dance studio."

The onlookers laughed.

"And so the prize goes to Jasmine Sanchez and Romeo Calhoun!"

Calhoun looked like he couldn't decide how to react—mortified that his real name had been so publicly revealed, or happy that his hard work had paid off.

"Romeo?" said Scooter in disbelief. "*Romeo?* Are you kidding me? That's what the *R* in 'R. J.' stands for?"

"Yup," I replied, then shouted "Way to go, Calhoun!"

Calhoun glanced over at me and smiled again.

After giving out the eighth grade prize—someone from Hatcher's wrestling team and his partner—it was time for the final category: most improved.

"This was also a tough decision," said Mr. Abramowitz.

"Knowing where these students started six weeks ago, and how far they've come, we feel they each deserve recognition. So how about another round of applause for all of this year's Cotillion members?" The crowd responded with enthusiasm, and then Cha Cha's father continued, "That being said, we would like to recognize one set of dance partners who got off to a *truly* rocky start"—my heart did a hopeful little skip at this—"but who have come through with flying colors: Truly Lovejoy and Scooter Sanchez."

Hatcher pulled his white gloves off and stuck his forefingers in his mouth, whistling shrilly. Scooter grabbed my hand and towed me across the dance floor. Mr. Abramowitz passed us each an envelope and shook our hands. Mrs. Abramowitz gave me a hug. "Well done, Truly," she whispered.

Dazed, I followed Scooter back to where my friends were waiting. How was this possible? Dancing was at the top of the list of things I wasn't good at.

"Hey, you know, about 'Truly Gigantic' and all," Scooter said uneasily.

That snapped me out of my daze. "Don't start," I warned him.

He shook his head. "No, I'm not—I mean, well, I'm sorry."

I stared at him. Two apologies in one evening? What on earth had gotten into Scooter?

"Truce?" he said.

"Uh, okay, I guess," I replied.

The music started up again, and the audience crowded onto the dance floor. My parents were among them, my father gamely resting Captain Hook on top of my mother's shoulder. My father said something and my mother threw back her head and laughed, the light glinting in her strawberry-blond curls. She looked really pretty tonight.

I saw Aunt True dancing with Mr. Henry, and Danny with Calhoun's older sister, Juliet. Meanwhile, the boys from my class made a beeline for the refreshment table, leaving us girls standing by the wall.

"Figures," said Cha Cha.

"Cowards," added Jasmine in disgust.

We watched the dancers, and a few minutes later Hatcher wandered over to join us.

"So, does that make up for yesterday?" he asked me, pointing to the envelope in my hand.

I considered his question. Cotillion was hardly a 100 Individual Medley. "Maybe a little," I admitted.

He smiled at me, then turned to Cha Cha. "May I have this dance?"

My mouth dropped open. My brother wanted to dance with the girl he called "the kazoo"?

"Sure," said Cha Cha, and he led her onto the dance floor.

Franklin reappeared, cramming the rest of a vomit bar into his mouth. Mumbling something, he held his hand out to Jasmine. She smiled a braces-free smile at him, and they joined my brother and Cha Cha. One by one my classmates were whisked away until I was left standing there all by myself.

I reminded myself that I didn't like to dance. That I wasn't any good at it. Okay, maybe not as bad as I used to be—I was holding a prize for most improved, after all—but still.

That didn't make me feel any better.

It wasn't so much that I *wanted* to dance, it was just that *not* dancing was worse. Way worse. Not dancing meant I was a wallflower. Not dancing meant I'd probably end up an old cat lady, like Belinda Winchester.

Who happened to dance by just then with Augustus Wilde. She'd traded the shorts I'd seen her wearing earlier for jeans and a red plaid flannel shirt. A plastic bag was looped over one of her wrists. I watched, incredulous, as Captain Romance gallantly dipped and twirled the former lunch lady, his red cape and silver hair streaming behind him.

*Are you kidding me?* I thought.

"Truly?"

I turned around. It was Calhoun. "Hey," I said.

"Would you like to dance?"

My mouth dropped open for the second time that evening. "Uh, sure," I managed to squeak out.

"You snooze, you lose," said Calhoun, his dark eyes gleaming in triumph. This time he wasn't talking to me, though. He was talking to Scooter, who was standing behind us with two cups of punch and a shocked look on his face.

Across the room, Aunt True beamed and gave me two enthusiastic thumbs up.

*No*, I wanted to tell her, *it's not what you think!*

Or was it?

The music shifted to a waltz, and Calhoun swung me smoothly into the *one, two, three* rhythm. I focused intently on not stepping on his toes. I really didn't want to step on his toes, for some reason.

We passed my brother and Cha Cha, and then almost bumped into Ella Bellow, who was dancing with Lou from the diner.

"It shouldn't be much longer before I can move in," she told him loudly, so that he could hear her above the music. "It's the perfect spot for my new shop."

Wait, what was Ella Bellow talking about? I steered Calhoun a little closer.

"I feel badly, of course," she continued. "You never like to see someone's business struggle. But it's certainly worked in my favor."

I came to an abrupt stop. Ella was talking about Lovejoy's Books!

I pulled away from Calhoun and marched over to her. "You're the one who took it!"

Ella Bellow looked at me in surprise. Then she stopped dancing too. "What on earth are you talking about?"

"*Charlotte's Web*! I overheard you just now, and you

practically admitted it!" I told her, my voice rising. The couples around us spun to a stop. "You had us special order that book about starting a new career in your retirement, and you've been prowling around the bookshop for weeks now, snooping. You're just waiting for us to fail so you can take over our space!"

"I most certainly am not!"

"You took it!" I shouted at her. "You need to give it back!"

Ella looked shocked. "How dare you accuse me of such a thing!" she sputtered.

My parents and Aunt True were making their way toward us through the crowd now.

"What's going on?" asked Belinda Winchester, dancing by with Augustus Wilde.

Ella pointed to me. "She just accused me of stealing from the bookshop! As if I'd ever do such a thing!"

The music had stopped by now, and everyone in the room was staring at me.

"Stealing what?" said Belinda.

"*Charlotte's Web*!" I replied.

Belinda looked puzzled. "How could anyone steal *Charlotte's Web*?" she said. "It's bolted to the wall."

It took me a minute to realize she was talking about the bronze sculpture in the library.

"I'm talking about the *book*," I told her. "The autographed first edition that was in the cabinet in our shop."

"Oh," said Belinda. "No one stole that. I have it right here." She reached into the plastic bag she was carrying and pulled it out.

A gasp went up from the crowd. My father stepped forward.

"Where did you get that?" he demanded.

"From Andy," she replied mildly. "He gave it to me for my ninth birthday."

"Wait a minute, you're the 'Bee' in the inscription?" said Aunt True.

Belinda Winchester nodded.

"Who's Andy?" asked my father, his head whipping back and forth as he tried to keep up with the conversation.

"E. B. White," said my sister Lauren. "It was in my book report, remember?"

"See? I told you I didn't steal anything," Ella Bellow said triumphantly. She turned to me. "And just in case you're wondering, Miss Think-You-Know-It-All, I have absolutely no designs on Lovejoy's Books. Bud Jefferson is going to rent out half his space for my new shop."

Once again, I'd gone and put my big foot in my mouth. I was Truly-in-the-Middle-of-a-Mess.

"Truly, I think you owe someone an apology," my father told me sternly.

My shoulders slumped. "Yes, sir," I said. I turned to face

the postmistress. I'd been so sure she was the thief! "I'm really sorry."

Her mouth pruned up. "As well you should be."

"Show's over, folks!" my father announced. He took me by the arm and hustled me over to a corner of the room, near where Annie Freeman was being interviewed by a *Patriot-Bugle* reporter about winning yesterday's spelling bee.

"And then this boy from West Hartfield messed up on a trick question," Annie told him. "The *P* is silent in P-T-A-R-M-I-G-A-N. Which is a bird."

One that happened to be on my life list. I'd been lucky enough to spot it when we lived in Colorado.

It took us a while to get everything straightened out. Once Belinda explained that she'd grown up in Maine, and that her family lived on the farm next door to E. B. White, it all made sense—the lunch-lady entry in the yearbook that talked about lobsters, the news report about her trip back to the seacoast to visit her sister, the cats named after Fern and Avery Arable in *Charlotte's Web*. Only two things still puzzled me.

"How did you manage to lose the book in the first place?" I asked her.

Belinda shrugged. "Things go missing," she said. "And things get found." She rummaged in her plastic bag again, emerging this time with a kitten and a half-eaten vomit bar. She took a bite—of the vomit bar, not the kitten.

The other thing I didn't understand was how Belinda

could possibly not have known that we all thought the book was stolen. It had been all over the news.

Except she didn't own a television, and she never read the newspaper. Plus, she had her earbuds in most of the time, listening to her music. Somehow, she'd managed to miss the whole thing.

The mystery was solved, at least, but not in a way that was going to help the bookstore. No way could my father and Aunt True use the book to pay off the bank loan now.

"Erastus Peckinpaugh, do you want to ask me something or not?" Aunt True said suddenly. Startled, I looked over to see the man in the green jacket—only tonight he was wearing an ordinary suit—hovering behind her.

"Punkinpie?" said Pippa. "That'th a funny name."

My mother turned around too. "Professor Rusty! How nice to see you here."

The man in the green jacket—the stork—was Professor Rusty? And Professor Rusty was Erastus Peckinpaugh? I felt something in my brain stir and come to life. Where had I seen that name before?

"Out with it already!" Aunt True put her hands on her hips as she turned to face him, tapping the toe of one of her red cowboy boots. "I'm tired of you creeping around like some silly high school boy. Do you think I haven't noticed you lurking outside the bookstore these past few weeks?"

And then Annie spoke up again behind us. "Finally, I got

the winning word," she told the reporter. "'Thespian.' T-H-E-S-P-I-A-N. It means actor."

Snick! The last puzzle pieces fit together as neatly as a sudoku puzzle. I leaned over to my friends.

"I know where the final clue is," I whispered.

# CHAPTER 37

We ran straight to the bookshop.

"There's something I need to check on," I told my friends as we clattered up the stairs to Aunt True's apartment. The key was still under the mat where she always left it, and I unlocked the door and led everyone inside. "Don't let Memphis out."

"Thespian" had been Annie Freeman's winning word, and Aunt True and Erastus Peckinpaugh had both been in the Thespian Club back in high school! I'd seen it in my aunt's yearbook.

The scrapbooks were still piled on the coffee table, where Lauren and Annie had left them. I started leafing through them, and it didn't take me long to find what I was looking for. "Ha!" I said triumphantly, showing my friends the program for *Much Ado About Nothing*.

"Hey, that's the show my parents starred in," said Calhoun, spotting their names. "My mom has a copy of that program too."

"Yes, but check out their understudies," I said, pointing to the cast list, which confirmed my suspicions.

My friends' mouths fell open when they saw the names: True Lovejoy and Erastus Peckinpaugh.

"My aunt and Professor Peckinpaugh—Professor Rusty, the guy in the green jacket—were Beatrice and Benedick too. Unofficially, of course."

I pointed to the prom picture on the opposite page. "Now check this out—"

"Whoa, that's some hair," said Scooter.

"Whose, her aunt's or her date's?" asked Calhoun.

"Both of them," said Lucas, and everybody laughed.

"Erastus Peckinpaugh is my aunt's old boyfriend," I said, pulling out my cell phone. "Don't you get it?" I scrolled through the pictures on it, hoping I hadn't deleted the one I'd taken on our field trip to the covered bridge. Nope, there it was. I enlarged the bit that showed the graffiti on the rafter. "See there, inside that lopsided heart? Where it says 'E and T Forever'? That's got to be Erastus and True! That's the exact place she chose for her yearbook picture, and I think it's their meeting spot."

My friends stared at the program and the picture, digesting all this information. Then Scooter looked up and grinned.

"What are we waiting for?"

Two minutes later, we were running down the road that led out of town, the only light to guide us the full moon above and the faint beams below from the flashlight apps on our cell phones.

We heard the river before we saw it. It was flowing freely again, thanks to the thaw, and as we approached we heard a loud *CRACK*, followed by a tremendous splash, as a great chunk of ice crashed from the falls into the water.

"Cool," said Scooter, aiming his light in the river's direction. "It's like the *Titanic* or something."

We jogged through the mouth of the covered bridge, our footsteps echoing in the dark as the sound bounced off its wooden floor and walls.

Jasmine giggled nervously. "Spooky," she said.

I shone my light up at the rafters, trying to remember where I'd been standing when I'd seen the graffiti. "It was somewhere in the middle, I think," I told my friends. "Can you guys all shine your lights up here too?"

They did, and it didn't take long to spot what I was looking for. "There it is! See? That heart with 'E and T Forever' inside? This has to be their meeting place."

"The envelope's probably taped to the top of the rafter, just like it was in the steeple," said Lucas.

"I'll take a look." Scooter climbed up onto the railing.

"Watch out!" cried Jasmine, grabbing her twin's lower legs to steady him. The X-shaped crosspieces along the wall of the bridge left too many wide gaps for comfort.

Scooter batted her away. "Relax, Jazz, I've got it."

Grasping a crosspiece with one hand, he stretched his other up toward the rafter. I glanced down at the moon's reflection in the river and shuddered. It would not be fun to take a nosedive into that dark, frigid water.

"I can't quite reach," Scooter said finally. "I'm not tall enough."

"I'm the tallest," I said as he hopped down. "Let me try."

"No, Truly, don't," begged Cha Cha. "Please."

"I'll be careful," I assured her. "Don't you want to know if it's up there?"

I hoisted myself onto the railing. The soles of my new heels were slick, and I edged my way cautiously along until I was standing directly under the graffiti. A sharp gust of wind made my coat and dress billow around my legs. I shivered. The tights I was wearing offered little protection, except perhaps for keeping Scooter from singing any more ditties about my underpants.

Holding tight to a crosspiece, I stretched up on tiptoe and reached for the rafter, just the way Scooter had done.

"There's something here!" I said after a moment of fumbling around.

"Is it an envelope?" Jasmine's voice was shrill with excitement.

"I think so—hang on a sec." I took off my mitten with my teeth and picked at the edge of whatever it was with my fingernails. "Got it!" I mumbled triumphantly a moment later, my mouth full of wool. "It's an envelope!"

I waved my duct-tape prize in the air in triumph, then handed it down to Jasmine. The others crowded around as she held it under the beam of Cha Cha's flashlight app.

I was climbing down to join them when my left shoe slipped.

"Whoa!" I cried. My arms windmilled as I tried to regain my balance. For a heart-stopping split second I teetered on the railing. And then my big feet betrayed me once again. Or, rather, my big shoes did. Both of them slipped out from under me completely and I landed on the railing with a spine-jolting bounce, then toppled through a gap between the crosspieces.

And then—well, then I did the Polar Bear Swim.

The last thing I heard before the river closed over my head was Cha Cha and Jasmine screaming. The next thing I heard was me screaming. Or what would have been me screaming, if I'd had breath enough to scream. The frigid water had knocked every scrap of it out of me.

I'd never felt *anything* that cold.

I thrashed in the icy current, gasping and choking. I couldn't think, I couldn't see, and worst of all, my jacket was dragging me down. Somehow I managed to wrestle myself out of it. The river swept it away under the bridge, and then it started to sweep me away. I panicked. Flailing blindly in the water, I smacked my hand against one of the pillars that held up the bridge and grabbed at it frantically, trying to get a grip on one of the stones in its base.

I clung there for a few seconds, trying to catch my breath. Somewhere far above my friends were shouting, but I barely heard them. I was too focused on not being swept away again. My shoes were long gone by now, and I jammed my ice-numbed toes and fingers into the crevices between the rocks, scrabbling clumsily as I pulled myself onto the base of the pillar.

Slowly, painfully, I began to inch my way up, collapsing in tears when I finally reached the top of the pillar's rough, narrow ledge. Only a minute or so had passed, but it felt like an eternity. My head ached. My teeth were chattering like a woodpecker on a tin roof. I was even colder now than I had been in the water, if that were possible, thanks to the bitter wind.

"Truly!"

Someone was calling my name.

"Here!" I croaked. "I'm here!" I looked up and saw Calhoun leaning over the wall of the bridge.

"Scooter and the girls ran for help!" he hollered down.

"We called nine-one-one, too," added Lucas, who was beside him.

I gave a feeble nod.

Calhoun stretched out his hand. "See if you can reach up and grab hold!"

I eyed the distance between us and shook my head. I didn't want to risk slipping again. The ledge was so narrow!

"Come on, Truly!" he urged.

With Lucas holding on to Calhoun's belt for all he was

worth, Calhoun stretched even farther down toward me.

"Bravery comes in all sizes," Aunt True had once said. I took a deep, raggedy breath. Did it come in mine?

I absolutely truly hoped so.

Shaking, I rose to my knees.

"You're almost there," Calhoun called down in encouragement as I forced myself to my feet and reached an arm up overhead. "A little to the left."

His left? My left? My knees were knocking and I was afraid my legs were going to collapse under me. I waved my hand back and forth. My fingertips grazed something. Or someone.

"That's it!" Calhoun shouted. "I nearly had you!"

It was my height that saved me. That and my Truly Gigantic, size-ten-and-a-half Amazon feet. Summoning every ounce of strength that I had left in me, I stretched myself up on tiptoes as high as I could and reached for Calhoun one more time.

"Gotcha!" he cried.

I promised myself right then and there that I would never, ever complain about being tall again.

It was agonizing. I was afraid to move even a fraction of an inch, for fear I'd plunge back into the river, dragging my friends with me. My toes, my legs, my fingers—my entire body was cramped with cold. I ventured a glance downward, which was a bad idea.

*This is definitely at the very top of the list of things I'm not good at*, I thought, closing my eyes to block out the terrifying sight of the dark water flowing swiftly past.

My arm felt like it was being pulled from its socket. *What am I good at, then?* I listed the things that came to mind: Swimming. Bird-watching. Sudoku. Window displays at the bookstore. And pre-algebra, thanks to my father's tutoring.

My father.

*Lovejoys can do anything*, he'd tell me if he were here.

Even this?

I wasn't so sure.

And then, finally, I heard a siren in the distance, followed by the sound of voices shouting my name. Footsteps pounded on the wooden floorboards of the bridge overhead. There were more shouts directly above, and then a voice I recognized. I opened my eyes and looked up to see that it was my father. A great sob of relief burst from me.

"Hang on, Truly!" He anchored himself to an eyebolt with his hook and reached down to me with his good hand.

"Don't let go, Dad!" I begged him as his fingers closed around my wrist. "Please don't let me go!"

"Never," he told me. "Cross my heart and hope to fly."

# CHAPTER 38

"I'm really, really glad you went with Captain Hook tonight, Dad," I said later, when we were safely back at the Town Hall. The music had stopped and people were milling around everywhere. They'd burst into spontaneous applause when the rescue vehicles finally pulled up out front.

"Me too, honey," he replied, putting his good arm around me and kissing the top of my head.

The rescue was a bit of a blur. My father held on to me until the fire department arrived and pulled me to safety. I was shoeless, of course, and practically blue with cold, and I'd gotten pretty bruised and scraped up too. But at least I was alive. The firefighters bundled me into blankets and made me take off what was left of my wet, tattered dress so I wouldn't get hypothermia, and then they took me directly to my mother.

She started to cry when she saw me. "You're safe!" she kept repeating, hugging me tightly as if to assure herself that I wasn't going to go flinging myself from another bridge at any moment. "My brave girl!"

I shook my head, which was buried in her shoulder. "It was Dad," I told her. "Dad's the one who's brave. He didn't let go, and neither did Calhoun and Lucas."

I smiled at my two friends, whose faces were pink from all the praise they'd been showered with. Lucas's mother had him in a death grip, though. The poor kid would probably never be allowed out of the house again.

My mother kissed the top of my head. "What were you thinking, sweetheart, going down to the bridge like that?"

"We were looking for something," I told her.

"This," said Cha Cha, pulling the duct-tape-covered envelope out of her jacket pocket.

Erastus Peckinpaugh, who had been hovering at the edge of the crowd that surrounded me, looking more stork-like than usual, suddenly froze.

My mother's forehead puckered. "That trash was worth risking your life for?"

"It's not trash; it's for Aunt True," I told her. "From Professor Rusty—I mean Professor Peckinpaugh."

At this, Pippa, who had barnacled herself to my leg the second I climbed out of the fire truck, finally let go. "Punkinpie! Punkinpie! Punkinpie!" she chanted, twirling, and the people gathered around us started to laugh.

Cha Cha took out the envelope and passed it to my aunt.

"You really should read the other letters first," I told Aunt True. "But they're back at home."

We explained about finding the envelopes, and the quotes that were on the letters. Calhoun recited a few, and when he stumbled, his dad stepped in to help him. Aunt True listened silently as we told her how we'd followed the clues, casting a glance up at Professor Peckinpaugh now and then.

"Astounding," she said when we were done. "You did this all on your own?"

My friends and I nodded.

"Please read the last letter to us," begged Jasmine. "We have to know how the story ends."

"Why not?" said Aunt True. Opening the envelope, she drew out the faded piece of paper inside. "'For B,'" she began. "'When I said I would die a bachelor, I did not think I should live till I were married.'"

"Is that it?" asked Cha Cha. "Just another Shakespeare quote?"

"No, there's more. It also says, 'True, will you . . .'" My aunt's voice trailed off. She looked up at Professor Peckinpaugh, her eyes wide with surprise.

"True, will you what?" I reached for the letter, but Aunt True clutched it to her chest. Wait a minute, had Erastus

Peckinpaugh just asked my aunt to marry him?

Aunt True shot to her feet. "Why didn't you say something, Rusty?" she demanded, advancing on the bushy-haired professor. "After I left town you never wrote, you never called—I never heard from you again!"

"I thought you'd followed the clues and found the letters, and you weren't interested," he protested, taking a step back.

"How could I *possibly* have followed the clues?" Aunt True sputtered. "You hid them in a book that didn't belong to you, and that I never found! What were you *thinking*, Rusty?"

Erastus Peckinpaugh looked miserable. "I was trying to be clever," he told her. "I knew that *Charlotte's Web* was your favorite book, and when I saw it lying there on the floor that day at the bookshop it seemed like a good idea. You were always the one who tidied up at night; I figured you'd find it right away."

Aunt True shook her head. "You should have just mailed the letter to me. At least I'd have gotten it that way."

Professor Rusty sighed. "I was planning to. I'd even picked out a stamp to remind you of all those Civil War reenactments I dragged you to."

Cha Cha and I exchanged a glance. Another piece of the puzzle solved.

"The point is, I didn't even *see* the stamp!" Aunt True snapped.

He glanced at her ruefully then hung his head. "I just

assumed you would, just as I assumed you'd put two and two together."

"What, and get *five?*" Aunt True threw up her hands.

Dr. Calhoun winked at my friends and me. "'There is a kind of merry war betwixt Signior Benedick and her,'" he quoted in a whisper. "'They never meet but there's a skirmish of wit between them.'"

Aunt True and Professor Peckinpaugh were still bickering as we gathered our things to leave. On the way out, we passed Ella Bellow, who was collecting her coat from the big rack near the door.

"Hold on a minute, what's this doing in there?" she demanded as a fuzzy white head poked out from one of the pockets. "This doesn't belong to me!" Ella's voice rose in alarm. She spun around, sweeping the crowd with her eyes. Her gaze narrowed when she spotted Belinda Winchester. "Did you put this creature in my pocket, Belinda?"

"Don't look at me; it isn't one of mine," Belinda replied. Turning away from Ella, she gave Lauren and me a mischievous smile. "And that's not a lie," she murmured. "Technically speaking, it isn't one of mine. I didn't give birth to it."

My sister and I giggled.

In the end, Ella Bellow went home with a kitten, and the rest of us went home with both mysteries solved at last.

# EPILOGUE

The January thaw lingered for three more days after my dramatic rescue, or what everyone in town was calling "a truly big splash."

That was the headline that had appeared on the front page of the *Pumpkin Falls Patriot-Bugle* the morning after my rescue. I was mortified at first, but the publicity really gave our bookstore a boost. The news wires picked up the story of the brave wounded-warrior-turned-bookseller who'd saved his daughter, and while Dad isn't thrilled being in the spotlight— he's been giving interviews to the media right and left ever since—he's definitely happy about the effect that the rescue had on our store's bottom line.

The Winter Festival Committee gave me an honorary blue ribbon for the Polar Bear Swim, which I pinned to the bulletin board above my desk, and Principal Burnside held a special assembly at school. He commended Calhoun and

Lucas for their part in the rescue, and me for what he called my "valor and panache" (I think that's another way of saying "bravery"), even though, as he pointed out sternly, we had absolutely no business being at the covered bridge in the first place without adult supervision.

Lots of people have been stopping by the bookstore to meet Dad and check up on me, both locals and tourists passing through. And just like Aunt True predicted, they sample our mini pumpkin whoopie pies and end up buying books.

So everything worked out for the best in the end.

The warm west wind that blew into town along with all the publicity carried with it the promise of spring. It melted the snow sculptures and released the frozen river from the grip of the ice, and ensured what Annie Freeman says will be a S-T-U-P-E-N-D-O-U-S maple syrup harvest this year.

I've been spending lots of time in the backyard since that night at the covered bridge, making friends with more of my grandfather's chickadees. I also added a cedar waxwing and an evening grosbeak and a ruffed grouse to my life list.

There would be more birds to add, come spring. Spring meant the return of meadowlarks and barn swallows, orioles and towhees, tanagers and buntings. And out on Lake Lovejoy, there would be osprey to watch diving for fish.

It might not be so bad to be stuck here in Pumpkin Falls, I decided, come spring.

Plus, my birthday was just around the corner, and that

meant Mackenzie's visit. I was looking forward to introducing her to my new friends.

"You know, I could have saved myself a whole lot of trouble if I'd just given that envelope to Aunt True in the first place," I mused to Cha Cha and Jasmine, stepping carefully around a puddle of slush as the three of us made our way downtown after school one afternoon.

"Yeah, but if you had, we might not all be friends," Cha Cha replied.

"And there'd be no Pumpkin Falls Private Eyes," added Jasmine.

They had a point. I was going to miss our adventures, but a town this small couldn't have any more mysteries to solve, could it?

"And don't forget the bookstore," added Jasmine. "You were the one who saved it."

That was a bit of an exaggeration. Yes, I'd inadvertently found *Charlotte's Web*, and yes, our business had gotten a boost from all the news about "a truly big splash." It still wasn't enough to turn the tide, though. What really turned the tide was Belinda Winchester.

She may look homeless, but it turns out Belinda invested her lunch-lady earnings shrewdly over the years, and she's rich. Her earnings support her kitten rescue, and she also fessed up to being the anonymous donor who gave the

*Charlotte's Web* sculpture to the local library years ago.

When Belinda realized what losing that autographed first edition meant for our family—and when she learned about the deadline hanging over our heads—she offered to become a silent partner in the business. Or maybe not-so-silent, since she's working part-time at the bookshop now. She knows everything there is to know about mysteries, so Dad and Aunt True have put her in charge of that section. She's as happy as a clam.

Aunt True also took her shopping for some new clothes, which is kind of like the blind leading the blind if you ask me, which nobody ever does. At least Belinda doesn't look like such a bag lady anymore. Well, except for the kittens. She almost always brings one or two along with her to work.

Dad says he still thinks Belinda Winchester is odd, but Aunt True reminded him that while books bring people together, it's people who bring communities together.

"A community is like a family," she told him, "and every family has a few odd ducks. The important thing to remember is that they're still family."

Belinda Winchester is definitely an odd duck, and so is Ella Bellow. We all kind of wish Ella had moved to Florida, but she's opening a knitting shop across the street from us next month instead. The sign is already up over her half of Earl's Coins and Stamps. She's calling it "A Stitch in Time," but Dad calls it the "Stitch and Snitch," since he says it's destined to be our town's new gossip central.

Ella also decided to keep her new kitten. She named it Purl, or as Annie Freeman tells everyone, "P-U-R-L, like the knitting stitch."

On the night before winter swooped in again, I heard something outside as I was getting ready for bed.

*Tu-whoo! Tu-whoo!*

I crossed to the window, threw it open, and leaned out to listen more closely. There it was again—*Tu-whoo! Tu-whoo!*

I held my breath. Could it be? I looked up at the full moon—an owl moon!—that hung in the sky. Its light reflected on the sodden snow below and shone through my window, puddling at my feet in a silvery glow.

I looked over at the picture book displayed on my shelf and thought of the father who takes his child owling.

Which in my case has never happened.

*What if I rewrite the story?* I thought. *What if in my story, the girl asks her father to go owling instead?*

"Dad!" I called, grabbing Gramps's barn coat and wool hat and stuffing my feet into my sneakers.

He didn't answer, so as I clattered downstairs, I reached for my cell phone and called him. A moment later, I heard the sound of his ringtone from the kitchen.

It was the theme song from *The Magnificent Seven*!

And right then and there I knew for sure that our family was going to be okay.

And that's exactly how it all happened, absolutely truly, cross my heart and hope to fly.

# AUNT TRUE'S
# MINI PUMPKIN WHOOPIE PIES

## Cookies

½ cup butter, softened

1 ¼ cups sugar

2 large eggs, at room temperature, lightly beaten

1 cup pumpkin

1 tsp. vanilla extract

2 T. molasses

2 cups all-purpose flour

1 tsp. baking powder

1 tsp. baking soda

1 tsp. ground cinnamon

½ tsp. ground ginger

½ tsp. ground cloves

¼ tsp. ground cardamom

¼ tsp. salt (only if using unsalted butter, otherwise omit)

## Filling

4 ounces cream cheese, at room temperature

6 T. butter, softened

½ tsp. vanilla extract

1 ½ cups powdered sugar

Preheat oven to 350° F.

FOR COOKIES: Cream butter and sugar in a large bowl. Add eggs and beat well. Add pumpkin, vanilla extract, and molasses; beat until smooth. In a separate bowl, whisk flour, baking powder, baking soda, and spices. Add to pumpkin mixture and stir well. Using a teaspoon-size cookie scoop (or a heaping teaspoon), drop onto greased or parchment-lined cookie sheets.

Bake for about 12 minutes, until the cookie springs back to the touch, or a toothpick inserted into center comes out clean.

Cool on baking sheet for 5 minutes, then transfer to wire rack to cool completely.

FOR FILLING: Beat cream cheese, butter, and vanilla until fluffy. Gradually mix in powdered sugar and beat until light and fluffy. Generously frost the flat side of one cookie with filling, then top it with the flat side of another one to make a "sandwich." Repeat with remaining cookies and filling.

# MISS MARPLE'S PICKS

*The Borrowers* by Mary Norton

*Charlotte's Web* by E. B. White

*Cinderella* by the Brothers Grimm

*Frog and Toad Are Friends* by Arnold Lobel

*Jane Eyre* by Charlotte Brontë

*Little House on the Prairie* by Laura Ingalls Wilder

*A Little Princess* by Frances Hodgson Burnett

*The Long Winter* by Laura Ingalls Wilder

*Mary Poppins* by P. L. Travers

*Millions of Cats* by Wanda Gag

*Mrs. Piggle-Wiggle* by Betty MacDonald

*Owl Moon* by Jane Yolen, illustrated by John Schoenherr

*Pride and Prejudice* by Jane Austen

*The Wolves of Willoughby Chase* by Joan Aiken

# ACKNOWLEDGMENTS

Heartfelt thanks to Ellen Ingwerson and Clara Germani, whose expert knowledge of competitive swimming helped keep me out of deep water; and to MG (R) Lee Baxter for guidance on all things military. Any errors that managed to slip through the net are entirely my own. And a great big shout-out to my friend Victoria Irwin and to René Kirkpatrick and the entire staff at Eagle Harbor Book Co. on Bainbridge Island, Washington, for letting me play in their sandbox one long winter weekend. The world is absolutely truly a better place with bookstores like this one in it!

# Did you LOVE reading this book?

## Visit the Whyville...

IN THE MIDDLE BOOK HIVE

## Where you can:

- ⬡ Discover great books!
- ⬡ Meet new friends!
- ⬡ Read exclusive sneak peeks and more!

## Log on to visit now!
### bookhive.whyville.net

Jr. Lela's

Whyville

a Numedeon, inc. property